D1082063

with me in seattle book 2

Fight
with me

KRISTEN PROBY

Fight With Me
Book Two in the With Me In Seattle Series
Kristen Proby
Copyright © 2013 by Kristen Proby

Second Edition 2016

All Rights Reserved. This book may not be reproduced, scanned, or distributed in any printed or electronic form without permission from the author. Please do not participate in or encourage piracy of copyrighted materials in violation of the author's rights. All characters and storylines are the property of the author and your support and respect is appreciated. The characters and events portrayed in this book are fictitious. Any similarity to real persons, living or dead, is coincidental and not intended by the author.

The following story contains mature themes, strong language, and sexual situations. It is intended for adult readers.

Cover Design by
Sara Eirew

Cover image used under license from
Shutterstock.com

Interior Design & Formatting by
Christine Borgford, Perfectly Publishable

For *Tanya*. Your support and friendship mean more to me than you will ever know. I love you, bff.

books by
KRISTEN PROBY

WITH ME IN SEATTLE SERIES:
Come Away With Me
Under The Mistletoe With Me
Fight With Me
Play With Me
Rock With Me
Safe With Me
Tied With Me
Breathe With Me
Forever With Me

LOVE UNDER THE BIG SKY SERIES,
available through Pocket Books:
Loving Cara
Seducing Lauren
Falling for Jillian

THE BOUDREAUX SERIES:
Easy Love
Easy for Keeps: 1001 Dark Nights Novella

Easy Charm

Easy Melody

Easy Kisses

THE FUSION SERIES:

Listen to Me

Close to You

Blush For Me ~ Coming Soon

prologue

Summer

My back hits the wall with a light thud, and Nate's face is buried in my throat, his hands on my ass, skirt hiked up around my waist, pulling me up so he can cradle his still-covered erection in the apex of my thighs. I pull the hair tie out of his thick, inky-black hair and run my hands through it, holding on to him. I've never seen his hair down before. He always ties it back at the nape of his neck, and it's so sexy. It falls just above his shoulders, framing that impossibly handsome face of his that makes my insides quiver and my mouth go dry every time he looks at me.

But he's never looked at me the way he is right now, in the semi-dark hallway in the middle of his apartment, just outside his bedroom. His gray eyes are burning as he rocks his pelvis against mine.

"Do you know how beautiful you are, Julianne?" he murmurs. "I need you naked, now."

He picks me up, hands still braced on my ass, and I wrap myself around him. He carries me into his bedroom, and I'm suddenly standing before him, and we are a tangle of arms and greedy hands, pulling and grasping clothes, flinging them haphazardly about the room. He doesn't turn the lights on, so I can't see him anymore, but oh, those hands. I don't know how many times I've sat in a meeting, watching these beautiful, large hands, and now they're on me.

Everywhere.

His mouth is on mine, his hands in my blond hair, and he's kissing me with a fervor that makes my knees weak. He's a really good kisser. Excellent.

Fucking amazing.

He picks me up again, cradling me in his arms this time and lays me down on the bed. The sheets are soft and cool against my naked backside, and I wish I could see him in all his naked glory. I've been day-dreaming about a naked Nate since he became my boss almost a year ago. I have a feeling there is a fine, fine body lurking under all those expertly tailored business suits.

Nate follows me onto the bed, and I run my hands up his stomach, over his chest, and up to his shoulders.

Holy fuck, he's built, and his skin is warm and smooth and . . . *wow.* His hands are cradling my face, kissing me tenderly now, biting and nib-bling my lips, and then he leans on one elbow at the side of my head and sends his other hand down my neck, over my breast, teasing the taut nipple with his fingers, and farther south, slowly finding his target.

"Oh God." My body bows off the soft sheets as he slips two fingers into my pussy, and his thumb gently circles my clitoris.

"Oh, you are so wet. And so fucking tight. Jesus, how long has it been for you, honey?"

Really? He wants to know this now?

"Longer than I care to think about," I respond and lift my hips up into his hand. Oh God, what this man can do with his hands!

"Shit, I want you. I've wanted you since I first laid eyes on you." His lips find mine, demanding and probing, licking and sucking, his tongue mirroring what his delicious fingers are doing down south, and I'm completely swept away. I've wanted him just as long.

"We shouldn't do this," I whisper unconvincingly.

"Why not?" he whispers back.

"Because . . . Oh God, yes, right there." My hips are circling, and I skim my hands down to his ass. His hard, muscular, oh-so-sexy ass.

"You were saying?" he whispers, nibbling down my neck.

"We could both be fired. No-frat policy."

"I don't give a fuck about anyone's policy right now." His lips close over my nipple, and I lose all conscious thought. Nate licks and sucks his way down my belly, paying close attention to my navel, before heading farther south, kissing my freshly waxed—thank God!—pubis and finally planting that tongue right *there.*

"Fuck!" My hips buck up off the bed, and I feel him grin before he pulls his fingers out of me, spreads my thighs wider and kisses me, deeply, his tongue pushing and swirling through my folds and inside me. I push my fingers into that glorious thick hair and hang on, and when I think I just can't take any more, he licks up to my clit and pushes a finger inside me, making a *come here* motion, and I come undone, shuddering and digging my heels into the mattress, pushing my pussy against Nate's skilled mouth.

As I surface back to Planet Earth, I hear Nate rip open a foil packet, and he is kissing his way back up my body, sucking on each nipple, and then kisses me. I can taste myself on his lips, and I moan, wrapping my legs around his hips, lifting my pelvis, ready for him to fill me, but he doesn't, he's just braced on his hands above me, his cock cradled between my thighs. His breathing is ragged, and I wish with all my might that the lights were on so I could see his gray eyes.

"Nate, I want you."

"I know."

"Now, damn it."

"You are so fucking hot," he whispers and lowers himself to brush his lips on my forehead.

"Inside me." I reach between us and grab his erection. Holy hell, he's hung. He's hard and smooth, and he hasn't rolled the condom on yet. I pull up the length of him, to the tip, and . . ."Holy shit, what is that?"

He chuckles and leans down to gently kiss me. "It's an apa," he whispers.

There is a metal bar with two small balls, one at the top and one on the underside, in the end of his penis, and I'm completely thrown. Nate, my suit-wearing, conservative-looking-except-for-the-long-hair-thing boss, has his *penis pierced?*

"A what-a?" My fingers trace it, and then I run my forefinger around the tip of him, and he sucks in a breath through his teeth.

"An apadravya. Fuck, honey."

"Why would you get this?" I ask, unexpectedly turned on and curious. I wish I could see it!

"You're about to find out." I hear the smile in his voice and then feel him reach between us and roll the condom down his impressive length. He kisses me again, more urgently, and buries his hands in my blond hair. I raise my hips and feel the tip—and those metal balls—at my entrance, and he slowly, oh so slowly, eases inside me.

Oh. My. God.

I can feel the metal rub against the walls of my vagina, all the way deep inside me, and he stops, buried in me, his mouth continuing to move over my own.

"Fuck, I love how tight you are." His words make me squeeze him and hold him, my legs wrapped around his lean hips, hands in that glorious hair.

He starts to move his hips, sliding in and out of me, and the sensation is unlike any I've ever known. I feel the metal, his impressive cock, his mouth doing crazy things to mine, and I feel my body quicken as a thin coat of sweat covers me. He picks up the pace and rotates his hips, just enough to make me completely lose my mind.

"Come on, honey, let go." And I do, violently. I cry out as Nate pushes into me, harder, once and twice, and then succumbs to his own release.

"Oh fuck!"

I JUST FUCKED my boss.

Nate pulls out of me and removes the condom, then tosses it on the floor beside the bed.

"Are you okay?" he asks.

No. "Yes."

"Do you need anything?" He runs his fingers down my cheek, and

I again wish that the lights were on, yet I don't because I'm now feeling shy, and I never feel shy. His voice is distant, like he doesn't quite know what to do with me now, and to be honest, I don't know what to do with me either.

"No, thank you."

Oh God, what did I just do? I just had to have the most mind-blowingly fantastic sex of my life with the one man in the world I just can't have. When he asked me to join him for a drink here at his place after dinner out with colleagues, I should have said no, but I couldn't. I've wanted to get my hands on him from day one, but our company has a very strict no-fraternization policy, and I've had a long-standing policy of my own: no fucking co-workers.

And yet, here I am, blissfully sated, and not just a little ashamed, in my sexy boss's bed in his swanky thirtieth-floor apartment.

Fuck.

"Do you want me to turn the lights on?" Nate asks and starts to move away from me, but I put my hand out, gripping his arm to stop him.

"No, it's fine."

"You don't sound like yourself. Are you sure you're okay?"

"I'm fine. Tired, probably too much wine." Those two glasses that I sipped while drinking in Nate's deliciousness have definitely not affected my head, but it's the only excuse I have. We're acting weird with each other now, and I hate it. I don't know what I expected. I don't know him that well. He's always been professional and polite, and until tonight I had no idea that he found me the least bit attractive.

He's got a very convincing poker face.

Nate kisses my forehead and pulls the covers over us, then turns me away from him and curls up behind me.

"Go to sleep. We'll talk in the morning."

Talk? Talk about what?

I don't answer, I just lie still and wait until his breathing evens out, then wait another ten minutes to make sure he's asleep. I carefully slip out from under his heavy arm—Geez, he's muscular! Those suits he wears are very deceiving. I fumble my way to the wall, praying I don't trip and fall on my ass, waking him up, and follow it to the doorway. Turning on the hall light, I gather my clothes quickly and dress, grab my purse from Nate's large, professionally decorated, gorgeous living room, and leave.

I call a cab from the lobby of the prestigious downtown Seattle condo building and wait for my ride back to the parking garage of our office building so I can get my own car.

When I finally get home to the house I share on Alki Beach with my best friend, Natalie, I see a strange Lexus convertible in the driveway and lights coming from the kitchen at the back of the house.

"Nat?"

"I'm in the kitchen!"

"Do you have company?" I am so not in the mood to meet Nat's new friend.

"Yeah," she calls back.

"Okay, going to bed. See you tomorrow." I climb the stairs to my bedroom, closing the door behind me, and take a long, hot shower. My skin is still sensitive from my romp in Nate's bed, and his scent clings to me, all clean and musky and sexy, and I can't help but regret, just a little, leaving. Perhaps there could have been more fun during the night before the harsh light of day settled in.

And along with it, The Talk.

No, thank you.

I really don't need to have Nate spell out all the reasons why this was a one-night indiscretion. I certainly don't think I can handle the awkwardness of the morning after. It's better to just pretend like it never happened and get back to business as usual.

I pull on pink panties and a white cami and dig my phone out of my purse on my way to bed. There are no messages or texts.

He's probably as relieved I left as I am.

I lie awake all night, trying to figure out what I'm going to say when I call in sick to work tomorrow.

one

Late Spring

I love my job. I love my job.

   God, sometimes, I hate my job. I read the terse e-mail from my boss, Nathan McKenna, once again and swallow hard.

Friday, April 26, 2013 13:56
From: Nathan McKenna
To: Julianne Montgomery
Subject: Working Late

   Julianne,

   I need you to work late with me tonight, possibly into the weekend. Please gather all the files on the Radcliffe account and meet me in my office at 6 p.m.

   Nate

   Damn it! For eight long months I've managed to steer clear of my boss, and I know I've been incredibly lucky that I haven't had to work alone with him after-hours, but we recently lost the other junior partner in our department, and that leaves just me and Nate.

   Large, beastly butterflies have taken up residence in my stomach.

   Since that one night last summer, Nate and I have maintained a level of professionalism that I'm very proud of, despite the fact that whenever I see him I feel a pull of electricity that makes my thighs clench. I did invite him to double-date with Nat and I for one of Nat's husband's movie premieres, but I managed to keep that night completely platonic.

It almost killed me.

Since then, it's been for the greater good of keeping a job that I enjoy that I steer clear of Mr. Sex-on-Legs.

Not that he's been clamoring to get me back into bed. The morning after *The Best Sex in the History of Mankind*, after I snuck out of his bed, he had been pissed. He'd called and texted, wanting to know what the hell happened, and I'd avoided him like the plague for a good two weeks, telecommuting from home and taking vacation time.

Then, he just stopped. All personal communication halted, and when we are together during business hours, he is the epitome of cool professionalism.

There are days that it pisses me the hell off.

And now, because the moron who had been in our department couldn't take the demanding schedule of our job and quit, I have to work alone with Nate.

Fuck.

I sit back in my chair and look at the time. Five thirty. I pull my glasses off and toss them on my desk and hang my head in my hands. So much for spending the weekend with a pint of ice cream and a good book.

I can do this. Pull it together, Montgomery. I've posed naked in magazines. I've had dinner with gazillionaires and hung out with movie stars. I have four older brothers who tease me incessantly and taught me how to kick ass.

I can handle the sexiest man I've ever seen in my life for a few hours without ripping my clothes off and having my wicked way with him.

I think.

Probably.

I pull myself together, check that all my calls and e-mails are set to forward to my iPhone, and go to the bathroom to prepare myself for this evening.

I'm happy with what I see in the mirror. My long, light-blond hair is still holding the loose curls I rolled into it this morning. My makeup is subtle and professional, setting off my blue eyes. I smooth on a fresh coat of nude lip gloss, straighten my simple cranberry-colored dress and skim my eyes over my slender figure. I was blessed with excellent genetics. I'm not as sexily curved as Natalie, but I was blessed with decent boobs, a perky ass, and a figure that got me onto the pages of *Playboy* magazine. Three times. I work out hard to maintain my shape.

Content with my reflection, I walk briskly in my black Louboutins to my office, gather the files Nate requested, along with my phone, and walk down the corridor to his office. His personal assistant, Mrs. Glover, is sitting at her desk. She's an older woman with gray hair and shrewd brown eyes. Her smile is deceiving. She scares the hell out of me with her sharp efficiency and her crazy ability to anticipate Nate's every move.

"Hello, Ms. Montgomery, you can go on in."

"Thank you." I nod at her and smile and head for his office, knocking twice and then opening the door.

"Come in, Julianne. Thanks for staying." Nate looks up from his computer and nods, his face completely blank.

"Sure."

Nate's office is vast, with large-scale, dark office furniture. The chairs sitting in front of his desk are plush black leather. There are shelves from the floor to ceiling with hundreds of books and files, meticulously put in order, no doubt by the efficient Mrs. Glover. Behind his desk are large windows with a view of the Space Needle and the sound.

It's beautiful.

I'm not sure Nate even pays attention to it.

I perch at the edge of one of the black chairs and set the files on Nate's desk, expecting him to get right to the point.

"How are you?" he asks, his voice soft.

"Um . . . fine, thank you." What the hell?

"I'm sorry about the short notice." He leans forward and braces his elbows on his desk, lacing his fingers, and keeps steady eye contact. God, those gray eyes are distracting. Almost as distracting as his hands and the delicious way he . . .

Enough.

"It's part of the job." I open a file and try to pretend that my cheeks aren't flushed. "So, what's up with this account?"

"How are Natalie and Luke?"

"They're fine." I sit back in the chair now and eye him speculatively. Why are we having a personal conversation? "Natalie is due in just a few weeks."

"That's great. Good for them." Nate grins, that elusive, sexy, melt-my-panties grin, and I find myself returning it. His hair is pulled back off his face, as usual. His chiseled jaw is freshly shaved, and he's wearing a black suit with a black shirt and blue tie. He never takes his jacket off to roll up the sleeves, and I briefly wonder why, then remind myself to get back to the conversation at hand.

"Yeah, they're excited. I'm hosting the baby shower next weekend."

"I promise not to make you work next weekend." He winks at me, and I about fall out of my chair.

Who is this man, and what has he done with my boss?

"So, about the account?" I ask as Mrs. Glover knocks on the door.

"Dinner's here, sir."

"Thank you, Jenny, bring it in." Nate rises and takes two large bags out of Mrs. Glover's hands. "That's all for today. I'll see you on Monday."

"Have a good weekend, sir. Ms. Montgomery." She nods to both of us and then exits the office, closing the door behind her.

"I had Chinese delivered. I got you your usual." He smiles and resumes sitting in his chair, unloading bags. He seems very happy with himself this evening, much more approachable and friendly than he has been since last summer.

What's his game?

"Thank you," I reply, realizing that I'm starving. I load a plate with rice, sweet and sour chicken and egg rolls, and we dig in, eating in silence for a few minutes. I feel Nate's eyes on me, so I decide to put my big-girl panties on and take the initiative.

"So, what's up with this account?" I ask again and take a bite of chicken.

"I don't have any idea. I just wanted to have dinner with you, and this is the only way I can see you."

Holy fucking shit.

I stop chewing, my eyes wide, and I just stare at his perfectly sincere face. "Excuse me?"

"You heard me."

I frown and set my plate carefully on his desk. "So, we're not working on this account?"

"No."

"I don't understand."

Nate lays his chopsticks down, wipes his mouth with a napkin and sits back in his chair, watching me carefully.

"I just wanted to share dinner with you, Julianne."

"Why?" And why does he insist on calling me Julianne?

He frowns again. "Do I have to spell it out?"

"I guess so."

"I like you. I enjoy your company." He shrugs, looking lost and a bit insecure. I'm so not used to seeing emotions on his beautiful face.

"But you're my boss."

"So?"

"So, we could both be fired."

"It's just dinner, Julianne."

"You're not looking at me like you just want dinner, Nate."

He cocks his head, and a smile kisses his lips. "How am I looking at you?"

"Like you'd like to fuck me on this desk." Holy. Fuck! Did I just say that?

Nate's smile disappears, and his eyes narrow. "Watch your mouth."

I swallow hard and blink rapidly.

"There are many places that I'd enjoy fucking you, including this desk, but right now, I simply want to enjoy a meal with you."

"Watch your mouth," I whisper, and his smile is back.

"Telling your boss what to do?"

"Somehow, I don't think we're having this conversation in a boss/employee context." I shake my head and stare at the man before me. "What is this? Why now?"

"Eat."

"I'm suddenly no longer hungry, thanks."

"Just humor me, Julianne."

"Why do you call me Julianne?" I ask and pick up another piece of sticky chicken.

"It's your name." His eyes are on my mouth, and I smile to myself as I grab an egg roll and bite off the end.

"Everyone calls me Jules."

"Not me."

"Why?" I ask again.

"Because Julianne suits you." He shrugs and takes a bite of his food.

"But I prefer Jules."

"Okay, Julianne." He winks at me and grins broadly before taking another bite of food.

"I'll bet when you were small your teacher sent home a letter to your parents saying, 'Doesn't play well with others.'"

Nate laughs, and my gut clenches. "Probably."

I realize I've cleaned my plate, and I throw it in the trash and bag the leftovers. "Okay, I ate. Thanks for dinner. Have a good weekend." I rise to walk out the door, but Nate leaps up and stops me.

"Don't go yet."

"Why not?"

He licks his lips, shoves his hands in his pockets and rocks back on his heels. "Stay with me this weekend. At my place."

I think I've entered an alternate universe. Or I'm on *Punk'd*. Yes, that's it. *Punk'd*. I start looking around the room, behind me, up in the corners of the room.

"What are you looking for?" he asks as he follows my gaze.

"The cameras."

"What cameras?"

"I have to either be on *Punk'd* or I'm being set up to be fired."

Nate laughs, a low chuckle that tickles my insides. "Why do you say that?"

"Because, you've shown no signs of attraction toward me in months, which is fine with me, and if I stay with you this weekend, we could both lose our jobs."

His smile is gone, and his wide gray eyes go glacial. "Number one, I don't give a fuck about the no-frat policy here. Any relationship I choose to have, in any capacity I choose to have it, is none of their business. And number two . . ."

He grips my chin between his thumb and forefinger and pulls me to him, slides his lips over mine, softly kissing me, persuading my lips open, and I'm reminded just how well this man can kiss.

He must have taken classes at some point.

I melt against him and brace my hands on his narrow hips. His fingers weave through my hair, and as this kiss goes on and on, my body relaxes against him in relief that he still finds me attractive, and in pure unadulterated lust.

"I definitely find you attractive, baby." He whispers the words against my forehead and plants a soft kiss there.

He caresses my cheek with the backs of his fingers, and his gray eyes have softened. "So, what do you say? Spend the weekend with me?"

two

What in the hell am I supposed to do? Nate's gray eyes are gazing into mine, and I see a hint of nervousness that I've never seen on his striking face before. He's always so self-contained, so confident. It's one of the things I'm most attracted to about him. I've felt pulled to him from day one, and not just physically, although he is something to write home about. He's also the smartest man I've ever met, and there is something here that I can't deny.

But . . . and there's always a *but* . . . he's my boss. And the last time I spent time with him at his place, it ended in disaster.

"I don't want to make things hard for us here," I find myself muttering.

"Things are already hard for us here. We've been struggling for eight months to pretend that there's nothing between us, and we both know it's a lie." He pulls away from me and shoves his hands back in his pockets, and I know he's giving me some space, letting me decide.

I shake my head and look down at my shoes, planting my hands on my hips.

"Unless *you* aren't interested in *me*, and if that's the case, I sincerely apologize."

I whip my head up at the chill in his voice and find his eyes narrowed on my face, searching. This is it, he's given me an out.

Tell him you're not interested. Walk away, Jules.

But I can't. I just . . . can't. And it fucking pisses me off that I'm feeling vulnerable and confused.

"I don't know what to do," I whisper and close my eyes.

"Don't overthink it," he whispers back.

Natalie is right. Whispering is sexy as hell.

"Let's just spend a few days getting to know each other better," he says. "If we decide there's no chemistry, fine, we'll get back to business as usual, no hard feelings." He reaches out and runs his knuckles down my cheek again, and his eyes warm, and I know I'm sunk. "I'd like to spend a few days with you, away from here."

I turn away from him and walk to his windows, looking out at the twinkling lights of the city. I want this. Two days with Nate, not worrying about saying or doing or looking at him in an inappropriate way, just being myself. Maybe we'll hate each other by morning.

I doubt that.

I take a deep breath and turn around. He's standing there, his hands still in his pockets, looking sexy as sin in that suit, his face completely sober, his eyes searching mine, and I know I can't resist what he's offering.

"I'll meet you at your place in two hours."

A smile tickles his lips. "I can pick you up."

"No, I'd rather have my own car." He frowns, and I explain further. "If you hate me by morning, I don't want to be dependent on you for a ride home."

"I'm not going to hate you, Julianne, but if that's the way you want it, fine. I have one condition."

I raise my eyebrows. "What's that?"

"You will not run out on me this time. If you decide you want to leave, it will be after you've discussed it with me first so I don't wake up to any surprises."

"Okay," I murmur. "Did I wound your fragile ego that badly?" I ask sarcastically.

"No, you hurt my feelings, and that doesn't happen often. I'd rather not relive it."

Oh.

Before I can respond, he walks to his desk and gathers his keys, wallet and the leftovers, locks up his desk and grabs a briefcase. "Let's go."

YOGA PANTS, TANK, Nikes. Extra underwear, bras, jeans, T-shirts.

Jesus, Jules, you'll only be gone for forty-eight hours, and that's if you're not completely sick of each other by tomorrow.

I survey my small suitcase, and then grab my new strapless gray dress with pink stilettos, handbag and accessories. Maybe we'll go out.

I throw in some toiletries, jewelry, and makeup. Then I shove my iPad into the Louis Vuitton handbag that my obsessively generous brother-in-law got for me and load everything into my little red car.

Good Lord, it looks like I'm moving in.

Aren't I? For the weekend, anyway.

Before I can chicken out, I lock up the house and drive back into the city to Nate's condo building in downtown Seattle. He texted me the address, but I remember the way. How could I forget?

I park underground in the extra space he owns, grab my small gray suitcase and purse and head for the elevator.

Dear God, I'm going to throw up.

I watch the numbers above the door climb as the elevator ascends to the thirtieth floor, and as each floor passes, anticipation and nervousness grip my chest. I'm not convinced that this is a good idea. Yet here I am.

I take a deep breath and ring Nate's doorbell. He answers quickly, opening the door wide and standing back to let me in. He's changed into soft faded blue jeans and a long-sleeved white T-shirt, his hair loose and pushed back from his face, just screaming for my fingers to be buried in it, and I'm glad that I had the foresight to change into blue jeans and a simple black T-shirt myself.

"I was afraid you'd change your mind." He smiles gently at me, his gray eyes warm.

"No need to worry, here I am." He takes the handle to my suitcase and sets it aside, closing the door, and then pulls me into him, his arms wrapped around my shoulders. I brace my hands on his lean, jean-clad hips, and we just stand here, looking at each other.

"Thank you," he murmurs.

"For what?"

"Agreeing to spend the weekend with me." He leans down and kisses my forehead gently, and I frown. This is a new side to Nate. I like it. How many more sides to him will I meet this weekend?

"Well, I've always found you to be pretty persuasive." I smile up at him, and I see the humor in his eyes.

"I'm happy to hear that." He steps back and links my fingers with his. "Let's get you settled."

Still holding my hand, he wheels my suitcase behind us and leads me through his condo. It's really spectacular. The floors are all a honey-colored hardwood. The front door opens up into a great room with tall ceilings and large windows with a great view of Seattle and the sound. The furniture is lush and inviting, in brown and red tones. The kitchen is to die for, and I can't wait to get in there and cook.

Cooking is a passion of mine.

This kitchen gives me a girl hard-on. Seriously.

Six-burner natural gas stove, with a grill, double oven and warming drawer, two sinks, lots of light-colored granite counter space, and a huge refrigerator.

"Can I cook for you this weekend?" I ask as we pass by the kitchen.

"You cook?" he asks, looking back at me with surprise.

"I love to cook." I smile. "Do you?"

"I do, too. Perhaps we can cook together?"

"Okay."

He turns away from me again, leading me from the room, toward the bedrooms. God, he's something to look at. Especially in jeans, which I've never seen him in before. His shoulders are so broad, and his T-shirt hugs the muscles across his back. His jeans fall off his hips in that sexy way that toned men have that make women sit up and drool.

And I don't know what it is about a sexy man barefoot in jeans, but holy shit.

Are we seriously going to jump right into bed? No, *Hey, would you like a drink? Or would you like to watch a movie?*

Just, *Welcome to my home, get in my bed?*

Nate leads me down the hall and points out a guest bathroom and an office. Then he walks right past his bedroom and stops at the door at the end of the hall. He opens the door and walks in, and I follow, completely confused.

"This is my spare bedroom. You're welcome to use it while you're here." He places my suitcase on the ottoman at the end of the beautiful, queen-size bed. The headboard is black swirly wrought iron, and the bedding is blue and green, matching the nautical-themed artwork on the walls.

"I'm not sleeping in your room?" I ask and cock my head, studying him.

"You're welcome to sleep in my room if that's what you want, but I don't want to assume anything. I told you that I wanted to spend the weekend with you to get to know you better, and that's the truth. If you sleep with me, I won't be able to keep my hands off you, and if there is no sex this weekend, I'm okay with that."

I raise an eyebrow. "You're okay with no sex?"

"It'll kill me because all I've thought about for the better part of a year now is getting your beautiful body naked, in the light this time so I can see you, but there's time for that." He walks back to me, those beautiful gray eyes on mine, and runs his fingertip down my cheek. "You are so lovely, Julianne. I love your gorgeous blond hair and your blue eyes. And I so enjoy your smart mouth."

Holy. Crap.

But then my snarky side rears her ugly head for a moment. We haven't slept together since last summer, and I know, just by looking at him, that he wouldn't lack for willing bodies to bang, should he so choose.

He leads me out of the bedroom and back into the great room.

"Would you like something to drink?"

"Water would be great." I need to keep a clear head while I'm processing all of this. No sex? With Nate? Why stay here then?

"I have a question," I say.

Nate crosses the living space to the kitchen and pulls water and a beer out of the fridge and saunters back over to me. "Shoot."

He passes me the water, and we both sit on a soft, light brown couch. I kick my flats off and pull my feet up under me and settle in.

"If you don't want to have sex with me, why am I staying over-night? We could just meet up during the day."

His fabulous gray eyes turn arctic, and I know I've said the wrong thing.

"I didn't say I don't want to have sex with you. I said it's up to you. And I want you, here, for a full forty-eight hours. I don't want you to run away from me this time."

He takes a pull off his beer and glares at me.

Okay.

"Any more questions?" he asks with a raised eyebrow.

"One. How many other women have you fucked since I was here last?"

three

H oly fucking shit! Why did that just come out of my mouth?

Because I want to know.

Nate's eyes go wide and then pissed off again. "Julianne, if you had been paying attention to me over the past year, you'd have noticed that I'm not interested in any woman, for fucking or otherwise, except you."

Oh. Really?

He pulls his sleeves up to his mid-forearms and runs his hands through his hair in frustration, and my eyes zero in on his right arm.

"What is this?" I scoot closer to him and can't help but run my fingers down his arm.

"A tattoo." A smile tickles his lips, and I smile back at him.

"Does it go all the way up your arm?"

"Yes. It's a sleeve."

Oh my God, it's sexy. It looks tribal, and it swirls around his forearm, from just above his wrist, disappearing under his shirt.

"So, my conservative-looking, suit-wearing boss has a tattoo and has his penis pierced?" I ask with a smile.

Nate laughs and takes another pull on his beer. "Yes. You didn't seem to mind the piercing, if memory serves correctly."

And just like that my panties are soaked, and I am on fire. No, I didn't mind at all.

"No, I don't mind it." I smirk. "I just didn't expect it. How long have you had this?" I run my finger down his arm again, and Nate grabs my hand and kisses it, then links his fingers with mine and rests them in his lap.

"Since my early twenties."

"Were you a bad boy?" I ask, teasing him.

"Oh, I think I still am on occasion." He's grinning, a full-out grin, and it just takes my breath away.

"You don't smile enough," I murmur.

"I don't?"

"No, you have a great smile."

"Thank you. Want to know a secret?"

"Definitely."

Nate's still grinning, and he has an edgy, bad-boy sparkle in his sexy gray eyes. He props his gorgeous feet on the ottoman in front of him, crossing them at the ankle.

"Most of my front teeth are fake."

"What? Why?"

"Because they got knocked out."

"Oh my God! Were you in an accident?" What the hell happened to him?

Nate laughs, and I'm completely confused.

"No, I used to fight."

"Fight with whom?"

"With other guys who signed up for it."

"I'm lost." I'm frowning at him. What the hell is he talking about?

"I used to be a UFC fighter, Julianne." He's still smiling, delighted with himself.

"You do MMA?" I ask. I shouldn't be surprised. That's exactly the kind of body he has.

"You know mixed martial arts?" he asks, his eyebrows raised almost to his hairline.

"Nate, I have four older brothers and a father. Not only did they all teach me how to protect myself, they made me sit and watch that crap or play it on the Xbox all the damn time. It's much to their dismay that I wear makeup and love pink."

"So, you're a badass, Miss Montgomery?"

"I am, Mr. McKenna."

"Wanna prove it?" He's smiling again, delighted with me, and I'm smiling back at him. Who knew sitting and talking with Nate could be so easy?

And who knew we'd have so much in common?

"Right now?"

"No, tomorrow. Come to the gym with me."

"I don't know." I shake my head. "I might really hurt that pretty face of yours."

"You think my face is pretty?" He kisses my knuckles, one by one, then leans over and kisses my cheek.

"You know your face is pretty."

"I know *your* face is pretty."

"It's just a face," I respond and shrug. I have always received a lot of attention because of my face, and my body. It's just genetics.

Nate narrows his eyes at me, his mouth forming a hard line. "Julianne, your beautiful face is only out-matched by what's inside you."

What the fuck? No one, *no man anyway*, has ever said anything about what's inside me. Unless he was referring to his dick.

I gasp and feel my eyes go wide. This is why I'm drawn to him. He completely throws me off-kilter.

"Well, aren't you the charmer?" I ask, trying desperately to lighten the mood.

Nate smiles again. "So, are you coming with me or not?"

"If you think you can take me, sure, I'll come with you."

"Did you bring workout clothes?"

"Yes."

"Good."

"So . . ." I look around his beautiful apartment. "Did you decorate this yourself?"

Nate laughs, and I feel the pull in my belly. I love his laugh. "No."

"It suits you."

"You think?" He raises an eyebrow and looks around at his beautiful home.

"Yeah, it's masculine but inviting, and comfortable. And the kitchen is sexy as hell."

"Sexy suits me, does it?" he asks and kisses my knuckles again, sending shivers down my back.

I shrug and raise an eyebrow. "You have your moments."

"Well, speaking of my sexy kitchen." Nate rises gracefully from the couch and pulls me with him. "How would you like some dessert?"

"Dessert?" I echo lamely. Watching him walk is making me crazy. He's so graceful. He clearly takes care of that body. I can't wait to see what he can do at the gym tomorrow.

"I have chocolate cheesecake." He smiles back at me, and I gasp.

"That's my favorite."

"I know."

"How do you know?"

"Because at every business dinner, you always order it for dessert." He motions for me to sit on a stool at the breakfast bar and pulls the cheesecake out of the fridge.

He pays attention to what I order at dinner?

"So I was a bit of a foregone conclusion tonight then?" I cock my head and smile sassily at him and can't help but enjoy watching him squirm.

"No, nothing you do is expected, Julianne, but I was hopeful, and prepared, just in case." He cuts the cake and pulls two white dessert plates out of a beautiful dark mahogany cabinet. He joins me, and we dig in.

"Oh sweet Jesus, that's good." I lick my fork and close my eyes. Diving back in for a second bite, I notice that Nate isn't moving. "What's wrong?"

"You are so sexy." His eyes are burning with lust, and my body starts to hum under his hot gaze.

"I love chocolate," I murmur and take another bite. "It's my vice. I don't drink much, I'm not big on junk food, but chocolate is not safe from me. If you don't hide that cake, I'll have it polished off by morning."

"I don't mind as long as I get to watch you eat it."

I laugh at him as I take another bite, and he digs into his own piece. He nods appreciatively and licks his lips.

Oh my, those lips. He's so good with those lips.

"Am I seriously sitting in your kitchen eating chocolate cheesecake?" I ask. I can't believe I'm here. "If someone had told me this morning that this is where I'd be tonight, I'd have told them to seek medical attention."

"Is it that much of a hardship?" he asks, and I can hear the hurt in his voice.

Oh no! I don't want to hurt his feelings!

"Not at all. Just a surprise. This is just the last thing I expected."

"I'm glad you're here," he murmurs, looking down at his plate, then he turns that hot gray gaze back to mine.

"Me, too," I reply and take the last bite of cake. "Feed me cheesecake like this, and I'll never leave." I laugh and gather my empty plate and take it to the sink, rinse it and place it in the dishwasher. Nate joins me, taking care of his dish, and then leans back against the counter, watching me.

"My fridge will now forever be full of chocolate cheesecake." He smiles warmly, and heat slowly spreads through me at his flirty statement.

"Don't make promises you can't keep," I quip and hop up onto his counter, dangling my feet and watching him. God, he's a sight to behold. I love seeing his hair hanging loose, and I definitely want to see more of that tattoo.

I wonder if he has more of them.

I lick my lips at the thought of exploring that hot body in the light. Yes, I know exactly where I'll be sleeping tonight, and it's not in the spare bedroom.

"That's a promise I can keep, honey. I didn't want you to leave last time." He frowns and crosses his arms over his chest. "Speaking of, why did you?"

Oh. We're going to have this conversation now.

"I couldn't deal with the morning-after regrets."

"What morning-after regrets?"

"You said you wanted to talk in the morning, and I naturally assumed that meant we'd have the 'this was a one-time deal' talk, and to be honest, I was saving us both from that uncomfortable conversation." I bite my lip and close my eyes, feeling the humiliation all over again.

"That's not what I was going to talk with you about, Julianne."

My eyes find his, and I grip the edge of the smooth countertop. "It's not?"

"No." He shakes his head and closes his eyes and swears under his breath. "When I woke up and you were gone, it pissed me off. Then you wouldn't speak to me for days. You finally asked me to go out with you and your friends, and I thought we had a good time, but then you went back to being professional and cool again. I know you're giving me all the signs that you're not interested, but I can't seem to stay away from you."

"I like my job, Nate. I worked hard to get it. And I enjoy working for you. You're so good at what you do, and I'm learning from you. I can't jeopardize my career because my boss is hot and I'm attracted to him."

Nate smirks and then runs his hands through his hair in frustration. "It's none of anyone's business if we see each other outside of the office."

"But someone will find out, and then it could be over for both of us."

"I have very good lawyers, Jules."

Jules? He just called me Jules!!

I shake my head and look down at my swinging feet. I want him, and by some miracle he wants me, too. Can we pursue this, whatever it is, and keep it away from work?

"Hey," he murmurs and pushes away from the counter to stand between my thighs. He wraps his arms around my behind and hugs me to his chest. He's so tall that I'm only a few inches taller than he is sitting up here. "Don't worry so much about this, honey. It'll work out."

I gaze into his earnest eyes, my blue to his gray, and run my fingers through his soft, long black hair. For the first time in eight months, my world feels right. I want to see where this goes.

I want him.

I lean down and brush my lips across his gently and nibble the corner of his mouth. I lean farther and bury my nose in his neck and inhale the musky, clean scent of him, and against my better career-woman judgment, I cave.

"I'm sleeping with you tonight," I whisper.

"Thank Christ," he whispers back.

four

Nate pulls me against him, cups my ass in his hands and lifts me in his arms. I wrap my legs around his waist, my arms around his neck and hold on tight.

"I want you. Now." It's not a request. His lips are on mine, searching, hot, and I weave my fingers in that thick hair as he carries me through his apartment and to his bedroom.

"Lights on," I murmur against his mouth, and he grins.

"Fuck, yes." He flips a switch on the wall as we pass through the doorway, and both the lamps on his end tables come to life. I can see his room now, in the light, and it's simply amazing. Gray walls, white linens, large white furniture. It's masculine and clean and classy.

It's so Nate.

He crawls onto the bed with me still in his arms. I love how strong he is. I rest my hands on his arms, reveling at how the muscles move and flex as he lays me on the cool linens. He's braced above me, his hands planted on either side of my shoulders, his hips cradled in mine, and he leans down and moves that amazingly talented mouth over my lips.

Fuck, he can kiss!

I run my hands down his back and pull his T-shirt up to his chest. I want him naked.

Now.

He sits back on his heels and pulls the shirt over his head, and I gasp as I sit up, bracing myself on my elbows. The sleeve tattoo on his right arm not only goes up to his shoulder, but over across his right chest area, too. With trembling fingers, I trace the swirly tribal design, over his chest, around his nipple, and up over the top of his shoulder and down his arm.

"It's beautiful," I murmur and look up into molten gray eyes.

His gaze is searching mine, a slight smile on his lips, patiently letting me explore with my fingers.

I'll explore it with my mouth before the night is over.

I glance down to his left side, and I abandon his right side and trace another tribal design that curls down his rib cage, disappearing into his pants.

"Take your pants off," I murmur and look back up into his eyes.

"I'd rather get you naked, baby." He tucks my hair behind my ear.

"Oh, trust me, you will, but right now I'm on a treasure hunt. This is much more fun with the lights on." I continue to follow the beautiful design with my fingertip. He kisses me quickly, chastely, then stands and shucks his pants and boxer-briefs, and then the finest specimen of man I've ever seen stands before me.

I feel my jaw drop as I skim my eyes up and down his perfect body. Holy hell. He's all tanned skin and toned muscle, and he's breathing rapidly. That tattoo on his left side falls down over his hip and onto his upper thigh. It's sexy as I don't know what, and I am itching to get my fingers on it.

And then my eyes zero in on his impressive erection—*holy Moses, what that thing does to me*—and I gasp at the silver metal in the tip. The jewelry felt bigger than it is, and I don't even want to think about the process it took to get it there.

Suddenly feeling overdressed, I sit up and pull my shirt over my head, throwing it on the floor. Nate just stands there at the edge of the bed, his hot gaze locked on mine, and I lie back and shimmy out of my jeans and kick them to the floor with the rest of our clothes. I'm lying on the bed in just my pink bra and matching panties, and I smile up at Nate and do the *come here* motion with my index finger.

"Jesus, Julianne, you are so beautiful." His voice is rough with emotion. I've heard those words hundreds of times, from other men, photographers, my friends, but they've never meant what they do to me right now. With this man.

"So are you. Are you going to join me, or what?"

"You're quite demanding, aren't you? I'll have to do something about that." He smiles mischievously and crawls onto the bed, climbing on his hands and knees until he's hovering over me the way he was before, and starts kissing me in the slowest, most tender way. He's not just kissing me, he's making love to me with his mouth. And, oh my God, it's sending electricity through me.

I hitch my left leg up around his hip, and he grabs my ass and grinds his cock against my panty-covered center, sending sparks all the way up my spine.

"Oh God, Nate," I whisper, running my fingernails down his back. My hips are moving in a delicious rhythm against him, our breathing loud and ragged.

"Baby, I can feel how wet you are through your panties." He's kissing my jaw now, over to my neck, and then he sucks gently on my earlobe.

"I want you," I murmur.

"God, I want you, too." He pulls my bra straps down and pushes the material down my torso, unleashing my breasts. His delicious mouth closes over one, gently suckling, and his fingers gently pull the other, and with his cock rubbing back and forth over my clit through my panties, I'm about to come undone.

"Fuck, Nate, you'll make me come."

"That's the point. Come for me, beautiful." He rocks those hips again, and his lips close over my other nipple, and I just fall apart beneath him, crying out as my body shudders.

As my breathing calms, and I'm able to open my eyes again, I see Nate braced above me, his elbows on the bed beside my head. He's brushing my hair back off my face, and his eyes are warm and happy.

"Are you on birth control?" he asks.

This could be a mood killer.

"Yes," I whisper.

"I don't want to use condoms with you, baby. I know it sounds irresponsible, but I promise you there hasn't been anyone for me since before you and I were together the first time."

I shake my head. I want to feel him. Just him. And I trust him completely, which is so new, but we've known each other for a long time, and I respect him. "Me either."

"Really?" His eyes widen in surprise.

"No, no one. Did you think there was?"

"I just assumed . . . you're so amazing . . . Thank God."

I push him onto his back and straddle him. He reaches down and rips—literally rips—my panties in two and throws them on the floor.

"Didn't like those?" I ask with a smile.

"They were in my way," he responds and grins.

I raise my hips and, holding him in my hand, slowly guide him inside me.

Oh. My. God.

I need to kiss whomever invented the apadravya. A lot. It feels incredible, having those two small balls massage the walls of my vagina.

"Fuck, you're so tight." Nate's jaw is clenched, his hands cupping my ass, and I lean down and gently kiss him and rest my forehead on his, bracing myself on his shoulders.

I slowly start to move, up and down, and the sensation is just . . . so good.

"Oh, Nate," I whisper against his mouth.

"Yes, baby," he whispers back, and I sit up, and start to really ride him, hard. He raises his hips in a counterrhythm, bucking me up and down, and I'm lost in him. I throw my head back and revel in the bliss of Nate being inside me, and I start to feel my body tense, my legs start to shake, and Nate suddenly sits up and wraps his arms around my waist and his mouth around my nipple, and I come undone, shattering around him.

He grips my hips tightly and pulls me against him, hard, and cries out my name as he empties himself into me.

Our breathing is ragged as I rest on his lap. He's still inside me, and

I push my fingers through his soft hair. I lay my forehead against his and smile.

"Well, that was . . . wow."

He chuckles and runs a hand down my back, from the nape of my neck to my ass. "That was definitely wow. Are you okay?"

"Hmm."

"Is that a yes?"

"Hmm."

He laughs and lifts me off of him and sets me down on the bed. He switches off one of the lights, turns down the covers and tucks us both in, pulling me against him. I lie with my head on his chest and use my finger to trace the outline of his tattoo.

"You don't have any tattoos," he murmurs.

"No, I'm allergic to needles."

"Huh?" He pulls back so he can see my face, and I grin.

"I'm scared shitless of needles. Natalie had to get me stinking drunk in college just to get my ears pierced. So if you prefer girls with body art, I'm not your girl."

He chuckles and kisses my forehead. "You're my kind of girl, with or without body art."

"Yours are beautiful," I murmur.

"Thank you. Do you want me to turn the light out so you can sleep?"

"I like having the lights on so I can look at you," I whisper shyly.

"Go to sleep, honey." He hugs me close, and I close my eyes and drift.

I CAN'T SLEEP. It's two a.m., and I'm wide awake. Nate is sleeping peacefully on his side, facing me. The sidelight is still on, and I can't help but stare at him. His face is relaxed, his dark eyelashes lying against his cheeks. He's just so handsome.

And I'm restless.

I slip from the bed, out of the room and down to the spare

bedroom, where my suitcase and purse still are. I pull on some pajamas, grab my iPad and iPhone out of my purse and go into the kitchen.

Chocolate.

I help myself to a slice of the decadent chocolate cheesecake and check my iPhone. No messages. Good. I fire up the iPad and perch on a stool, nibbling on the second-most-delicious thing in the world, ranking just below the very sexy Nate.

Suddenly my phone chirps with a text. It's from Natalie. At two a.m.?

Can't sleep. So uncomfortable! Are you awake?

I smile and call her. I've missed her so much since she moved out of our place and into Luke's house just up the street from me. I don't get to see her as often as I used to.

"So, you are awake?" she asks drily when she answers.

"Yes, can't sleep. You?" I take another bite of cake.

"I'm so damn uncomfortable. This baby has something against letting me breathe these days. And she thinks my bladder is a trampoline."

I can hear the joy in her voice, and I grin. "I can't wait to meet her, Nat."

"Me either. Only a few weeks left. Can you believe it?"

"No, it's gone so fast. Are you excited for the shower next weekend?" I ask.

"I'm excited to see the family, but you know I hate it when you guys spend money on me, Jules. We don't need anyone to give us gifts. You know that."

I roll my eyes. I am never going to win this argument with her. She makes me crazy. "We love you, Luke and that precious baby girl. We want to spoil her. So shut up and be grateful."

"Don't be a bitch," she responds, making me laugh. "How are you?"

"I'm fine. But I have a confession." I have to tell her. She's my best friend.

"What?"

"I'm at Nate's apartment."

"What?" she squeals.

I explain about his e-mail this afternoon and dinner in his office and how I ended up here. There is just silence on the phone, and I think I've lost her.

"Nat?"

"I'm here. Fuck, Jules, do you know what you're doing?"

"I know that I like him, Nat. I don't know what's going to happen, but frankly I'm so tired of pretending that I'm not attracted to him. It'll work out." I bite my lip and push my cake away.

"I hope it works out the way you want it to, sweetie. Just be very careful. This could have disaster written all over it."

"Trust me," I respond sarcastically, "I'm aware."

I hear Luke's deep voice in the background and Natalie's response. "I'm fine, my love, just can't sleep. Jules, I'll call you this weekend. Luke's awake now."

"Good, I do not want to hear you two go at it over the phone." I roll my eyes again and exhale. "I love you, girl."

"Love you, too. Good night."

I put my phone down and rest my head in my hands. I told her the truth. I am tired of pretending. I'm not a great actress. But I'm going to have to continue to act at work like there is nothing going on between us. Can I do that?

Do I have a choice?

"Julianne! Fuck, Julianne!"

five

My heart slams into my throat as I twirl at the panicked shouts of Nate in his bedroom. I hear him lunge off the bed, and his feet are hitting the floor hard as he runs into the great room. He comes to an abrupt stop when he sees me across the room on the stool. His eyes are raw, feral, and he's panting, standing there in all his naked glory.

He plants his hands on his naked hips and takes a deep breath.

"I thought you left," he murmurs.

Holy shit.

"I'm here. I just couldn't sleep." I cross to him and wrap my arms around his waist, linking my fingers at the small of his back, and lean my cheek on his chest. "I didn't think it was really that big a deal if I got up for a while."

I feel his lips move against my hair, and I think I hear him whisper, "You have no idea, do you?" But when I lean back to gaze up into his gray eyes, his face is calm.

"Are you okay?" he asks.

"I'm fine. I raided the cheesecake and spoke to Natalie for a minute. The baby is trying to kill her." My hands are running up and down his strong arms, soothing him.

"Trying to kill her?" He raises an eyebrow, and I'm relieved to see the humor in his eyes.

"She's forty-seven months pregnant. She can't breathe or lie down and has to pee every three minutes. She texted me and asked if I was awake so I called her." I lean in and kiss his sternum, and he kisses the top of my head. This, being here with him, feels so good.

"Forty-seven?" he asks with a raised eyebrow.

"She's been pregnant forever," I respond defensively. "I miss her," I murmur and shrug, looking back up at him. "I don't get to see her very often these days."

"You'll get to see her next weekend."

"Yeah, it'll be fun. And as of this week I'm on call twenty-four/ seven." I grin up at him.

"Why?" He cocks his head and hooks a stray piece of hair behind my ear.

"Because I get to be there when the baby is born. Someone's got to keep Luke sane. Poor guy." I bounce a little and clap my hands, grinning. "I can't wait."

"What if she needs an IV?" Nate asks.

"Jesus, you're mean. I never would have pegged you for mean."

He laughs, a belly laugh, and I can't help but join him. "I'll leave the room for that part, smart-ass. So this is my official warning, for work: I may have to leave at a moment's notice if I get The Call."

"That's not a problem. If I'm not available, just let Jenny know, and she'll get me the message."

"Okay, thanks." I kiss his sternum again, circle my arms around his lean waist and hug him to me. "You're a nice boss."

"I'm so happy you think so," he says drily, making me smile.

"Are you cold?" I ask, nuzzling his chest with my nose.

"Not particularly, but my bed was cold when I woke up without you." He's combing his fingers through my hair. Yum.

"I'm sorry. I didn't want to wake you, and I was wide awake, so I got up. I won't leave again, Nate." I tip my head back and gaze up into those beautiful eyes. His messy hair is framing that to-die-for face, and the beginning of dark stubble covers his chin.

Fuck, he's amazing.

"Okay, thank you." He leans down and frames my face in his large hands and sweeps his lips over mine, gently, caressingly. He nibbles the side of my lips before settling in and kissing me long and slow and deep, as if his life depends on it, as if he'll never get to do it again. "Come back to bed, baby. Let me make love to you."

He lifts me effortlessly in his arms and moves across the room to his bedroom, still kissing me tenderly. He lays me on the cool sheets and covers my body with his and makes slow, sweet love to me, getting lost in me, and taking me with him.

I SMELL COFFEE. And bacon. Is Natalie cooking? Did hell freeze over? I roll onto my side and stretch and open my eyes and frown.

This is not my room.

Then I remember. The e-mail, dinner, coming to Nate's apartment, the cheesecake, the sex . . . Oh, the sex.

I sit up and wince. I'm a little sore, but that's to be expected. I haven't had sex in almost a year, and Nate's . . . well, Nate's big. I smile to myself and climb out of bed, pulling on my discarded pajamas from the night before, and wander out into the great room.

Nate is at the stove with his back to me, and I pause a moment to take in the gorgeous. He's wearing pajama pants that hang low on his hips, and he's shirtless, his hair tied back off his face. His tattoos are such a distraction, and they give him a bad-boy look that I so was not expecting. Who knew that under those conservative suits was a rough, tattooed, pierced fighter?

It's fucking hot.

He's moving about his sexy kitchen gracefully, with cool confidence. I can't remember the last time someone cooked for me, aside from my mom when I was a kid, or Luke when he and Nat invited me over for dinner last month.

But those don't count. They're family.

Daughtry is singing about it not being over from Nate's sound system. His voice is gritty, and sexy, and so appropriate to describe the hot man in the kitchen.

I saunter into the room, wrap my arms around Nate's waist and bury my nose in his back between his shoulder blades. God, he smells good. Body wash and sex and Nate. It's a heady combination.

"Good morning, beautiful." He turns in my arms, grabs my face in his hands, and kisses me in the only way Nate can.

"Good morning, hot stuff." I grin up at him and run my fingers down his face.

"Coffee?" he asks.

"God, yes. Please." He laughs and pours me a cup, adding just the right amount of creamer and sugar, and my eyebrows climb into my hairline. "How do you know how I take my coffee?"

"I pay attention." He shrugs, hands me the mug and turns back to the stove.

What else does he know?

"Can I help?" I ask and take a sip of coffee. Mmm . . . perfect. I could get used to this.

"It's just about done. Egg-white omelet okay with you?" he asks.

"Perfect. You'll work the bacon off in the gym when I kick your ass today." I put my sassy smile on and lean against the counter, sipping my coffee.

"I look forward to it, baby." He grins back at me and winks. We settle in at the breakfast bar and dig in.

"Mmm . . . good," I mumble around the food in my mouth.

He grins down at me and digs into his own plate. We eat in companionable silence, then I hop up and clear our dirty dishes and load them into the dishwasher. I turn, and Nate's watching me, his chin resting in his palm.

"What?" I ask.

"I could have done that."

"You cooked. I don't mind." I shrug and lean back against the sink.

"You look good in my kitchen."

"It's a sexy kitchen," I murmur and grin.

"So I've recently been told by a very sexy woman."

Oh, flirty Nate is fun!

"Really? Do I know her?"

"I think so. She has gorgeous, long blond hair, the bluest eyes I've ever seen, and a killer body." His eyes soften on mine, and he continues, "And she is so smart, funny as hell, and a very loyal friend. Oh, and her work ethic is infuriatingly solid."

Wow. What the hell do I say to that? I blink at him and open my mouth, then close it again. I cross my arms over my chest and look down.

"Look at me," he whispers, and I raise my eyes to his. "Whether you believe it or not, Julianne, you are a very special woman, and I'm thankful that you're here."

"I think you're special, too," I whisper and offer him a smile.

"Come on." He climbs off his stool and holds a hand out for me to join him. "Let's go to the gym before I strip us both naked and we spend the day in my bed."

"DO YOU HAVE a leather jacket?" Nate asks as we ride down the elevator to the garage.

"No," I respond.

"We're going to have to get you one." The elevator stops, and we walk out.

I wonder why he thinks I need a leather jacket. I'm wearing my black yoga pants, a tight sports bra and fitted black tank, and because it's spring and still cool in Seattle, a denim jacket. Nate is in long workout pants, a black sleeveless muscle shirt, and a black leather jacket. He has a folded black bandanna wrapped around his head, keeping his hair out of his face. I spot his shiny black Mercedes and my little red Lexus.

"Do you want to take my car or yours?" I ask.

"Neither," he responds and keeps walking. He stops next to a sleek, black motorcycle. It's long and lean, with chrome tires and handlebars.

"This is yours?" I ask, my eyes wide.

"She is." He offers me a wolfish grin. "You'll need leather so we can ride her often."

"It's not summer yet," I respond, backing up a bit.

"It's not raining today. We'll be fine." He eyes me and sees my apprehension. "If you'd rather not, we can take my car."

He looks so hopeful, how can I say no?

"No, it's fine. I've never ridden on one before."

"Well, I'm glad I'll be your first, Miss Montgomery." He swings a leg over the seat and settles in, pulling the bike upright and clicking back the kickstand. He holds his hand out to me to help me on.

"What about my purse?" I ask.

"Oh, here." He opens a satchel on the side, and I slip my bag down in it, then climb on behind him. The seat is surprisingly comfortable. He passes me a black helmet and helps me secure it before fastening his own. "Hold on to me, around my waist. Lean into the turns. Just sit back and enjoy the view, Julianne. I've got you." He kisses me briefly, and my belly tightens.

Fuck, he's hot. All these new sides of him that I'm learning are so damn fun and sexy. And so unexpected!

He revs the engine and backs us out of the parking space, and then we're flying out of the garage and onto Sixth Avenue. I squeal and wrap my arms around him tightly, smiling wide. What an adrenaline rush! I feel the rumble of his laugh against my cheek as I hug up against him and watch the people on the sidewalk fly by. The wind is cool, but it feels so good against my cheeks.

Nate swerves into a parking lot not far from his condo building, and I can't help but be disappointed that the ride isn't longer. He parks, and I climb off, smiling at him.

"How was that?" he asks, taking off his helmet.

"So fun!" I respond and remove my own helmet, hand it to him, then secure my ponytail. "I'm shopping for a leather jacket this week."

He laughs and climbs off, retrieves my handbag out of the satchel, and leans down to kiss me.

"I'm glad you liked it. Come on. If memory serves, you think you can kick my ass." He leads me toward a nondescript building. It looks pretty new, but there are no signs on it, and a passerby would just assume it's some kind of warehouse.

"Where are we?" I ask.

"My gym." He opens the door for me and ushers me inside.

Holy shit, this isn't any gym I'm used to. It's one huge room, with a loft above. There are treadmills and ellipticals in the loft. Around the perimeter of the main room are punching bags suspended from the ceiling, mats for sit-ups and push-ups, free weights and medicine balls. Metal bars are also suspended from the ceiling for pull-ups.

On one side, there are large tractor-size tires, and men are flipping them over, then jumping through the hole and flipping them again.

Holy shit. This isn't just working out. This is a sport.

In the center of the place is a ring. Two men are inside, wearing protective headgear, white tape around their fists, sparring.

"Jesus, Nate, I've never seen anything like it."

"This is where I've always trained."

"When you fought?" I ask.

He grins mischievously down at me and winks. "Yes, and I still work out here."

"How often?"

"Five days a week, when possible." He grabs my hand and pulls me into the room, and I realize that I'm the only woman here.

"Well, look who's here! Hey, son!" A large, well-built older man walks over and pulls Nate into a man hug, slaps him on the back and steps back, smiling wide. His face is handsome. His nose has obviously been broken a few times. He has dark hair, and he's solid muscle.

"Hey, Dad, I'd like you to meet Julianne."

Six

D ad? Did he just say Dad?

I plaster a smile on my face and hold my hand out. "Pleasure to meet you, sir."

"Call me Rich. Everyone does." He winks at me, and I immediately see the family resemblance.

"Please, call me Jules. Everyone does, except your stubborn son."

A look passes between Rich and Nate that I don't understand, but Rich quickly recovers and grins at his son. "She's got you pegged, son. What are you two going to do?"

"I'm going to kick his ass," I reply before Nate can speak, and both men look down at me, surprised, and then laugh again.

"I guess she's going to kick my ass, Dad."

"Good luck with that." Rich winks at me and then wanders back to the ring to yell out orders to the fighters.

"You could have warned me that I'd be meeting your father," I murmur as Nate takes my bag and jacket and hangs them on a coat tree near the door along with his own.

"Yeah, but then you wouldn't have come." He turns to me, his hands on his hips, prepared for a fight. And I'm suddenly in the mood to give him one.

Maybe it's all the testosterone I'm surrounded by.

"I don't do well with half-truths, Nate."

"Look, I'm sorry. I wanted to be here with you today. It'll be fun. My dad owns the place. He was my trainer and my manager when I fought, so of course this is where I work out." He shrugs and looks around the gym.

I eye him for a moment, enjoying the view. "Where do you want to start?" I ask.

"You still want to work out?"

"Yes, we're here. Let's go."

"Okay, let's warm up with the jump ropes and see what you can do." He grins and leads me over to a mat, handing me a jump rope.

Should I mention to him that my brother Will used to make me train with him for football season?

No.

Nate sets his watch timer for two minutes, and I jump easily, using the form my brother taught me. Nate watches me, also jumping with ease. I'm hardly panting when the two minutes are up, and inside I'm smug. I keep a bored, bland look on my face.

"Next?" I ask.

"You've done this before," he murmurs.

I shrug and drop the rope on the mat. "What's next, ace?"

"Can you do a pull-up?" he asks, his eyebrow raised.

"I can do one or two," I respond and smile. I have to call Will later and thank him profusely for being such a hard-ass. Thanks to him, exercise comes easily to me, and my body is in excellent shape. I love to sweat.

Nate guides me over to the metal bars.

"Do you need a boost?" he asks.

I look up at the bar. It's probably about seven feet off the ground. "I think I got it," I respond.

"Ladies first." He motions for me to go first. I rub my hands down my pants, then hop up, gripping the bar. I find the space between my hands that I like and begin to pull myself up, using a style Will taught me that he uses in CrossFit. As I come down, I push in an arc away from the bar, then swing back up, pulling the bar under my chin.

God, this feels fantastic!

I manage twenty pull-ups, then drop to the mat, shaking my arms and panting.

"Your turn." I plant my hands on my hips and look up at Nate, who is gazing at me with a huge smile plastered on his handsome face.

"What?" I ask, but I know I just shocked the shit out of him. I glance around to find all the men in the gym are watching me, their mouths dropped.

"Who trained you?" he asks.

"My brother." I shrug like it's no big deal. "Your turn, ace."

"Okay." He's still smiling as he leaps up and easily begins raising and lowering that sexy body up and down on the bar. His arms—holy Moses, those arms—flex and bunch with each repetition. I wish he'd take his shirt off so I can watch his chest. He effortlessly executes forty pull-ups and then drops to the mat.

"Not bad." I smirk and jump back up, gripping the bar. I begin the push and pull again, loving the burn that's moving through my arms, shoulders and back. After twenty I drop back down to the mat.

Without speaking, Nate hops up and completes forty pull-ups.

"Warmed up?" he asks, panting and sweating, and I just want to lick him.

"Yes."

"I want you in the ring."

I raise an eyebrow at him. "There's quite an audience here right now, Nate."

He laughs and grips my hand in his, pulling me toward the ring. "That, too, but for now, I want to spar with you."

Rich meets us at ringside and hands me headgear, helping me fasten it in place as Nate takes care of his own.

"You've got some upper body strength going on there, girl." Rich grins down at me, and I can see the unspoken questions running through his handsome head.

"My brother plays for the Seattle. He used to make me train with him." I smile at him as he wraps my hands in white tape.

"Wait," Nate interrupts. "Your brother is Will Montgomery, the football player?"

"Yeah." I grin, so unbelievably proud of my big brother. "He's a good workout partner, but he's brutal."

"I didn't know that." Nate has stopped taping his hand and is gaping at me.

"You don't know everything, ace. Are you going to stand there with your mouth hanging open all day, or are you gonna man up and take an ass-beating?"

The whole gym erupts in laughter, including Nate, and he grips my shoulders and pulls me in for a rough kiss, then pushes me away and finishes taping up.

"Good luck, son. Make me proud." Rich laughs and steps over to the side of the ring, leaning on the platform, ready to watch the show.

Thank you, brothers of mine, for making me take martial arts and self-defense classes, and for kicking my ass every time Mom wasn't in the room. The training is about to pay off.

Nate and I circle each other, his eyes full of humor. He thinks he'll take me down easy. Of course, he's bigger, stronger, and well-trained, but I have a few tricks up my sleeve, and I'll get a few good shots in before he takes me down.

I let him advance first, knowing he's not really going to hit me. As he reaches for me, I grab his arm, pivot, and stomp on his foot, jab my elbow into his stomach and roll us both onto the ground, me landing on top, then quickly roll off of him and back onto my feet. The guys who have gathered around the ring cheer, and Nate rises gracefully off the ground, grinning.

"Good one."

"Thanks." I grin back at him.

The next few minutes are the same, me using all the tricks my brothers and teachers taught me to defend myself. We're not throwing punches. We're grappling, and it's so sexy and fun! Finally, after a few minutes, Nate lifts me and pushes me up against the corner of the ring. His gray eyes are shining, staring into mine with lust and excitement and, if I'm not mistaken, admiration.

"You are so hot," he whispers, panting harshly, so only I can hear.

"Come on, McKenna!" a muscular, bald black man yells from ringside. "Stop dry-humping her against the corner and let her kick your ugly ass!"

I laugh and wrap my arms and legs around Nate. "Yeah, McKenna," I whisper.

He spins quickly, and suddenly we're wrestling around on the ground. I manage to squirm out from under him briefly, but then he pins me again, lifting my hips and legs off the ground, and I know I've lost.

"Shit," I mutter as someone slaps the ring and calls the match. Nate rolls off me and helps me up, then pulls me into his arms and kisses me fiercely.

I climb out of the ring, and Rich meets me once again to help me out of the headgear and to cut the tape off my hands. "Not bad, baby doll."

"I have four older brothers. I had to learn to defend myself against them. Mom couldn't always be there to referee." I grin at Rich. I like him already.

The crowd thins again as all the guys go back to their own workouts, and Nate joins us. "Ready to go?"

"Sure."

"You come back anytime, girl." Rich hugs me—hugs me!—and smiles at Nate. "You can come, too, if you must."

"Gee, thanks, Dad."

THE RIDE BACK to the apartment is no less exhilarating than the ride to the gym was. My body is still sensitive from our rigorous workout, and the humming of the bike between my thighs is doing delicious things to my core. I wrap myself around Nate. My nipples pucker against his back, and I squeeze his thighs with mine.

He inhales sharply and curses, and I smile. "Thank God this is a short trip."

He pulls into the garage and into his parking space. It's fairly dark down here, the only light coming from fluorescent overhead bulbs. It's deserted.

I climb off, and we take our helmets off. Then before he can lower the kickstand, I climb back on, straddling his lap.

"Hey." His eyes widen, and he grabs my ass to steady me.

"Hey, yourself." I lean in and kiss him, my hands on either side of his face, and he pulls me more snuggly against him, rubbing me against his erection still hidden in his workout pants.

"I want you," I murmur against his lips.

"Here?" he asks.

"Fuck, yes."

"Jesus, you never fail to surprise me, baby." He's supporting the heavy bike, and us, with his strong legs braced on either side. He reaches between us and rips my yoga pants at the seam of my crotch. *Holy fucking shit!* My panties are next, and before I know it, he's lowered the waist of his pants and is filling me.

"Oh God, yes." I lean back and brace my hands on the handlebars of the sexy motorcycle, wrap my legs around his waist, and he guides me up and down his beautiful cock with his hands cupping my ass.

"Fuck, baby." His teeth are clenched. He pulls one hand around and presses on my clit with his thumb, and I explode around him, pushing down on him, and he finds his own release, shouting my name. I hear it echoing in the parking garage, and I smile smugly, looking up into his hot gray eyes.

"I've never had motorcycle sex before." I lean up, wrap my arms around his neck and kiss him. He's still inside me, but anyone watching would just assume we're making out on his bike.

"Me either." He chuckles against my lips, lifts me off of him and pulls his pants up. I stand next to the motorcycle and wrap my jacket around my hips, knotting it at my waist. That should get me upstairs.

"I'm going to have to go shopping this week. You're tearing up all of my clothes." I laugh as we walk onto the elevator, and Nate pulls me into his arms, hugging me close.

"I'll replace them." He kisses my forehead, and I smirk.

"No need. I don't mind."

"Did you bring a dress?" he asks.

"Yes, why?"

"I'd like to take you out tonight." He runs his hand up and down my back, and I feel like purring.

"Okay."

"Good, let's go shower."

seven

I study myself in the mirror and grin. I've pulled my blond hair into a loose bun behind my left ear. My eye makeup is smoky and sexy, setting off my blue eyes, and pink lip gloss is smoothed over my lips.

It will probably be kissed off before we leave the condo.

My dress is light gray and strapless, with a sweetheart neckline. It's gathered between my breasts and has soft ruffles that fall down the length, just above my knees. I have pink diamonds in my ears, a birthday gift last year from Natalie, a pink bracelet on my right wrist and pink Louboutin heels.

Grabbing my gray clutch bag, I toss in my phone, lip gloss, money, debit card and driver's license.

Time to knock Nate's socks off.

Coldplay's *The Scientist* is playing. Nate is not in the great room or the kitchen, and I know he's not in his bedroom or master bathroom, because that's where I just came from.

Huh. Where is he?

I wander back down the hall and see the light on in his office. Leaning against the door frame, I watch him work. I love his work face. His eyes are narrowed, watching the computer screen, and he's quickly tapping on the keys, most likely sending an e-mail.

He looks absolutely mouthwatering in black jeans and a snug-fitting royal-blue button-down shirt with the sleeves rolled up to just below his elbows. I love seeing the tattoo on his right arm. His hair is loose, because I asked him to leave it down while we were scrubbing each other in the shower. A shower that took about four times longer than it should have because we couldn't keep our hands off each other.

It's like my birthday and Christmas all rolled into one when he's naked, and he seems to feel the same way about me.

"Am I keeping you from work this weekend?" I ask, smiling at him.

His head jerks up and those gray eyes go wide as he looks me over from head to toe.

"No, nothing important." He pushes back from his desk and saunters over to me, his warm gray eyes holding mine. "You are stunning."

"Thank you. You look incredible yourself." I run my fingers through his hair, and I don't care that I have a goofy grin on my face. "I like your hair down."

"Do you?" He bends down and softly kisses my neck, just below my ear. "You take my breath away, Julianne."

"I'm glad." I kiss his chin and adjust one of the buttons on his shirt. "Where are we going tonight?"

"There's a great seafood place down on the waterfront."

"Sounds good."

He kisses me, sweeping his lips across mine, and then lays his forehead on mine. "Let's go."

DINNER HAS BEEN enlightening and delicious. We have talked like old friends, and I've learned even more about Nate's childhood, growing up as an only child with just his father. We've avoided talking about work, so I decide to broach the subject.

"So, what's going to happen Monday?" I ask and take a sip of wine as we wait for dessert.

"I'm assuming we'll be at work," he comments and eyes me apprehensively.

"You know what I mean."

"Well, let me ask you this." He takes my hand and examines my French-tipped fingernails. "Is this a one-weekend thing for you? Do you want to go back to having a purely professional relationship at the stroke of midnight tomorrow?"

No! Is that what he wants? The thought makes me sick. I've learned so much about him in the short twenty-four hours we've been together, seen such an amazing new side to him. I enjoy his no-nonsense conservative side at work, and I can't get enough of the bad boy I've met today.

"No," I whisper. "That's not what I want."

He exhales deeply and kisses my fingers, relief evident on his gorgeous face. "Me either."

"So, what do we do?"

"We continue having an amicable, professional relationship at work, and whatever happens outside of the office is our business." He shrugs like it makes perfect sense. Like it's so easy.

"I'm not a good actress."

"Oh, I don't know, you've done well enough for the past eight months." He sits back and takes a sip of wine, not letting go of my hand, his eyes hooded.

There is no choice. If we give any clue at work that we're intimate, we'll both be fired. If we decide to never see each other again, I'll be devastated and brokenhearted. Neither option is appetizing.

"Okay. Business as usual."

"Excuse me." Our waiter approaches the table, and I smile up at him. "Aren't you Jules M from *Playboy*?"

I feel the blood drain from my face. I'm never recognized, ever. It's been five years since I last posed in that magazine, and it has to be now, when I'm with Nate, that some kid remembers seeing me in a magazine his dad probably had hidden under his bed.

I throw on my fake smile and wink at him. "I am."

Nate releases my hand, and I cringe on the inside.

"Wow." The waiter blushes and smiles back at me. "I thought I recognized you. I don't want to bug you. I was just curious. Your dessert should be ready in a second."

"Thank you, Derrick," I reply smoothly, reading his name tag. He nods awkwardly and walks away, and I take a deep breath and meet Nate's eyes across the table.

"I guess I should mention that I posed in *Playboy* a long time ago,"

I murmur.

"I guess you should," he responds. His voice has gone colder, and I cringe, on the outside this time.

"It's not something I'm ashamed of, but it doesn't come up often anymore. It was a long time ago." I shrug and watch his expression, which doesn't change.

"Why did you do it?" he asks.

"Well, Natalie used to take a lot of photos of me. She still does. The biggest part of her business is boudoir and couples photography. She got into it in college, and I was the one she practiced on."

"Go on," he says after Derrick places our desserts on the table.

"So, there was a talent scout in Seattle one weekend, and I grabbed a few of the photos she took and went there to see what they thought. One month later I was in LA at a studio posing for the magazine." I shrug again and fidget with my silverware. "It didn't pay very well, but I didn't need the money anyway. I guess it made me feel sexy, and girlie, which was important to me because I'd always been around so many boys, and it was fun. The photographer was very professional, as was everyone else on the set. I got to stay at the Playboy Mansion a few times and hang out with the other girls and Hef, and there were celebrities around. For a twenty-one-year-old, it was glamorous and exciting."

"But?" he asks, prompting me to continue.

"But, I didn't like the crude guys that would approach me when I was out with Nat. One guy cornered me in a bathroom hallway in a bar one night, and well, let's just say he had a hard time taking no for an answer." I swallow and look down at my clenched hands. "I beat him to a bloody pulp." Nate's hand flexes into a fist on the table, and I raise my eyes to his. "I literally put him in the hospital."

"Good," is his only response.

"I decided that posing those few times was enough. It's something I'll always have, but not something I need. I'm shocked that kid recognized me." I shake my head and close my eyes, wishing Nate would give me a clue to what he's thinking.

"Please say something," I whisper when it feels like minutes tick by without a peep from him.

"I don't like it." His voice is quiet and cold, and my stomach clenches in fear.

"That's understandable," I mutter, my head down. I focus on the tablecloth, running my fingers over it, steadying myself for him to say he's done. This is a deal-breaker for him. He thinks I'm a whore.

I've heard all those things before.

"I think you're incredible."

What? I whip my head up, my eyes searching his. My mouth is open in shock.

"What?"

"You heard me."

"You don't think I'm a whore?" Seriously?

His eyes go arctic. "Don't you ever fucking say that again."

"I'm sorry, I just . . ."

"Just what?" he snaps.

"I've heard it before," I whisper and look down again.

"Look at me." His voice is softer, calmer, and I raise my eyes to his again. "You are a brilliant, lovely woman, Julianne. You had a wild streak in college. That's something I can identify with." He raises an eyebrow, and a smile tugs at the corners of his lips.

"The problem I have," he continues, "is that other men have seen your beautiful body."

"I wasn't a virgin when I met you," I remind him.

"No, you weren't, and I can deal with that, although I admit it makes me a little crazy. But knowing other men have seen you, and fantasized about you, makes me want to put each and every one of *them* in the hospital, starting with our young waiter."

Oh. I don't know why that touches me, and I'm mortified to feel tears prick the backs of my eyes. I blink rapidly and try to find my equilibrium. He never fails to surprise me.

"So . . ." I swallow and grip his hand in mine. "So, you still want to see me?"

"Of course." He frowns like it's an absurd question.

I nod and look down at my chocolate cake. "Can we get these to go?"

"Great idea." He signals for the waiter and requests boxes for our delicious-looking desserts.

He's quiet on the ride back to his apartment, but he keeps a hand on my thigh, as though he just can't stop touching me, and I breathe a sigh of relief.

He still wants me!

I glance at his sexy motorcycle when I climb out of his car, and I smirk, remembering this afternoon. He smiles down at me and kisses my hand. "I'm looking forward to doing that again," he murmurs.

Oh, me, too!

"Do you want dessert?" Nate asks me once we get inside the apartment.

"Yes," I respond and smile up at him, running my fingers through his soft black hair.

"I'll plate these for us." He starts to turn away, but I grab on to his shirt and turn him back toward me.

"That's not what I meant," I mutter. Those beautiful gray eyes darken and look down at my lips as I pull my bottom lip between my teeth.

"No?" he whispers back and runs his fingers down my cheek. I shake my head and take the bag containing our dessert out of his hand. I walk over to the fridge, my pretty pink shoes clicking on the hardwood, and my gray dress floating around my thighs, making my skin hum. I stow the containers and turn back around, and Nate is standing right behind me.

"Oh!" I gasp, startled.

"Dessert should be eaten in the kitchen," he murmurs and cups my face in his hands, nibbling my mouth and pushing me back against the stainless steel fridge.

"It should?"

"Yes, no food allowed in the bedroom."

I smile and tilt my head to the side as he slides those amazing lips over to my ear and down my neck. I run my hands down his back and pull his shirt out of his pants, gliding my hands up his smooth, warm skin.

"You feel good," I whisper.

He groans and lifts me, pivots and sets me down on the countertop, stepping between my thighs. My fingers find their way into his hair, and I gaze up at him, a smile tickling my lips. "You're so handsome."

He smiles shyly and shakes his head and leans down and nibbles my bare shoulder.

"Hmm." Oh, that feels good.

He pushes his hands under the hem of my dress and up my naked thighs, to my hips.

"You're not wearing panties?" His eyes are wide as they search mine, and he grins wolfishly.

"I figured, what's the point? You'll just rip them off me anyway." I giggle, and he drops to his knees, hitching my legs over his shoulders.

Whoa!

He scoots me to the very edge of the counter, and I have to grip it so I don't fall. "I'm going to fall," I gasp.

"No, you won't, baby." He hikes my skirt up around my hips and parts my thighs. "Jesus, look at you."

"Nate." I squirm, and he smiles up at me.

"I think I'll have you for dessert, Julianne."

And with that he leans in and runs his tongue up over my labia and to my clit, then back down again and sinks into me, kissing me deeply, those talented lips kissing and coaxing my most intimate lips, his tongue working its way in and out of me in a perfect rhythm. I clutch his hair in my fingers and throw my head back, reveling in the way his amazing mouth feels on me.

God, I missed having him do this to me, and he only did it once before!

I feel his thumb on my clitoris and push my pelvis against his mouth as electricity shoots through me, through my limbs to my toes, and up my spine.

"Oh fuck, Nate."

He sucks my lips into his mouth and presses harder on my clit, and I unravel, completely coming apart at the seams. He rains soft kisses on my inner thighs, then suddenly he's standing before me, his pants unzipped, and his beautiful cock is hard and ready for me. I reach down and run my finger around the head and over the silver balls that I've grown to really, really love.

Really fucking love.

He sucks air in through his clenched teeth, and I push him away from me to hop off the counter, still fully clothed. I push him against the refrigerator and kneel, taking his cock in my hands and pushing up and down, loving how smooth and hard he is.

"Oh God, Jules, you don't have to do this."

I look up into his blazing gray eyes and frown.

"You called me Jules."

He gives me a cocky grin and shrugs, and I reward him with a grin of my own.

I resume massaging his cock and swirl my tongue around the tip, then over, tasting a small bead of dew. I like the way the apa feels against my tongue. I look up at Nate's face, elated at the raw lust in his eyes, and lick his shaft, from his scrotum to the tip, then sink my mouth over him.

"Holy fuck."

It takes me a second to get accustomed to the piercing, but then I find a rhythm, up and down, pushing my lips over him, sheathing my teeth behind them.

I push down until I feel those silver balls at the back of my throat and thank God that I don't have much of a gag reflex. Pulling back up, I swirl my tongue around the shaft, over the head, then sink back down. I repeat this over and over. Nate's breathing is labored and ragged, and I feel so sexy.

Finally, I feel him start to tense, and I move a bit faster.

"Stop, baby, I'm going to come."

Fuck that!

"For fuck's sake, Jules, stop." He pulls me up into his arms and kisses me voraciously. I can taste me and him on our lips, and I groan.

"In me. Now," I murmur, and he pivots so I'm now against the fridge, and he lifts me, his hands cupping my ass, and pushes swiftly into me.

"Oh God, baby." His face is buried in my neck, and I wrap my arms around his shoulders.

"Yes," I whisper.

He sets a fast, punishing rhythm, rocking in and out of me, and I know this won't last long. My muscles tense and clench around him, and my legs grip him more tightly to me, and I bear down, coming again, gripping on to his shoulders for support. He slams into me, hard, twice more and then tenses, and I feel him erupt inside me.

"Fuck," he whispers and rests his forehead on mine.

"Wow," I respond.

"Jesus, you have an incredible mouth." He's still panting, and I run my fingers through his hair and offer him a Cheshire cat smile.

"So do you, ace. You make me crazy."

eight

"Are you sure you have to go home?" Nate asks as he leans against the doorway of the spare bedroom, watching me pack my bag. I wrap my pink Louboutins in tissue and place them in the suitcase.

"Yeah, I do. I have laundry to do, and I need to get ready for my workweek." I smile over at him and am caught off guard at how gorgeous he is. I'm still getting used to seeing him dressed casually. He's in a soft gray T-shirt that shows off his muscular biceps where they cross over his impressive chest. God, I love that tattoo on his right arm. His faded blue jeans hang low on his hips. He's barefoot, and his hair is loose.

I catch his gaze, and a slow, sexy smile spreads across those beautiful lips. He knows I appreciate what I see.

Boy, do I.

"When will I see you again?" he asks.

"In about twelve hours, ace." I smirk as I add the last of my things to my suitcase and zip it up.

"You know what I mean, smart-ass."

"Dinner tomorrow night?" I ask.

"I have that business meeting late tomorrow." He runs his hand through his hair with a scowl. "Do you have plans for your birthday?"

My gaze shoots back up to his in surprise, my eyes wide. "How do you know when my birthday is?"

"Jules, we work in the same office. A birthday card circulated around for you last week. Not to mention, I have access to your personnel file."

"Well, that's just . . . creepy."

"Birthday cards are creepy?" His silver-gray eyes are laughing at me, and I can't help but giggle.

"No, you reading my personnel file is creepy."

"I love your laugh."

"Don't try to sweet-talk your way out of this, ace." I plant my hands on my hips and try my best to look stern. Nate pushes away from the door and saunters to where I stand by his spare bed. He takes my face in his big hands and tenderly kisses my forehead.

"I just wanted to know more about you, Julianne."

Oh.

"So do you have plans for your birthday?" he asks again.

"No."

"Good. I'd like to be with you for your birthday."

I rest my hands on his jean-clad hips and lean my forehead on his sternum. His hands glide back against my cheeks and into my hair, and we stand like this for a long moment, neither of us wanting me to go.

"I would enjoy that. Thank you," I murmur.

I feel him grin against the top of my head, and I straighten to look up at him. "Would you like to come to my place Tuesday night for my birthday? We can just stay in, watch a movie, or whatever."

He frowns and brushes his thumb across my lower lip, sending electricity through me. "You just want to stay in?"

"Yes. I just want to spend it with you. I don't need anything else."

Nate leans down and kisses my lips softly, then rests his forehead on my own. "If that's what you want, baby, that's fine with me. I'll bring dinner with me."

I grin up at him. "Okay."

"Are you sure you have to go?" he asks again, brushing his fingers through my messy hair.

"I'm sure. But I'll see you in the morning."

He frowns and looks down at my lips, then back up into my eyes. My breath catches at the vulnerability I see there. "What is it?" I ask.

"Work's just going to be different tomorrow. Thank you for giving me this weekend, Julianne. I've wanted it for a long time. I don't think I want it to end."

I run my fingers down his stubbled cheek. "Thank you, Nate. For everything. I had a great time."

I step closer to him, wrapping my arms around his torso, and rest my belly against his pelvis. I have to lean my head back to look up into his sober face. He continues to hold my head in those amazing hands, his fingers threaded in my hair. He stares into my eyes for a long time, a wide array of emotions passing over his face, and I'm mesmerized by him.

Finally, I lean in and kiss his chest and rest my cheek against him, hugging him tight. He wraps his arms around my shoulders and rocks me back and forth, kissing the crown of my head and breathing me in.

"Drive safely on your way home," he murmurs, making me smile.

"I will." I pull away and reach out to grab my suitcase, but Nate waves me aside and lifts it himself.

He takes my hand in his empty one, and we walk through the apartment and down to my car. He stows my bag in the back seat and kisses me chastely. "Call me when you get home."

"Okay. See you tomorrow, ace." I flash him a sassy smile, start my little car, and wave as I pull away.

Traffic is light on this Sunday evening, so it doesn't take me long to get home. I unpack my suitcase and start a load of laundry and then grab my phone out of my handbag.

A text is waiting for me.

I had a great time this weekend.

I grin and respond. *Me too.*

After a few moments, he responds. *Are you home?*

Yes. Home safe. Laundry in. What are you doing?

I walk into the kitchen and grab an apple and a bottle of water and settle on the couch, flipping on the TV to watch one of my reality TV shows.

Just working for a bit.

I smile as I picture him sitting at his desk, all sexy in his T-shirt and jeans. I'd love to distract him while he works. Yes, that makes the to-do list for the not-too-distant future.

You work too much. I send the text and watch in fascination as a fight breaks out on my TV between two annoying housewives. I don't know why I watch this shit. I'd never admit it to anyone, and the only reason Natalie knows about my housewives addiction is because she shares it with me.

We will take this secret to our graves.

My phone chirps. *I wouldn't be working if you were still here.*

I grin. *No? What would you be doing if I were there?*

He responds almost immediately. *Kissing every inch of your amazing body.*

Oh my. My face splits into a wide smile, and I curl my feet up under me as I settle in for some sexting with my man.

Only if I can return the favor. I would love to trace your tattoos with my mouth.

I love to trace your pussy with my mouth.

Holy fuck!

Mmm . . . you're good with your mouth, ace.

The housewives are still screaming at each other on the TV, so I mute it. My phone chirps.

Come back here, and I'll show you just how good with my mouth I can be.

Oh, I'm so, so tempted.

I thought you had work to do?

You are always more important than work, baby.

Damn, he can be so sweet.

I don't really want to sleep without him, with or without the sex, but I need a little distance. This is so new. I don't want him to burn out on me. And I have to get my head on straight for work tomorrow.

Ditto, I reply. And then: *Heading to bed early to recover from the amazing sex this weekend, and to dream of you. Will see you in the morning.*

Good night, beautiful. Sleep well.

But I don't. I toss and turn most of the night, wishing I were with Nate.

Fuck, I have it bad.

IT'S MONDAY MORNING. My five-mile run this morning before work did nothing to calm my nerves of going back to the office after my amazing weekend with Nate.

I fire up my computer, and while it wakes up, I go in search of coffee to try to wake myself up, too. I walk into the employee lounge, and standing by the coffeemakers, pouring himself a cup, is none other than Nate. Fire surges through me, and it's a shock to see him back in his sharp business suit, hair pulled back, looking all professional and . . . hot.

I'm thankful that his back is to me so I have a moment to paste a neutral look on my face and approach him as I would have seventy-two hours ago.

"Good morning," I say, proud of myself for maintaining a pleasant, normal tone.

Nate turns to look at me, and a moment of heat flares in those gray eyes before they go cold. He stirs his coffee, throws away the tiny red and white straw and nods at me, not meeting my eyes. "Julianne."

With that, he turns on his heel and walks to his office.

I face the coffee, my back to the room, and close my eyes tightly. Okay, that hurt. I know I have to get used to it. Nothing can change for us here. But seeing the chill in his eyes, knowing I can't touch him . . . *fuck.*

I pour my coffee and head back to my own office to find an e-mail from Nate waiting for me, asking me to compile some data on an account and ship it back to him ASAP.

Then I pull my phone out of my handbag to check for any messages, and there is a text, from Nate, received two minutes ago.

Good morning. You look amazing in that black dress. I wanted to fuck you in the break room, but I think that would be frowned upon.

Oh my God! I giggle, and my hurt feelings disappear.

You look delicious this morning. Almost forgot how hot you are in your suits. Of course, you're hot out of your suits, too, ace.

I missed you last night.

I sigh at this last text.

Missed you too. Did you sleep okay?

I bring up the Internet on my computer to start the work Nate requested when my phone chirps.

No.

Oh.

I'm sorry to hear that. Do you have any available time around lunch? I'd ask Mrs. Glover, but this isn't a professional request.

I dig into my research, then realize it's been at least ten minutes since my last text. I frown, wondering if he's going to respond, when my phone chirps.

I just cleared thirty minutes at 12:30. Told Jenny I need a lunch meeting with you.

My desk phone rings.

"Jules Montgomery," I answer.

"This is Mrs. Glover, Jules. Mr. McKenna is requesting a lunch meeting with you at twelve thirty." She sounds polite and brisk.

"Thank you, Mrs. Glover. I'll be there."

She hangs up, and I pick up my cell phone.

It's a date.

COULD THE MORNING have gone any fucking slower? Every minute was excruciating as I sat watching the clock, wishing time would pass. Finally, at twelve twenty-five, I shut down my computer and lock my desk, grab my iPad and walk with purpose to Nate's office.

"You can go on in, Jules." Mrs. Glover smiles at me, and I walk through Nate's office door, thankful that there are no windows looking out into the reception area, and close the door behind me. I silently turn the lock.

"So." I turn to face him and smile, enjoying the sight of him sitting behind his desk. His eyes are warm as he watches me cross the room toward his desk.

"So," he replies.

"Just to clarify, you are not my boss right now."

"Okay."

I walk around his desk, and he swivels in his chair so he's facing me, looking up at me. A smile flirts at the corners of his lips, and I can't resist him. I lean down, planting my hands on the armrests of his chair and kiss him, pushing my tongue past his lips, teasing him and pulling back, and suddenly he's wrapped his arms around me and pulled me into his lap.

With one arm wrapped around my waist and one hand in my hair, he pulls me hard against him and takes control of the kiss. He's kissing me as though he's dying of thirst and I'm the first drink of water he's seen in days. It's thrilling, intoxicating, and I wrap my arms around his neck and hang on for the ride. After long minutes of being in Nate's arms, I remember what my original plan was for this lunch meeting, and I stand up off his lap.

"Where are you going?" He grabs for my hand, but I pull it out of his reach and kneel on the floor between his legs.

"Not far."

His eyes widen. "Julianne . . ."

"Shh." I press a finger against his lips to silence him. "Just sit back and enjoy, babe. Nothing like a blow job to brighten up a Monday."

I unfasten his pants and pull his large, hard dick out of his boxer-briefs and immediately wrap my lips around the head, teasing his apa with my tongue, and Nate's hips surge up in his chair.

"Holy fuck, baby!" He grabs my hair in his hands and holds on to me as I move up and down his beautiful cock, gripping him with my lips, sucking up on him and then sinking back down until I feel that metal in the back of my throat.

I moan against him and jack him with my hand while cupping his scrotum with my other hand. I've never felt sexier, more powerful, more in control, and I love it. I love making Nate mad with lust for me.

"Oh God, yes, Jules . . . suck it . . . Oh my fuck, baby." His naughty words urge me on, and I move faster, harder, until suddenly he stands, picks me up by my shoulders, bends me over and is suddenly inside me. He grips my hair in one hand, pulling me back until it's just this side of painful, and grips my hip tightly as he slams in and out of me, over and over, before grunting as his climax claims him, pulling me with him.

He slips out of me and steps back, and I feel the wetness ooze down between my legs.

Nate gasps. "That's the sexiest fucking thing, baby."

I grin and stand up, shimmy my skirt down, and kiss his chin as he tucks himself away and zips his pants. "Can I use your bathroom, please?"

"Of course, help yourself. He gestures to the door that leads into his private bathroom, and I walk inside and clean myself up.

I saunter back into his office and find him standing at his window, arms crossed, gazing out at the view of the sound and the Space Needle. I walk up behind him and wrap my arms around him, pressing a kiss to his back. "Looks like we've got about ten minutes left of this lunch meeting, Mr. McKenna."

He covers my hands with his own, and we stand there for a long moment until I finally ask, "What's wrong?"

"Absolutely nothing." He turns to me and presses a soft kiss to my cheek. "That was a nice surprise."

"If you keep sexting me the way you do, I'll give you a nice surprise every day." I wink at him, and he grins delightedly at me.

"How's your day so far, baby?"

"Long. Yours?"

"The same. Better now, though." He kisses me and sits in his chair, pulling me back into his lap. "I'm going to be in meetings the rest of the day, so I won't see you until tomorrow."

I wrap my arms around his shoulders and bury my face in his neck. "Okay."

"Come to my place after work. You can stay with me tonight." He's rubbing my low back in a rhythmic circle, and I want to purr.

"You have a late meeting, remember?"

"I want to come home to you."

I lean back and search his sincere eyes. I don't want to tell him no. Last night without him was horrible.

"I don't want to sleep without you," he whispers.

How can I resist him? "Okay," I whisper back and bury my face in his neck again, enjoying these last few minutes with him before we have to go back to work. "I'll be there."

nine

Today is my birthday.

I fire up my computer to get the workday started when there is a knock on my door.

"Come in," I call out.

Mrs. Glover comes breezing efficiently into my office, carrying a large bouquet of colorful mixed flowers. "These just came for you, Jules."

"Oh, thank you!"

She places them on my desk and leaves my office, shutting the door behind her. I greedily pull the small white card out of the bouquet and open it, praying they're from Nate.

They aren't.

Happy Birthday, baby sister. Have a good day. Love, Will

He's sweet. Will is the closest to me in age. I pick up my phone and send him a text to thank him for the flowers then get back to work.

An hour later, there is another knock, and Mrs. Glover comes back into the room, carrying a large bouquet of pink roses. "I think you should just leave your door open today, Miss Montgomery." Her tone is dry and full of humor, and I laugh.

"Good idea."

I read the card, knowing these are from Natalie. She always sends me pink roses.

Happy Birthday, best friend. We love you, Nat, Luke and Baby

Oh, that makes me cry. I love them, too. I fuss over the pretty blooms and set the bouquet on the windowsill behind me.

By noon I have six bouquets of flowers spread all over my office, with wonderful, sweetly written cards from my family.

None from Nate.

Maybe he'll bring me something tonight. I shrug. We've only been seeing each other for four days. He's not required to get me anything.

At twelve thirty, Nate comes walking through my door, looking every inch the successful businessman in his black suit and red tie. I hold my smile in when I glance up at him, and I can tell he's doing the same.

"Do you have a moment, Miss Montgomery?"

"Of course." He closes the door behind him, and I've never been so thankful that I don't have any windows out to the main part of the building.

"Hi," he murmurs and looks around my office.

"Hi," I respond, rising from my desk and coming around to him.

He gathers me in his arms and kisses me deeply, then pulls back and runs his fingers down my cheek. "How is the birthday girl?" he asks.

"I'm good. Feeling a little spoiled." I step back and gesture at all the flowers, and he smirks.

"All of your admirers?" He quirks up an eyebrow.

"Yes, my brothers, parents and Nat are my biggest fans." I smile up at him, and his eyes get serious as he sweeps the pad of his thumb along my lower lip.

"I think I rate up there, too," he whispers.

"Oh," I respond, mesmerized by the serious look in his eyes.

"I have something for you." He steps back and pulls an envelope out of his breast pocket.

My eyebrows climb to my hairline in surprise. "Why?"

"Because it's your birthday, Julianne." He looks at me like I'm stupid, and I flush in pleasure.

"Thank you."

"You haven't opened it yet."

He passes me the envelope, and I rip it open. There is a handwritten note inside, in his handwriting, and I grin up at him.

Julianne,

I am delighted to have the honor of sharing your birthday with you. I'm giving you the rest of the day off and have set up an account at Neiman Marcus that has no limit. Go shopping. Replace the clothes I ruined over the weekend, and be sure to find a leather jacket, along with anything else you want.

Happy birthday, Beautiful.

Yours,

Nate

Wow.

I smile and look up into his amused gray eyes.

"This is where I do the obligatory 'you shouldn't have.'" I kiss him softly and rub my nose against his.

"And I'll do the obligatory 'but I wanted to.'" He grins, delighted with me, and I hug him close.

He's come to be so precious to me in such a short time. Or has he always meant this much to me and I just couldn't admit it to myself?

"Thank you, so much." I whisper.

"You're welcome. I wanted to send you flowers, but it wouldn't be appropriate here."

Oh, that's right! No wonder.

"I understand. This is a very generous gift." I nuzzle his chest and hug him tighter.

"You'll get your other gifts tonight," he murmurs and kisses my hair.

"What?" I pull back and look up at him. "This is too much as it is, honey."

"Don't be ungrateful. If memory serves, you hate that quality in Natalie."

Oh. Damn him.

"I'm not ungrateful. I'm . . . overwhelmed."

He smiles warmly and kisses me again. "I have a meeting. Go have fun. I'm serious, get whatever you want."

I grin and jump up and down in excitement. "Okay, you asked for it."

He laughs, a full-out belly laugh, kisses me again, and leaves to go back to work.

Holy shit, so this is how Natalie felt when Luke treated us to a day of shopping for her birthday. No, Natalie hated it.

I'm going to love the shit out of it.

I NUDGE THE front door closed behind me with my foot, my arms and hands loaded down with bags from Neiman's and climb the stairs to my bedroom, throwing the bags onto the bed.

I did good.

Nate was very generous today.

I didn't go crazy. I replaced the underwear he ripped and bought some extra because they are sexy and will most likely meet the same fate as my other lacy panties. I splurged on a couple of pretty nightgowns, and the rest is a hot, black leather jacket, shoes and handbags.

Oh, the shoes and handbags.

Two pairs of Blahniks and one pair of Jimmy Choos that are, frankly, to die for. Nate also got me a Gucci handbag and matching wallet.

He really shouldn't have.

I laugh as I pull everything out of the bags and put it all away. The smallest bag has a tiny wrapped box in it, tied with a red bow, and I hug myself, excited to give Nate his gift.

This gift was paid for by me, of course.

I hear my doorbell and race down the stairs to greet my man.

"Hi." I smile up at his beautiful face. He's let his hair down—*yum*—and he's holding a large bouquet of red roses in one hand and a white plastic bag full of food in the other.

"Hi, gorgeous. These are for you."

"Thank you." I bury my nose in the soft blooms, inhaling their sweet scent and grin. "Come inside, make yourself at home."

I step back and lead him through the house to the kitchen so I can fuss over my lovely roses and put them in water.

"Plates?" he asks, and I point to the cupboard that houses the dinnerware.

I love this house, and I'm thankful to Natalie every day that she lets me live here, rent free. It's beautiful, with a fantastic view of the Puget Sound. The kitchen is state-of-the-art, though not quite as sexy as Nate's.

I arrange my flowers and put them on the breakfast bar where I can admire them.

"These are fantastic. Thank you."

"You're welcome." Nate leans down and kisses my cheek, then loads both our plates with Italian food.

We settle at the dining room table, and I pour us each a glass of red wine.

"So, did you have fun today?" Nate digs into his lasagna.

"I had a blast today. Thank you again."

He grins, looking exceedingly proud of himself. "You're welcome. What did you get?"

"Oh, you know . . . lingerie, shoes, handbags . . . the things girls love the most." I smirk and take a sip of my wine.

"I'm glad." He takes my hand in his and kisses my knuckles. "I'd love to go with you next time. You can try the lingerie on for me, and I can attack you in the dressing room." His eyes are shining with humor and lust, and my belly clenches.

"It's a date." I finish my food and push my plate away. "How was your day?"

"Business was uneventful but profitable." He winks at me and smiles.

I'm sure it was. He's very good at his job. "That sounds like a good day."

"It's much better, now that I'm here."

"Such the charmer." I wink at him and nudge his leg under the table, making him laugh.

I clear our plates and take them to the kitchen, then snag the small box off the kitchen island. "I have something for you."

"Oh?"

I set the box on the table and smile. "This was not charged to your account today."

He frowns at me and looks down at the box. "You didn't have to get me anything. It's your birthday."

"You don't always have to have an occasion to buy a gift." I roll my eyes at him. "I wanted to get you something."

His eyes soften for a moment, and then they burn with excitement. I can tell he's dying to see what's in the box.

"Open it."

"Okay." He pulls the ribbon off and unwraps the white paper. Inside is a small black jewelry box. He flips the lid, and nestled in cream-colored satin are two platinum cuff links engraved with his initials.

His face is completely blank. I can't tell what he's thinking. He hates them? I just don't know.

Then his face transforms into his big, panty-melting grin, and he pulls me into his lap, nuzzling my neck. "Thank you, baby. I love them."

"You had me worried there for a second." I run my fingers through his hair and enjoy being in his arms.

"I'm not used to getting gifts."

"Get used to it." I kiss his nose and then sweep my lips over his mouth, sweetly kissing him.

"Well, since we're giving gifts . . ." He shifts, pushing me back on his lap, and pulls a small red Cartier box out of his pocket.

Holy fuck.

"Nate, you've spent too much money on me today already."

"Stop." He rests his fingers over my mouth. "I've been waiting a long time to give you things, Julianne. Don't rain on my parade."

Oh, he's just so sweet.

I open the lid on the box, and nestled inside are princess-cut diamond earrings. They sparkle brilliantly, reflecting the light from the chandelier, and simply take my breath away. They are easily a carat each.

And way too expensive.

I shouldn't accept them.

But when I look up into his gray eyes, I see apprehension and maybe a little fear, and I know I can't tell him no.

"Thank you," I whisper, overcome. Tears begin to run down my cheeks, and I don't bother to try to stop them.

"Hey, what's wrong, baby?" He brushes my tears away with his thumbs.

"I'm just . . ." I swallow and turn my tear-filled eyes to his, and I know I have fallen in love with him. Not because of his expensive gifts, but because of how gentle and generous and kind he is, not to mention sexy as sin and smarter than any man has a right to be.

But it's too soon to tell him.

"I'm just thankful, and maybe a little overwhelmed by your generosity."

He kisses my cheek, tucks me under his chin, and I curl up on his lap, enjoying the feel of his strong arms around me, holding me to him.

"Get used to it, baby."

Ten

"Oh!" I sit up and kiss Nate quickly on the mouth and jump off his lap. "I have something else to show you. Wait here."

I can hear Nate's chuckle as I run up the stairs to my bedroom, pulling off my clothes along the way. I strip out of my black skirt, thankful that I wore my black thigh-high stockings today, my bra and shirt and grab my shiny new black leather jacket. I push my feet into my new black Jimmy Choo stilettos and take a look in the mirror. Hmm . . . hair's not right.

In the bathroom I brush my hair vigorously, giving it a wild look, and touch up my makeup, adding red lipstick.

I look like a hot rocker biker chick. It's a new look for me, and I am totally *working it.*

I walk downstairs, jacket unzipped, and find Nate finishing with the dishes. His back is to me. He's taken off his suit jacket, rolled the sleeves of his white shirt—yum, that tattoo—and his ass just looks so fantastic in those black slacks.

"Need any help?" I ask, getting his attention, and am not disappointed by the drop of his jaw when he turns and looks at me. His eyes go wide and dilate, and I smile smugly, my hands on my hips.

"I see you got a leather jacket," he murmurs as he slowly saunters toward me.

"I had orders." I shrug. "I'm good at taking direction."

"So you are." He stops about two feet away from me and rakes those hot gray eyes over my body, from my Choo-clad feet to the top of my blond head, then looks me in the eyes and takes a deep, deep breath.

"Fuck, you're beautiful."

I can't speak. I can't move. I can just gaze back into those lust-filled eyes, and the blood rushes south, pooling between my thighs. I bite my lower lip and reach out, bunching his shirt in my fist, my eyes still on his, and jerk him forward so his chest is just an inch from mine. His hands are still hanging at his sides, balled into fists. Our lips are inches apart, and I can't stop gazing into his eyes.

"Nate," I whisper.

"Yes, baby?" he whispers back.

"If you don't touch me, like thirty seconds ago, I'm not responsible for my actions."

His lips curve up into a half smile, and he exhales, his eyes moving down to my lips, then back to my own. His fingers lightly brush down my cheek, the pad of his thumb across my lower lip, and I bite that pad, gripping his wrist in my hand, and then gently suck it, rolling my tongue around it. His eyes close and teeth clench, and the next thing I know, he's kissing me like crazy and pushing me back into the living room.

"Jesus, you're so fucking hot." His face is against my neck, licking and biting, just under my ear, and it sends the most delicious tingles down my back. He parts the front of my jacket, exposing my breasts, and kneads one, brushing his thumb back and forth over my nipple, making it pucker and my back bow.

Nate lays me down on the couch and covers my body with his, hitches my right leg around his hip and grinds his still-covered erection against my center.

"Oh God." My hands dive into his hair, and I hold him against me, rubbing against him, feeling his lips and teeth on my neck, and it's pure bliss. "Nate."

"Yes, baby?" He rocks a little harder against me and kisses me tenderly, and I fucking come apart beneath him, writhing and pushing against him.

Holy shit.

Before I can recover, Nate has unzipped his pants, and I feel the tip of his glorious cock, and those magnificent metal balls, at my opening, and he slams into me, burying himself inside me.

I cry out, lifting my hips against him.

He stills and lifts his head, his molten gray eyes boring into mine. "Did I hurt you?"

"No, God, no, don't stop."

He growls and pulls out almost all the way, then slams in again, over and over. I feel my body tightening, and I try to hold it back, wanting this to last.

"You're so goddamn tight," he growls, his jaw clenched shut.

It feels so fucking good.

"Let go, baby."

"Not yet," I whisper back.

He bites my earlobe and starts to slam into me even harder, gripping my ass in one hand and pulling me tighter against him.

"Yes, now. Do it, babe."

And I can't stop. The orgasm pushes through me with such intensity I can't even feel my teeth. I grip his ass in my hands, and he cries out as he slams into me one last time, and I feel him erupt inside me.

"Holy hell, happy birthday to me," I murmur and feel him grin against my neck.

He rears back and pulls out of me, stands up and pulls me up into his arms, cradling me against his chest, and carries me up the stairs.

"Where are we going?" I ask, as I run my fingers through his hair.

"I'm not done yet. We're going to bed."

Holy shit.

THERE ARE MANY things that I love about my job. It makes me think, it's challenging, I'm surrounded by incredibly intelligent people. On the downside, it is fiercely competitive, and colleagues can be brutal. In my experience, women are especially catty. The men I've worked with have been driven and don't involve a lot of emotion in work. There's just no time for it.

But women are a different breed. What is it with women and drama?

I'm not here to make friends. I have friends. But having an amicable working relationship with my colleagues is preferable. This hasn't been a challenge for me, for the most part.

Until Carly Lennox.

Carly joined our firm last summer, and she hated me on sight. She's really good at plastering a fake smile on her pretty face in front of the bosses, but her eyes are cutting. She'd give her right tit to throw me under the bus. I've managed to ignore her for the most part because she works on a different team, and I'm thankful.

But then there are days that I just can't seem to avoid her.

I breeze into the restroom at five p.m. on Friday afternoon. It's the end of the workday, and Nate and I are going to spend a good portion of the weekend together, again. We've spent every night together since Monday, alternating between his place and mine. We take separate cars to and from work, leaving at different times so we don't attract any attention.

Pretending Nate is just my boss, acting professional and detached, has begun to wear on my nerves. I never realized before how often I see him throughout the day. A few days away from the office to just be *us* will be a welcome reprieve.

"Jules," Carly sneers as I walk into the large, plush restroom.

"Carly," I respond, smiling sweetly. My mom always says, Kill 'em with kindness. It seems to especially work with the bitchy Carly.

"Plans for the weekend?" she asks and smoothes pale pink lip gloss over her pouty lips.

She really is stunning, with naturally curly red hair, big brown eyes, and creamy skin. She's super thin, though, with no muscle tone and no boobs.

That's what you get when you're a bitch.

"Yes, I have a few," I respond, deliberately vague. "You?"

"Oh, I have a date." She smirks and looks around, as if she's about to confide a deep secret and wants to make sure we're alone. "With Nate."

What the fuck?

My face doesn't change. I apply my lipstick, smooth my tongue over my front teeth and smirk at her. "Good luck with that."

I saunter back out of the restroom, my mind whirling. Obviously, she's lying. I have no question that Nate is not seeing her. He spends every free minute with me.

So what's her game?

I shrug her off and head toward Nate's office. He's requested another "after-work meeting" so we can firm up tonight's plans.

And so he can see me.

It's really quite ridiculous how addicted we've become to each other. But it feels so damn good.

Entering his office suite, I see that Mrs. Glover isn't at her desk, so I just continue to Nate's office door, knock once, and before he can answer, I open the door and breeze right in.

"Sorry I'm late, Mr. McKenna—" The words stop, and my world tilts on its axis.

Nate is sitting at his desk, leaned back in his chair, looking up at a very beautiful brunette perched on the edge of his desk, her long legs crossed, black stiletto-clad feet dangling. She's wearing a simple, casual maxi dress.

Nate is scowling up at her. Her fingers are running down his face.

I want to claw her fucking eyes out.

Nate's gaze swings to mine when I enter the room, and for a brief moment there is a look of surprise, perhaps regret, then he's his cool, calm, professional self.

Mrs. Glover clambers in after me.

"I'm sorry, Mr. McKenna, I wasn't at my desk to ask Miss Montgomery to wait."

"That's okay, Jenny. Audrey was just leaving." He rises from his chair and comes around the desk.

The brunette jumps gracefully off his desk and smiles adoringly up at him, but he ignores her, his gray eyes pinned to mine.

I clear my throat and thank the baby Jesus that I've maintained a neutral, professional expression, conscious that Mrs. Glover continues to hover behind me. "I'm sorry to intrude. I thought we had an appointment, but I can see you're busy. I'll be leaving for the day."

I turn to leave, but he stops me. "One moment, please." He turns to Audrey and says sternly, "The answer is no. As always. Don't come back here."

She exhales in frustration and looks like a spoiled girl who doesn't like to be told no.

"Fine."

She glares at him and turns on her heel to stalk out of the room, pausing by me. She gives me a cold smile. "We haven't met." She offers her hand, and I take it before she says, "I'm Nate's wife, Audrey McKenna."

eleven

I feel the blood leave my face, but I don't flinch. It's the hardest thing I've ever done.

"Hello," I murmur and shake her hand, then step back, avoiding Nate's gaze. I can feel his eyes on me, silently begging me to look at him.

Fuck him.

"Bye, babe." Audrey waves at Nate and saunters out of the room, and I decide to make a hasty escape as Mrs. Glover watches.

"I really do have to go." I back toward the door. "Let's reschedule our meeting for Monday."

"Julianne . . ."

I vaguely hear him say my name, but I ignore him and walk quickly, and with all the dignity I can muster, with my head up, out of his office. I know he won't follow me, not with Mrs. Glover and anyone else still in the office watching.

I use this to my advantage, quickly gather my handbag and jacket and leave the office, just catching the elevator.

What in the name of all that's holy just happened?

Nate's married? *Married?*

How is that possible?

My hands start to shake, and I just need to get the hell out of here. Once in my car, I race out of the underground parking lot and fight downtown traffic. Tears have started to fall, and they piss me off because I never cry, and he's made me cry twice this week.

I hear my iPhone ringing in my handbag and ignore it. I can't talk to him. I don't want to hear his excuses.

I risked my career for him. But even worse than that, I risked my heart.

Fuck.

My phone continues to ring. He just hangs up then dials again. Finally, I rummage in my bag, pull out the phone and turn it off.

I don't want to go home. He'll just come there, and I don't want to see him, so I go to the only other place I can think of.

I need Natalie.

I guide my little red Lexus through the gate to Luke and Natalie's home and down to their beautiful, white, modern house. I ring the bell and frown. I hope I'm not waking Nat up from a nap. She's so pregnant. Luke made her stop working a few weeks ago, and she's been taking it easy.

Natalie answers the door, takes in my tear-streaked face and steps back.

"What's happened?"

"I can't talk about it yet. Give me a minute." I close the door behind me, and she holds her arms open for me. "How do I maneuver around this thing?" I ask and hug her over her baby bump.

"Where there's a will, there's a way, believe me." She hugs me close and strokes her hand down my hair. "What's going on, sweetie?"

I shake my head, pull back and rub her belly. "She's almost here."

Natalie smiles widely and covers my hand with hers. "I'm scared out of my fucking mind."

"You'll be fine. Luke and I will be there. I'll kick the doctor's ass if anything happens to either one of you."

"That's why I have you. You're the brawn in this operation."

We laugh, and I follow her through the great room into the kitchen. From behind, you'd never know she was pregnant. She's hardly gained any weight, mostly due to the horrible morning sickness she's had. Natalie is the most beautiful woman I've ever seen, and I've seen plenty of beautiful women. She has long, chestnut-brown hair and green eyes, and her body is kickin' with luscious curves.

But her heart is the most beautiful part of her. She is kind and generous to a fault. She thinks I don't know that she paid off my parents' mortgage last year. Of course I know.

"Tea?" she asks and fills a kettle in the kitchen sink.

"Please." I sit on a stool at the breakfast bar and hang my head in my hands, my thoughts returning to Nate.

"Hey, Jules." Luke smiles at me as he walks into the room from his office. He kisses me on the cheek then moves into the kitchen and wraps his arms around Natalie, kissing her deeply, his hands roaming to her belly.

"Jesus, guys, really? I just got here."

Luke pulls back and smiles smugly at me, and Natalie goes back to making tea. He really is a handsome son of a bitch, with messy blond hair and the bluest eyes ever. And he treats Nat like a goddess, so I can't help but love him.

"What's up, Jules? You don't look so good." He leans his hips against the counter and crosses his arms, frowning.

I shrug and look into the great room at all the baby gear. "There's a lot of pink going on here."

I see Nat and Luke share a worried glance, then they both look back at me. I'm so not getting out of here without spilling the beans, but I'm not ready yet. Maybe if I don't talk about it, it didn't happen.

"It's a girl, Jules." Natalie smiles at me and rubs her belly.

"I know. Thank God. I'm going pink crazy myself." I grin and feel my eyes widen when Natalie flinches. "What's wrong?"

"She's kicking the shit out of me."

"Oh, I wanna feel!" I run around the island and kneel before her. She guides my hands where the baby is, and I lay my head on her belly, listening.

"This would be so much more fun if you two were naked," Luke remarks, earning a slap from Nat.

"Shut up, perv," I mumble and caress the baby bump while Nat runs her fingers through my blond curls. Oh, how I've missed them.

Suddenly, the enormity of what happened in Nate's office hits me, and my loneliness for my best friend overwhelms me, and tears start to roll down my cheeks.

"Hey," Nat murmurs and continues to soothe me. "Jules, what is it? You never cry."

I shake my head again and feel the baby kick my right hand. Oh, I can't wait to meet her.

"Do you want me to leave?" Luke asks and starts to move away from the counter.

"No, stay." I sigh and sit back on my heels, still holding on to Natalie. I know they are confused and concerned, but they just watch me warily. Finally, without looking up, I whisper, "He's married."

"Excuse me?" Natalie backs away and grabs my hand, pulling me to my feet. Both she and Luke are frowning.

"Nate is married." I turn and go back to my stool at the bar.

They look at each other again and then back to me. "What happened?" Luke asks, his voice low, and I know he's in überprotective-brother mode.

I am surrounded by overprotective men.

"I walked into his office this afternoon, and there she was, all leggy and hot and perfect, perched on his desk with her hand on his cheek." I wince and squeeze my eyes closed at the memory.

"What did Nate do when you walked in?" Nat asks.

"Nothing. What could he do? She got up to leave and introduced herself to me as his wife and left. His secretary was in the room, and to maintain a shred of dignity, I left and came here." I shrug and gratefully accept a tissue from Luke.

"Has he tried to call?" Nat asks.

"Yeah, I turned off my phone."

"Hello, déjà vu," Natalie says drily.

"Shut up. Luke wasn't married, for crying in the night," I respond.

The man in question clears his throat. "I'm right here, you know. Jules, you should at least hear what he has to say. Before I break his jaw, and he can no longer speak."

"He used to be in the UFC. But thanks for the offer," I murmur.

"You're sure she said wife?" Natalie asks, her mind working.

"Yeah, and introduced herself as Audrey McKenna." I shrug and sip the tea Natalie sets in front of me.

"It's hard for me to believe that you guys have shared all you have over the past week, and he never mentioned her. You've been at his apartment, Jules."

"I know, it doesn't make sense. Trust me, no woman lives there. It's a total man's place." I shrug again and shake my head.

"Maybe they're separated?" Nat frowns and rubs her belly again.

"As long as there is no *ex* before *wife*, I don't give a shit where she lives," I mutter. "Besides, even if there were an *ex*, he should have told me."

Suddenly, the doorbell rings, and we all look at each other, our eyes wide.

"How do I know who that is?" I ask.

Luke clears his throat. "Um, Nate called right before I came out of my office and asked if you were here, and I thought I'd heard your voice, so I said yes, but I didn't know what was going on, Jules."

I glare at him. "Tell him to go away."

"No, don't." Natalie walks to me and takes my hand in hers. "Just hear him out, then if you don't like what he says, let Luke kick his ass."

The doorbell rings again, twice this time. Luke stalks to the door and opens it. He murmurs to Nate, and I can't hear what they're saying. After about thirty seconds, Luke steps away from the door and allows Nate to enter. His eyes search the room and find me, and he moves swiftly through the room, and suddenly he's right in front of me, his arms on either side of me, braced against the breakfast bar, but he's not touching me.

"Why did you run?" His voice is cold, matching his steel-gray eyes. He's winded, and he just looks . . . pissed.

"Well, let's see." I lean back against the counter and go for sarcasm. "I'd just been introduced to my boyfriend's *wife*, after catching her with her hands on him in his office. And the fact that I'm using the terms *boyfriend* and *wife* in the same sentence really fucking pisses me off."

"She's my ex-wife, Julianne. Do you really think I'd pursue a relationship with you if I was married to another woman? Do you really think so little of me? Jesus, you know me better than that."

I look frantically around the room, but Luke and Natalie have disappeared. Great.

"Apparently, I don't know much," I snap back at him. "You've never told me you were married. She introduced herself to me as your fucking wife, Nate."

"What could I do? Jenny was right there. If I'd tried to explain, it would have given away our intimate relationship."

"You didn't correct her."

"You didn't give me a fucking chance to!" He pushes angrily away from me and paces the room, rubbing his forehead. He takes his suit jacket off and throws it on the couch and continues to pace.

"We've been divorced for seven years. We were only married for two." He shoves his hands in his pockets and scowls at me.

"Do you have kids with her?" I whisper.

"Hell no!" He shakes his head and looks down, then back up at me. "I was fighting back then, and she was what we call a ring bunny."

Bile rises in my throat. "I know what a ring bunny is."

"Yeah, well, I was twenty and stupid, and she wanted a fighter on her arm." He shrugs. "I rarely speak to her."

"Why was she there today?" I ask.

"She comes around when she wants money."

"You support her?" I ask incredulously, and his gaze whips up to mine at my tone.

"No, not anymore."

"What does that mean?"

"I helped her out for a while." He frowns and looks down again, clearly uncomfortable.

"How long is awhile?" Do I really want to know this?

"Until I met you." His eyes meet mine again, and they soften, and there's the man I know and love.

"Why?" I whisper.

"Because if I keep giving her money, she'll never leave, and I don't want any skeletons from my past fucking this up." He takes a deep breath and eyes me warily.

"Well, apparently, she's still coming around," I shout.

"I told her no. You heard me. I said it in front of you for a reason."

"Did you sleep with her until you met me, too?" I ask.

"On occasion."

Fuck.

"Baby, I cut all ties with her when I met you. I've told you, you are the only woman I'm interested in."

"She has your name." I blurt it out before I know I'm thinking it. This is killing me.

"She never changed it." He shrugs again, looking lost.

I take a moment and just look at him, this handsome, smart, sexy man. I don't want another woman to have his name. It means that he once belonged to her, legally, and it tears me up inside.

"Look"—he rubs his forehead again—"I'm sorry that you found out about her that way. It was shitty. But it was nothing. She is nothing to me and has been for a very long time. I helped her out because I felt responsible for her, and I slept with her because she was convenient. I don't feel about her the way I feel about you. I never did."

I watch his face, his eyes, and my stomach starts to settle. He's telling the truth. Thank God.

"You guys can come out of hiding," I call out, and Luke and Natalie emerge from the hallway, hand in hand. I smirk at them.

"Hey, I had to make sure you didn't need me to kick his ass," Luke says with a grin.

Nate laughs. "You could try."

"You okay?" Natalie asks quietly, and I nod.

"So, the shower is tomorrow afternoon at my place." I stand and walk over to Nate, kiss his cheek and run my fingers down across his jaw, reassuring myself that everything is right again.

"Do you need help setting up?" Natalie asks.

"No, I'm having it done professionally. I hired a party planner."

"For a shower?" Natalie asks, her eyebrows rising.

"I have a demanding job, Nat. And it has to be perfect, so, yes, I hired it out." I grin at her and do a little happy dance. "I'm so excited!"

"I think I might have some work to do." Luke's eyes are wide, and he runs his hand through his hair.

"Oh no, you're coming." I point my finger and glare at him.

"This is really a chick thing," Nate says.

"Whose side are you on?" I ask.

"Luke's," he states matter-of-factly. "It's a chick party."

"He's the daddy." I plant my hands on my hips and glare at both of these stubborn men while Natalie laughs. "He has to go. Besides, my brothers and parents will be there, along with his family, too, so it's a co-ed party."

"Will there be pink?" Nate asks.

"The baby is a girl. Of course there will be pink." I look at him like he's being ridiculous.

"Chick party." Nate sneers.

"A chick party that you're now going to," Luke interrupts.

Oh no. My panicked eyes meet Natalie's, and she offers me a small smile.

"I don't know if that's a good idea . . ." I look around the room and over to Nate, and he's frowning at me.

"Why?" Nate asks.

"I don't know if I'm ready to introduce you to my family," I whisper.

"Why?" he asks again.

I shrug. "It's kind of soon."

"You just called me your boyfriend ten minutes ago."

"I just didn't know what else to call you." I shrug and turn away, and then find myself pinned to him, his hand twisted in my hair and the other at the small of my back, pressing me to him, and his mouth— oh, that mouth—is on mine, kissing me urgently. Then, just as fast as he started, he releases me and backs away.

"Oh my," Natalie mutters.

"Be there at two," Luke tells him with a smug smile.

Twelve

I 've been quiet all through dinner. Nate and I ordered pizza after returning to my house from Nat and Luke's. We threw in an action movie and settled on the couch in the loft with our cheesy, delicious pizza and a couple of beers.

But I can't stop thinking about the scene in his office earlier today. If he didn't tell me about an ex-wife, what else is he hiding?

While Nate watches the movie, I clear our plates and tuck the leftovers in the fridge.

"I'm going to take a shower," I murmur as I walk past him on my way to my bedroom.

"What's wrong, Julianne?" He catches my wrist and pulls me down next to him.

I shrug and shake my head. "I'm not sure I know."

"Bullshit. You're still pissed about today." He frowns as I pull my hand out of his and scoot away from him, needing to distance myself just a bit.

"I'm not exactly pissed, as much as still a little confused and disappointed. Why didn't you tell me you have an ex-wife?" I eye him speculatively, and he pushes his fingers through that glorious black hair, swearing under his breath.

"Honestly, I didn't think about it."

"Look, I get that she was a long time ago. I believe that you haven't slept with her since you met me, and I'm not accusing you of anything like that, Nate. But it was not a good feeling to walk into that office and see a beautiful woman with her hands all over you, not after everything we've shared over the past week. So, yeah, I'm still on edge about it."

"I apologized and explained."

"Yes, you did. What else are you going to have to apologize and explain about, Nate? What other dirty little secrets are you hiding?" I get up off the couch, needing to get into the shower and away from him for a few minutes, but he snags my hand again.

"Don't fucking run out on me again. I don't have any secrets from you. *She* is not a secret. She's just part of my past."

I look down into his silver-gray eyes and soften a bit. His face is tight with worry.

I pull my hand out of his grasp again, and he scowls, about to say something, but I brush my fingertips down his cheeks, hold his jaw in my hands and look at his face. I can feel my own war of words and emotions playing out in my head, moving across my own face. Finally, Nate takes my wrist in his hand and plants a kiss in the palm, looking up at me.

"Talk to me," he whispers.

I straddle his lap and rest my bottom on his knees. He links my fingers in his, and I stare down at them, resting in his lap between us.

"Hey," he whispers again, "Julianne, talk to me."

I look into his eyes and whisper, "I guess I finally realized today how much you could hurt me."

"Oh baby." He pulls me against him, wraps his arms around me, and I bury my face in his neck, breathing in his clean, sexy scent. "Same goes here. Watching you walk out of my office today, knowing that I'd hurt you, not knowing where you were . . . It tore me up. I am sorry. I promise, no more secrets."

He kisses my hair, and I kiss his neck, his smell intoxicating, and I just know that I need him, right now.

I nibble up to his ear, pushing his beautiful hair out of my path. His hands glide down my back to my ass, and he pulls me more tightly against him, pushing the erection in his slacks against my core.

"I need you," I whisper into his ear, and fire surges through me as he growls in response. Wrapping my arms around his neck, I nibble my way down his jaw and kiss him, lightly at first, just teasing his lips with my own. My eyes are on his, blue to gray.

He pushes one hand into my hair, tilting my head and directing the kiss, taking it deeper, as he spreads his other hand across my lower back, pressing me more tightly against him.

I sit back and pull my blouse over my head, and Nate makes quick work of my bra. When my breasts are freed, he takes one swollen, puckered tip into his mouth and pulls gently, then pays the same attention to the other breast. I can't help but lean back, pressing my center harder against him.

Finally, he stands, sets me on my feet and strips me of my pants and thong. I help him out of his work shirt and pants, and then he lifts me, his hands under my ass. I wrap my legs around his waist and continue kissing him with a desperate fervor. I can't get enough of this man's mouth. It's magic.

Nate walks us over to the wall, and as my back hits the cool surface, he lifts me slightly and rests the head of his cock against my opening.

"I can't take it slow this time, baby. I want you too much."

I clench my legs around his hips, pulling him into me, and he accepts the invitation. He pushes all the way in, hard, and the combination of his large cock and that amazing piercing is almost my undoing.

"Fuck, Nate," I whisper, and he grins against my mouth, and then leans back to look into my eyes. He pulls back and slams into me again, then stills and watches my face. I'm panting, my cheeks flushed with lust. "If you do that again, I'm gonna come," I whisper.

His grin widens, and he pulls back, then slams back inside me even harder, and rotates his hips in a circle, grinding the root of his cock against my clit, and I come apart at the seams, my body shuddering and clenching, my blood on fire, screaming his name.

"You needed that?" he whispers and plants tiny, sweet kisses all over my face, across my cheeks, down my jaw, my nose.

"Hmm," I respond.

"Open your eyes."

My gaze finds his, and he's smiling at me gently, brushing stray strands of hair off my temples.

"Are you okay?"

I kiss his lips softly. "I'm okay."

"Good, because I'm not done."

I realize that he's not only still inside me, but he hasn't come, and he's as hard as ever. My eyes widen, and I tighten my arms and legs around him as he pushes us off the wall and starts to walk up the stairs, his hands still supporting my ass.

"God, you're strong." I run my hands through his hair, loving that he can carry me so effortlessly.

"You're just small, baby."

He carries me into my bedroom and pulls back the duvet. He climbs onto the bed with me still in his arms and lays me down on the cool sheets, his body hovering over me.

"You needed it rough, but I need this." He laces my fingers in his and brings both of our hands above my head and starts to move inside me again, slowly, pulling all the way out and pushing all the way in again in a slow, easy pace.

His lips are driving me mad, nibbling the sides of my mouth, right under my ears, sending sparks through me and down my spine.

"Faster," I whisper, but he just smiles lovingly down at me and shakes his head.

"No, just like this."

He's worshiping me with his body, showing me without words what I mean to him, that he's sorry for earlier.

I pull my legs up his sides, and he shifts so I can rest my calves on his shoulders without letting go of my hands, and he leans into my legs, pushing even farther into me.

"Oh, Nate."

"Yes, baby."

This slow pace is killing me. I tighten my inner muscles around him, and he clenches his eyes shut. With each stroke, I clench around him, as hard as possible, until finally he starts to speed up.

"So fucking tight . . ."

Our hands are still locked together above me, my legs on his shoulders, and he picks up speed, thrusting harder and faster, sweat rolling down the side of his face. I feel his body tighten, and I know he's about to surrender to the climax building in him.

"Come, babe," I whisper, and his eyes snap open.

He kisses me hard and cries out as he comes, rocking his pelvis against mine as he releases into me.

"Oh God, baby." He lets go of my hands, letting my legs down, and buries his fingers in my hair. I wrap my legs around his waist and run my hands down his sweat-dampened back. He's kissing me gently, our breathing slowly returning to normal. He pulls back just slightly so he can focus in on my eyes and says, "It's only you, Julianne. It will only ever be you."

NATE'S IN THE backyard overseeing the crew setting up the tent for today's party, and I'm more than a little bemused. How did this happen? How did this amazing man muscle his way into my life and start helping me handle things?

And why doesn't it scare the shit out of me?

I put the finishing touches on my makeup and approve of my soft gray, wide-leg slacks, white button-up blouse and wide black belt cinching my waist. I'm wearing my black Choos, and my hair is in a loose chignon, makeup simple. Birthday diamonds wink at my ears.

God, I love fashion.

Once downstairs, I survey the kitchen and grin. There is always too much food at our family parties, and today is no exception, but the whole kitchen and dining area is full of soft pink and gray. Puffy tissue paper pom-poms hang from the ceiling, and the linens on the table and breakfast bar match. My dining room table boasts a gorgeous display of pink, frosted cupcakes stacked on several tiers, and the top tier is an eight-inch round cake frosted in white and covered in delicate pink flowers.

I walk out into the tent that is now an extension of the house and gasp. Oh, it's so pretty out here.

The party planner brought in heaters for the tent. It is spring in Seattle, after all. A faux floor has been laid so we don't have to walk on damp grass. There are tables and chairs scattered about with more pink and gray tablecloths, and long pink, gray and white sheets of fabric are draped from each corner of the tent and gathered in the center. More softly colored tissue pom-poms are suspended over the tables. White Christmas lights are woven through the fabric, giving the space a sweet glow.

Alecia, my new party planner, is getting a big, fat bonus.

"Are you happy?" Nate asks as he wraps his arms around my middle from behind and kisses my neck.

"It's so beautiful. Natalie will love it."

He smiles against my neck. "You're beautiful."

I turn and gaze up at him, running my fingers through his soft black hair. He's wearing a gray button-down, fitted shirt and black slacks. His sleeves are rolled up, giving me glimpses of that sexy tattoo.

I want to lick him.

"You don't clean up so bad yourself, you know." I smile and brush his lips with mine. "They'll be here soon. Are you ready for this?"

His smile fades as he sees the apprehension in my eyes. "Yes."

"They're going to like you. After they beat the crap out of you."

That brings the smile back, and he laughs. "Why are they going to try to beat me up?"

"Because you're a man, you've had your hands on me, and they love me. And I think it has something to do with owning a penis. It makes men want to beat the shit out of each other. I'm thinking about doing research on it." I shrug, trying to look nonchalant, but I'm really nervous.

Really. Nervous.

"Have they always beaten up your boyfriends?" he asks.

"I've never given them an opportunity." I shrug again. "I don't bring men home to meet them."

"Why not?" He runs his knuckles down my cheek.

"No one's ever deserved to meet my family before."

His eyes flare, and his hold on me tightens. "Julianne, I . . ."

"There you are!" My mom bursts through the back door of the house and into the tent, her arms open for me.

Gail Montgomery is a petite blond woman with a big heart and loud laugh. She's happy, kind, and I want to be her when I grow up.

"Hi, Mom!" I pull out of Nate's embrace and wrap my mom in a big hug.

"Your father and I pulled up at the same time as Will and Matt. They drove together." She swings her eyes to Nate and smiles wide.

"Mom, this is Nate." I smile reassuringly at Nate, but he's already kissing my mom's hand and laying on the charm.

Why am I surprised? This man charms people out of millions of dollars every day. He's going to be fine with my family.

"Mrs. Montgomery, what a pleasure."

My mom melts and gets a gooey look on her face, and I can't help but smirk.

"Well, hello, Nate. Please, call me Gail."

"Why is it so fucking pink in here?" Will pushes his way into the tent, hands on his hips, glaring at me.

"Because, douche bag, Natalie is having a girl." I punch him in the arm before I kiss his cheek. "I owe you," I whisper.

He looks down at me with a frown. "Huh?"

"I'll explain later. I have someone I want you to meet, and I want you to be nice."

Will isn't really the one I'm all that worried about anyway.

"Will, this is Nate McKenna." I step back and bite my lip. My brother is taller than Nate by a good three inches and is wide-shouldered, muscled, and strong. He's a freaking football player, for the love of Moses.

We have the same genes, so he's hot in a he's-my-brother-and-he's-gross-to-me-but-all-of-America-wants-to-bang-him kind of way.

It runs in our family.

"I enjoyed last season," Nate states as he holds out his hand for Will to shake. Oh, he's good.

"Yeah? Why's that?" Will asks and shakes his hand.

"Well, we kicked Green Bay's ass, you didn't get injured, and you helped me win a bunch of money during the playoffs. Next season looks promising," Nate replies.

"He can stay," Will declares and goes back inside to find food.

One brother down, three to go.

And my dad.

I need a drink.

Nate winks at me and slides his arm around my waist. "Stop worrying," he whispers.

"I'm not worried," I lie.

He laughs, and I lead us back inside so I can put some music on. Will is eating a bowl of spinach dip with corn chips and talking with our brother Matt. Matt is the most laid-back of my brothers, and I know he'll be polite to Nate. Matt gestures for Nate to join them, and I breathe a sigh of relief while I plug my iPhone into the sound system and bring up the playlist I made for today.

Adele starts to croon about finding someone like you, and I turn as Nat and Luke walk into the room.

Well, Nat waddles.

"I love this song," she says as she hands Luke her coat and hugs me close.

She's adorable in a black maternity dress and black flats.

I rub my hands over her belly and laugh. "You play Adele for this baby way too much. She's going to be born bitter and angry at men. Give the poor girl a fighting chance, Nat."

"Hey, Adele is brilliant."

"I agree, but start the baby out with something more optimistic."

"It's beautiful in here." Natalie kisses my cheek, and I grin.

"I know. Alecia, my new bff, is brilliant. Wait until you see outside." I glance over at Nate to make sure no one has killed him and hidden the body, but he's joking and eating with Matt and Will. My dad and Luke have joined them, and my dad seems relaxed and cool.

Maybe this won't be so bad after all.

"Nate seems to be enjoying himself," Natalie murmurs.

"So far, so good, but Caleb's not here yet."

"Oh," she says.

Yeah. Oh.

"Come on." I grab her hand and pull her out into the tent.

"Oh, Jules, this is just—" She stops and takes in the pretty party room and bursts into tears. "I love you so much."

"Nat, don't cry. Don't cry." I hug her close and rub her belly.

"I'm not sad. I'm so fucking hormonal I cry during Doritos commercials." She sniffs and wipes the tears from her cheeks. "This is really wonderful. I have a crush on Alecia now."

"Me, too," I say with a laugh.

We wander back inside, and I see that my brother Isaac, his wife, Stacy, and my niece, Sophie, are here. I scoop the sweet baby girl into my arms and blow kisses against her neck, making her giggle.

"Hey, Nate!" I call across the room and motion for him to come over. He excuses himself from the guys and joins me, placing his hand at the small of my back.

Isaac frowns and eyes Nate up and down, and I roll my eyes.

"Nate, I'd like to introduce you to my oldest brother, Isaac, his wife, Stacy, and my gorgeous niece, Sophie."

Sophie immediately holds her arms out to Nate, and he responds without hesitating, bracing her on his forearm and spreading his other big hand along her back to hold her steady.

Oh my.

"Wow," Stacy says with a laugh, rubbing her own round belly. She'll be having their second baby in just a few months. "That's a first. Soph's been going through a stranger-danger phase lately. She doesn't usually go to anyone she doesn't know."

"I'm good with kids." Nate shrugs and smiles at Sophie. "Hey, gorgeous." Sophie squeals with delight and slaps his cheek.

Is there no woman in the universe Nate can't charm?

Probably not.

"Where are Brynna and the girls?" I ask Stacy. Her cousin, Brynna, and Brynna's five-year-old twin girls recently moved back to Seattle from Chicago.

"The girls have colds, so she decided to keep them home," Stacy replies.

Isaac hasn't said anything. He's just watched Nate with his daughter, but he finally looks over to me and gives me a slight nod.

Nate has passed the test with three brothers and my father.

Maybe Caleb won't show up.

Luke's parents arrive along with Luke's older sister, Sam. His younger brother, Mark, is on a fishing trip up north, so he won't be joining us. I make more introductions as Natalie joins the boys around the food to chat and snack.

Nate keeps a firm grip on Sophie, who has laid her sweet little blond head on his shoulder, as he shakes everyone's hands.

"It's so nice to meet you, Nate," Luke's mom, Lucy, says and winks at me.

"Definitely great to meet you, Nate," Sam agrees and smiles at me with a look that says, *I so want details later.*

"It's a pleasure to meet you all. Julianne," Nate says and kisses Sophie's cheek before handing her back to Stacy, "should we move this party to the tent? There's more seating out there."

"Good idea." Now he's hosting this party with me.

Oh my God, we're a couple.

"Let's load up some plates and head out to the tent, you guys. It's heated, and there's a lot of seating."

Somehow, Goddess Alecia managed to have my sound system wired out into the tent as well, so the music follows us.

The gift table is overflowing with wrapped boxes and bags and bows, and Natalie catches my eye with a frown. I just smile sweetly and look away.

I'm spoiling this baby, damn it!

"Julianne," Will says in a sarcastic, sing-songy voice, "would you please hand me a napkin?" He winks, and I want to deck him.

Nate snickers next to me, not at all bothered by my brother's teasing.

"Julianne"—Matt's face is perfectly serious—"how is work going?"

"Fine," I spit out between clenched teeth, and my brothers laugh.

"So, Ju-li-anne . . ." Isaac stretches my name out, enunciating each syllable, earning a smack from Stacy. I want to kill them all. They know I hate it when people call me Julianne.

Except Nate.

"What?" I snap.

Nate links his fingers through mine and clenches tightly beneath the table, making me look up at him. His eyes are laughing. "Don't sweat this," he murmurs.

"Boys, leave your sister alone," Mom warns.

"We're not doing anything," Will murmurs with a sulk, and I bust out laughing. What are we, five?

Across the table from Nate and I, Luke is leaning over, whispering in Natalie's ear, and she's smiling softly. God, they're disgusting in public. But so in love. I need to stop worrying about Nate and my family. This party is for them.

"Presents!" I jump up and down in my seat and clap my hands.

"Jules." Nat frowns and swallows hard. "Can I just say thank you all so much and open them at home?"

"No." I pout. "This is the fun part."

"That's not a bad idea," Luke jumps in. "There's a lot here. It'll take all afternoon."

"I don't mind," Stacy agrees, and there are nods and agreements around the room.

"Well, hell," I mutter. "Okay, but will you just open mine? 'Cause I want to see your face when you see it."

"Okay." Natalie smiles, and I clap again.

My present isn't on the table with the others. It's too big.

"I'll be right back."

I run through the house and out to the garage, and thank God that I have that upper body strength Nate's dad mentioned last weekend, because this mother is heavy.

I manage to get back to the tent, and Nate jumps up to help me when he sees me come through the door.

"Christ, why didn't you ask me to help you?"

"I've got it."

"Jesus, Julianne, you'll hurt yourself. Give this to me." Nate wrestles the large wooden sign out of my hands, and I notice the grins of delight on the faces of my family as we walk around the table to Natalie and Luke.

"Okay, turn it around."

Natalie gasps, and her hand flies to her mouth as she reads the words that I painted on the rough wood. I know she has a thing for old barn doors, and inscriptions, and I decided to give her both.

I had the door cut down to three feet by four feet, and I sanded and stained it, and painted the inscription in dark gray and pink, the colors Natalie chose for the nursery.

"Read it," I murmur.

"*No one else will ever know the strength of my love for you. After all, you're the only one who knows the sound of my heart from the inside.*"

"Jules, where did you get this?" Luke asks.

"I made it." I shrug and grin.

"You made this?" Nate asks, surprised.

"Yeah, I can be crafty if I need to be." I flush and smile at Natalie. "Do you like it?"

She's started crying again, and I hope that's a good sign.

"Oh, it's perfect." She stands as quickly as possible, which isn't terribly fast, and I walk around to hug her. "Thank you."

"You're welcome. I love you."

"I love you, too."

"Caleb!"

I turn around at my mom's excited voice and find my brother glaring at Nate from the doorway.

"Who the fuck are you?"

thirteen

"Caleb!" I turn to march toward him, but Nate stops me with a hand on my shoulder. His eyes are locked on Caleb's, ice cold, but his face is completely expressionless.

If this is how he looked at his opponents in the ring, I'm surprised they didn't turn and run and cry for their mommy.

"I'm Nate McKenna." Nate steps forward and extends his right hand.

Caleb doesn't take it. He just keeps staring at Nate.

I frantically look around the room for help, but everyone is just watching the show, wondering what's going to happen next.

"Why are your hands on my sister?" Caleb doesn't move, his face also expressionless.

Fuck, I was afraid of this. Of all my brothers, Caleb has always been the most protective. He's a Navy SEAL. He can kill someone and make it look like natural causes. If you look "testosterone" up in the dictionary, there should be a photo of his handsome face rather than a definition. He's the same height as Nate and roughly the same build.

He's scary.

And he loves me.

Not a good combination.

"Caleb," I try again, but Nate puts his hand up to make me stop, and I frown at him.

"I am Julianne's date today," Nate states simply.

That's a good way to put it. I like it.

Caleb doesn't seem to.

"I think we should take this outside." Caleb turns toward the door, and Nate follows.

"With pleasure."

"STOP!" I scream and both men turn to me. "This is not about you, Caleb. Stop being a testosterony asshole."

He frowns and starts to yell back at me, but I walk over to him and kiss his cheek and whisper in his ear, "Stop. I love him. He's a good man. If he fucks up, you can kill him."

Caleb pulls back and looks into my eyes, then his face softens, and he tugs on my ear. "Okay." He looks back at Nate, then to our brothers, who seem to give him some kind of weird subliminal message that I've never been in tune with, and then extends his hand to Nate. "Caleb."

Nate takes it and grips it firmly. "Pleasure."

Caleb laughs. "Right. Sorry I'm late, guys. I've been packing."

"Where are you going?" Natalie asks, tears in her eyes again.

Jesus, she never turns off the waterworks these days. Is this what pregnancy does? Makes you a slow-moving, emotional wreck? Ugh.

"I can't tell you that." Caleb smiles at Natalie and hugs her close, rubbing his hand over her belly. He always did have a crush on her. "I'm afraid I won't be here when the bambino gets here."

"Oh." Natalie looks at me and back at him. I know how she worries for all of us. After losing her parents so unexpectedly a few years ago, she always worries. "Please, be careful."

"I'll be fine. Don't worry about me. I'll be excited to come home and meet . . . what are you naming her, anyway?"

Natalie and Luke look at each other and grin. "We're not telling," Luke responds.

"Fuck that, I won't be able to be reached for a good three months, so tell me."

Nate and I take our seats. He kisses my cheek, and I rub his thigh under the table.

"Watch your mouth!" Mom yells, and Caleb rolls his eyes at her. He's so gonna get it.

"It's a surprise." Caleb frowns at Nat, and we all laugh. "No one is allowed to get on the phone and call TMZ, got it?"

"Whatever. Spill it," Will calls out.

Natalie looks at Luke, and he grins and nods his agreement to tell us.

"Her name is Olivia Grace. Grace is for my mom." She rubs her belly and smiles, and I feel tears start to roll.

"Hey, you okay?" Nate asks and wipes my tears off my cheeks.

"Yeah, Natalie's hormone issues are contagious." I laugh and dab beneath my eyes with a napkin, careful not to smudge my makeup. "It's a beautiful name, sweetie."

"SO, NATE," MY father begins from the table next to ours, and Nate swivels in his chair to face him, "what is it that you do?"

I cringe inwardly. Of course this question was going to come up. Natalie and I share a look before I look back to Nate, who smiles at my father.

"I work with Julianne."

"What do you do there?" my dad asks.

"I'm a senior partner, sir."

Dad nods and narrows his eyes at me. "So you're her boss?"

"Yes," Nate states, his eyes not leaving my dad's.

The whole room has quieted now, and everyone is listening to the exchange. Dad's not being a jerk, but we all know this is the official inquisition.

Nate laces my fingers with his and squeezes gently, reassuring me.

"And what, exactly, is going on between you and my daughter, son?" Dad leans back in his chair and crosses his arms over his chest, his handsome face neutral but his eyes narrowed.

Without missing a beat, Nate states in a strong, sure voice, "A mutually respectful and loving relationship, sir."

Wow.

"Damn," Matt mutters, and I look around the room to see the girls grinning and the boys looking at Nate with respect on their handsome faces, and a wide smile blossoms on my lips.

My dad continues to eye Nate, sizing him up, then nods once and grabs his beer. "Okay then."

Dad winks at me, and I wink back, and we all return to our lunch, chatter breaking out again amongst my brothers.

"So, Jules, I get to surprise you now." Natalie wrestles her way out of her chair, smiling at me, and I look around the room, confused.

"Huh?"

"Well, it was your birthday this week, and we didn't get to throw you a party, so we're celebrating now." Natalie smiles smugly and walks into the house, Luke and Will following her, and I look around again to find everyone grinning at me.

"You're all in on this?" I ask.

"Honey, you didn't think we forgot your birthday?" My mom grins at me, and I frown.

"You all sent me flowers and texts and called me."

"Those aren't presents, kid. That's just what you do on someone's birthday," Will states as he walks into the room loaded down with gift bags.

Holy shit.

"This is Nat and Luke's party," I state firmly and shake my head.

"Jules, shut up," Natalie murmurs and leans down to kiss my cheek on her way back to her seat.

I look up at Nate, who is grinning delightedly at me. "Did you know about this?"

He shrugs. "Of course."

Well, hell.

Will sets the gifts on the table and takes his seat. "Open them, kid."

"Stop calling me that," I mutter, my usual response to his nickname for me.

"No," he responds with a grin.

I frown at the gift bags and look around at my family again to find everyone watching me. Finally, Nate chuckles and hands me a bag. "Open them, baby."

I work my way through the gifts, delighting in the new silver brace-let from Luke and Nat, a gorgeous scarf from Isaac and Stacy, and a wide array of generous gifts from my whole family. By the time I'm done, I have tears in my eyes and a wide smile on my face.

"Thanks, guys. This is fantastic, and unexpected." I loop my pret-ty new red scarf around my neck and slide the bangle bracelet on my wrist.

"We have one more thing," Natalie says and smiles at me.

"What?" I ask.

"A full day at the spa, you and Natalie, after the baby comes," Luke says with a smile.

"Nice! Thanks, I won't turn that down." I grin at Natalie, and she smiles back.

Suddenly, Nate places another small, gold gift bag on the table in front of me. I look up into his gorgeous gray eyes and frown.

"You already gave me a birthday present."

"Julianne, everyone is giving you gifts today. Do you think I'd come empty-handed?"

"But . . ."

"Stop," he murmurs and cups my cheek in his hand, making me look into his eyes. "I've already told you how I enjoy giving you gifts. Just open it."

I hold his gaze for a moment and then look inside the beautiful gold bag. Nestled inside is a red Cartier box.

"Nate . . ."

"Just open the box, please."

Inside is a beautiful, sparkling white and pink diamond tennis bracelet.

"Oh my," I murmur.

"Holy shit, that's beautiful!" Samantha exclaims.

"How lovely," my mom breathes.

Nate takes it out of the box and fastens it around my wrist, then kisses my hand. I cup his face in my hands and kiss him, tenderly, and his hands glide down my back to my waist.

"Watch your hands, McKenna," Caleb warns, making us all laugh.

"Thank you," I whisper.

WELL, NO ONE died. No one even got maimed.

All of the guests have finally left, and it took only three cars to load up all of baby Olivia's loot to get it back to Natalie and Luke's place.

I close and lock the front door and go search for Nate. The house is a mess, which I expected, and is another reason that I'm so glad I found Alecia. She's arranged to have a crew come in tomorrow to clean up and remove the tent and tables and chairs.

God bless her.

I find Nate in the kitchen, tossing paper plates in the garbage and stowing leftovers in the fridge.

"We'll be eating leftovers for a week," I comment, as I walk into the room and help him finish sealing the containers and place them in the fridge.

"Did you have fun?" he asks with a grin.

"After you were introduced to everyone, yes."

Nate wraps his arms around me from behind and kisses my hair.

"You didn't have to worry about me. I was fine."

"I know, it's just a nerve-racking thing. My brothers are good guys, but they're really overprotective, and I didn't want them to be douche bags."

He smiles against my hair and leans down to kiss my neck. "They were fine, baby."

"Well, I'm sorry about Caleb." Oh God, I love it when he kisses my neck like that.

"Caleb was protecting you. I'd do the same. No harm done. Besides, he and I had a long talk before he left, and we're good."

"You did?" I turn in his arms and search his handsome face. "I didn't notice that."

"You were doing girl stuff." He smirks and brushes his lips on my forehead. "Thank you for including me today."

"I didn't have much of a choice, did I?"

"Of course you did." He frowns and suddenly looks worried. "If you didn't want me here today, you should have said."

"No." I run my hands down his chest and back up to his shoulders, loving the way his muscles feel under my hands. "I was just nervous. I'm glad you met my family."

"I want to learn everything about you, Julianne." He runs his fingers down my face and gazes deeply into my eyes. "I plan to be around for a long time."

"Oh." What else can I say to that? He's so much more than I ever realized. He's the controlled businessman, the playful bad boy, and he's just so . . . sweet.

I wrap my fingers in his long, soft hair and pull him down to me, softly kissing him. His hands roam my back before settling on my ass and pulling me tightly against him. I moan and push closer, my breasts pressed against his chest.

"I think you've earned an award for good behavior," I whisper against his mouth.

"Really?" He grins delightedly and leans back to look down at me. "I think I like the sound of that."

"Oh, you're definitely going to like it." I pull out of his arms and take his hand while leading him to the stairs.

When we reach my bedroom, I turn on the sidelight and turn to him and slowly begin to strip. I take the wide black belt off first and toss it aside, followed by my slacks.

Nate's eyes are on fire, his arms crossed on his chest, and he's pulling at his bottom lip with his thumb and forefinger as he watches me undress. I unbutton my shirt but leave it on, open in the front, showing off my nude-colored bra and matching thong.

I walk to him, and he drops his arms to his sides, not touching me, and that's okay.

This is for him.

I pull his shirt out of his slacks and unbutton it, then push it off his strong, broad shoulders, letting it fall to the floor. I trace the tattoo on his right arm and shoulder with my fingertips and lean over and kiss the dark ink on his chest, smiling as he inhales swiftly through his teeth.

I'm just getting started.

My hands glide down his sides and make quick work of unfastening his belt and pants, slipping them down his hips and legs to the floor. He went commando today.

Holy shit.

I step back and let my eyes feast on his beautiful body. His hair is loose, his steel-gray eyes on mine. His breathing has quickened, and his hands are in fists at his sides, and I can see that it's taking every ounce of his self-control to not attack me.

Backing up to the bed, I make a *come here* motion with my finger and point to the bed. "Lie down, please."

A soft smile touches his lips as he wanders to me. He stops in front of me and cups my cheek in his palm, bringing my eyes up to his before rubbing my lower lip with his thumb. I kiss the soft pad, and he groans.

"How do you want me to lie down?" he asks, his voice raspy with lust.

"On your back."

He pulls back the covers and lies in the middle of the bed, braced on his elbows, watching me. I let my shirt fall to the floor, slip out of my bra and thong, and climb on the bed with him, my knees between his legs. I kiss his belly, his sternum, and then his lips, pulling back when he tries to deepen the kiss, then leaning in again and teasing him with just the tip of my tongue.

"You're making me crazy, baby," he murmurs, and I grin.

"You haven't seen anything yet, honey." I nip his chin, run my tongue down his neck, and glide my mouth and hands down his torso, settling back on my heels between his legs. His cock is full and hard, and I circle the tip with my finger, over the silver balls.

"I like this," I murmur, and he chuckles.

"Do you?"

"Hmm."

"I'm glad."

I run my finger down his length and over his scrotum, then back up to the tip.

"Jesus, baby, that feels good."

I lean down and follow the path my finger took with the tip of my tongue, and the bed shifts as he falls onto his back, growling.

"Fuck, seeing that little pink mouth of yours on my cock is so sexy."

It's about to get a lot sexier.

I swirl my tongue around the tip and sink down over him, and suddenly, his strong hands are in my hair, guiding me up and down, directing me where he wants me to go, and it's so fucking *hot*.

His hips are moving beneath me, pushing up into my mouth, and just when I think he's about to let go, he grips my shoulders, and I'm suddenly on my back with Nate over me, spreading me wide open and pushing into me, hard.

"Oh God!" My back arches, and his lips find a nipple, his arms wrapped around my waist, as he pushes into me, over and over again.

He pulls me up so I'm straddling him. His hands find my ass and raise and lower me over him, grinding deeply into me, his mouth still on my breast. I bear down and squeeze him, feeling those silver balls in my core, and I come apart around him, shuddering and convulsing.

"Fuck, yes," he cries out and pulls me down one more time as he erupts inside me.

I'M ON MY back again, staring at the ceiling, Nate wrapped around me, his cheek resting on my belly. We're still panting, coming down from our violent orgasms.

"That was fun." I grin and run my fingers through his hair. "Let's do it again."

"Jesus, Julianne, give a man a chance to recover."

"Don't be a pussy." I laugh as he bites my belly and climbs up my body, resting on his elbow to my right side.

He brushes the hair that came out of my bun off my face and kisses me sweetly, then bites my lip.

"Ow!"

"You have such a dirty mouth."

"I just call 'em like I see 'em."

He bites my lip again, more gently this time, and I sigh against his mouth.

"And you see me as a pussy?" he asks, deceptively softly.

"Hmm . . . maybe not."

He leans back and raises an eyebrow. "Maybe?"

"Probably not."

"I'll show you how much of a pussy I am, baby."

He's suddenly inside me again, and I'm tucked beneath him, and . . . *holy shit.*

fourteen

Cooking with Nate this past week has been a lot of fun. We get sidetracked a lot and burned the hell out of a perfectly innocent pork tenderloin when we lost track of time in the shower one evening, but it's exciting to be creative with him in the kitchen. Up until tonight we've either eaten out or cooked together, and I want to cook *for* him.

So I am.

It's Sunday evening, and we're back at Nate's place for the night. Alecia's cleaning crew did a great job at the house, but we decided to come back to Nate's condo so he can get some work done in his office.

Because I prefer to cook to music, I plug my iPhone into his sound system and crank it up. Yes, my cooking music tastes are a bit . . . juvenile. I prefer pop music to dance around the kitchen to. Britney Spears. Lady Gaga. Maybe a little Carly Rae Jepsen and her *Call Me Maybe*. In fact, that works. Carly starts to sing through the speakers hidden throughout the room, and I start to shake my ass while compiling what I need for dinner.

Hmm . . . I wonder what Nate would look like in ripped jeans? Good call, Carly.

I pour myself a glass of fruity white wine, take a sip and pull my hair up into a messy twist at the crown of my head. I'm still wearing gray yoga pants and a black tank top from our trip to the gym today. God, I love watching Nate work out. At thirty, his body is incredible. Hell, his body is incredible for a twenty-year-old.

I still didn't win in the ring today, but I knocked him on his ass twice, and that's a victory in my book.

I smile smugly and quarter baby red potatoes for roasting, plopping them in cold water until I'm ready for them. The chicken I'm roasting with lemon and basil goes in the oven when the bell rings, telling me it's warm enough. I'll round out the meal with roasted asparagus with garlic.

I have time for a shower, so I set the kitchen timer for one hour, grab my wine, and walk down the hallway to the master bedroom, passing Nate's office. His door is open, and he's at the desk with the phone cradled between his ear and shoulder, and he's typing furiously on his keyboard.

"No, fuck that, they'll never accept that offer," he snaps, but his eyes soften when he sees me in the doorway.

"Dinner's still a couple hours away. I'm hitting the shower," I whisper.

"Hold on, Parker." He pushes the receiver against his shoulder so Parker can't hear him. "Okay, baby. What is that noise coming out of my speakers out there?"

"Cooking music." I shrug innocently, blow him a kiss and saunter into the bathroom, stripping as I adjust the water temperature in his amazing shower. This bathroom is beautiful, and the shower is big enough to host a small orgy, with a large rainshower showerhead in the ceiling. It feels incredible.

Thankfully, Nate's sound system is wired throughout the whole condo, except his office, so I'm shimmying my hips and singing along to *Pocket Full of Sunshine* by Natasha Bedingfield as I lather up my hair. I lean my head back and let the hot water flow over me, rinsing my hair. The soapy lather falling down my back and over my breasts, bottom and legs feels so good on my skin, still sensitive from today's workout, and my hands glide over my breasts, the nipples puckering on contact.

Mmm . . . pity Nate has so much work tonight. I could use some company. He's very inventive in the shower.

John Mayer starts to sing through the speakers about my body being a wonderland, and my hands start to slide all over my torso, one wandering closer to the homeland.

I perch one foot on a bench built into the tile and slide my hand between my legs, pushing my fingers between my folds, and imagine that it's Nate's fingers making me crazy. My other hand plucks at a nipple, and suddenly, Nate is behind me, his body pressed to mine, his arms wrapped around me, and I jump, startled. I was so wrapped up in my little fantasy I didn't hear him join me.

"Don't stop," he whispers in my ear. "Keep touching yourself."

I shake my head and lean back against his chest, suddenly shy. He nibbles my neck and grabs my hand in his, guiding it back down between my legs.

"Want me to help?"

"Yes." I sigh and arch my back as he pushes my fingers through my folds again, rubbing back and forth and up over my clit, then back down to my labia.

"Oh God," I moan. It feels so good, and just a little naughty. I try to pull my hand away to let him continue on his own, but he grabs it again in a firm hold.

"You don't know what it does to me to see you pleasure yourself, Julianne." His words are soft, hypnotizing and so sexy, and I can feel his hard-on against my ass.

Our hands continue their assault, and he presses my palm against my clit and bites that spot on my neck, just behind my ear, and my body starts to shudder. I come against our hands, rocking and pushing against them, crying out his name.

Nate spins me around and pins me against the cold tile wall, leaning his torso against me, his cock pressed to my belly, and his lips are on mine, kissing me voraciously. I run my hands over his sides to his back and down to grip his very fine, very firm ass and squeeze.

"I need to be inside you," he growls and cups my ass to lift me. "Wrap your legs around me, baby."

I do, and he eases himself inside me, slowly, his forehead leaning against mine, gray eyes burning with lust and need. I tangle his wet hair in my fingers and hold on as he begins to move in and out of me, faster and faster, our breathing ragged and harsh. His eyes never leave mine as he pushes and pulls harder, faster, and I feel my legs clench tighter around him, another orgasm moving though me.

"Come on, baby, give it to me," he whispers against my lips, and his words are my undoing.

"Oh God, Nate!" I pulsate around him, milking his cock and those amazing silver balls with my pussy, and he bites his lower lip, then clenches his teeth as he falls over the edge, his hips grinding into mine, hands gripping my ass so tightly it must be bruising me, as he comes inside me.

He holds me there, against the wall, for a long minute, both of us gasping for air, gazing at each other. I rhythmically run my fingers through his hair, and he places his lips gently on mine, brushing back and forth, kissing me softly.

"You are so sweet," he murmurs. "You're mine, do you understand? No matter what happens. You. Are. Mine." His eyes and voice are raw with emotion, and I feel tears prick the sides of my eyes.

"Yes," I whisper. "I'm yours, Nate." Where is this coming from?

He shudders one more time and slips out of me, gently lowering me back to my feet. He cups my face in his hands and runs his nose down along mine before kissing me chastely and pulling away, shutting off the water, and leading me out of the cavernous shower to dry off.

"What in God's name is this music?" he asks with a scowl. Fergie is singing *Glamorous*.

"Hey, I love this song." I smack his ass as I walk past him to his bedroom to root through my suitcase for clothes.

"Your taste in music sucks, baby." He pulls a black T-shirt over his head and then steps into a pair of old worn blue jeans. No underwear.

"I like listening to happy music while I cook," I explain calmly.

"Rock is happy." He plants his hands on his hips and watches me pull on my jeans and a blue tunic top.

"So is this." I shrug and walk past him into the bathroom to blow my hair dry and secure it back in a ponytail.

"Why are you watching me?" I ask, feeling his eyes on me.

"I like watching you," he responds, leaning against the door frame with his arms crossed over his chest.

"Are you done working?" I ask.

"No, I have a few more calls to make."

"Do you need any help?" I feel guilty. I'm sure there's something I can do to help. He's my boss, for Pete's sake.

"No, I've got it. I'll have some things for you at the office in the morning."

"Okay." Happy with my hair, I turn and lean my bottom against the vanity and gaze at him. "Is this getting weird for you?"

He frowns, perplexed. "Is what getting weird?"

"Us, working together, practically living together." Fuck. Now he's going to think I want to live with him. "I mean, we don't really live together, but we're together all the time."

"Work isn't weird for me. We only see each other a few times throughout the day." He pushes away from the door and walks to me, leaning his hands on the vanity at my hips, bringing his eyes level with mine. "I want to be with you as much as possible outside of work. This is when we're *us*, with no pretenses. Is it weird for you?"

"I don't know." I shrug and lower my gaze to his chest, but he captures my chin in his fingers and makes me meet his stare.

"Look at me, and be honest. I don't want you to be uncomfortable, Julianne. Not about us."

"I'm not uncomfortable. I wouldn't be here if I didn't want to be. There are moments at work that are weird. I won't deny that." I run my hands up his strong arms and over his shoulders to rest them on his muscular chest. "You're my boss. If you decide to end this, you could also end my career. It's a sticky place to be for me."

He frowns again, his eyes so serious. "I know you have to trust me, Julianne. I have to trust you, too. It works both ways, you know."

That hadn't occurred to me. If I chose to end this, or if I was a bitter, scorned woman, I could ruin his career in a heartbeat. Not that I would ever do that. It's not my style.

The trust is on both sides, equally.

I stroke his cheek with my fingertips, and he closes his eyes briefly, then pins me again with those beautiful gray eyes.

Yes, I trust him.

"Don't worry," he whispers. "I wasn't kidding when I said you're mine. I will protect you with everything I have, baby."

"Ditto," I whisper and watch his eyes widen in surprise.

He pulls me into him, wrapping his arms around me and pressing my head to his chest, and I feel so loved. This is not sexual at all. I feel cherished.

Finally, I pull back and smile up at him, wanting to lighten the mood. "I don't want to burn the chicken. We've wasted enough food this week. You go work, and I'll finish up dinner."

"Okay." He kisses my nose and ushers me out ahead of him.

"I WON'T BE in the office this week." Nate strides into the kitchen, his face taut with frustration.

"What's up?" I ask and dish up our plates.

"I have to go to New York. Parker thinks I need to present this deal in person." He joins me at the table, and we dig in.

"He's probably right," I respond. Parker is a partner in our New York branch and knows his stuff. The deal they've been working on for the past two weeks is a tricky one.

"Business trips don't hold the same allure as they used to."

I look up at him, and he's frowning down at his plate.

"Hey." I take his hand and squeeze his fingers. "This is part of the job. You couldn't have a more understanding girlfriend in this area, Nate. I know this is part of who you are."

"I can't take you with me. I don't need your help for the work, and it would raise eyebrows."

"I know." I shrug and keep eating, proud of myself for maintaining a calm expression on my face. "When will you be back?"

"By Thursday. I'm leaving tomorrow morning."

"Okay. Need a lift to the airport?"

"Thank you." God, he's so serious today.

"Don't worry." I kick him playfully under the table. "I'll be here when you get home."

fifteen

I've discovered that work is easier with Nate gone. I'm only halfway through the workday, and I'm already more at ease. I don't have to worry about anyone noticing anything different between us, a look or coy smile. I pray to God no one can read my mind, because I'd be escorted to the sidewalk with all of my belongings in a box in the blink of an eye if they could.

Nate e-mailed me a list of things to do for him at this end to then send back to him via e-mail for his presentation in New York tomorrow. He'll be in the New York office preparing all evening.

He was really very cute this morning when I dropped him off at the airport. It makes me a little giddy that he didn't want to leave me and will miss me.

I'm going to miss him, too.

Sleeping alone for the next few nights doesn't appeal to me in the slightest. I got lucky with Nate. He doesn't snore or hog the bed, and he's a really good cuddler.

Who would have thought?

But in the office, I feel more relaxed with him gone.

I finish typing a very dry, professional e-mail to my handsome man with the completed requests he sent me this morning, expecting to receive an e-mail back with more revisions and requests.

Meanwhile, I pick up my iPhone and send him a sexy, nonprofessional text.

Hey, handsome. Did you land safely? Would have loved to join the mile-high club with you today.

I turn my attention back to a report I'm working on when my phone chirps with a response.

Arrived safely, baby. Wish you were here. We will take a trip soon. I promise.

I like the sound of that.

It's a date. Be safe, I'll talk to you tonight. xo

His response is a simple *xo*.

When did I turn into such a sap? I miss him already.

There's a knock on my door, and Carly Lennox breezes into my office, leaving the door open behind her, thank goodness. She's dressed in a black suit with the skirt too short and white shirt unbuttoned too low for my taste. This is an office, not a club.

"Hi, Jules," she purrs.

"Carly. What can I do for you?" What the fuck does this bitch want?

"Well, I could use some help with an account today. I'm trying to get some work done early because I don't want to work late. I have a date, and I figured us girls have to stick together." She smiles sweetly, but her eyes are shrewd.

I don't trust this woman, but I'm curious what her game is. She hates me. So I decide to play along.

"You have a date? That's great. Anyone I know?" I paste on the smile I use for people who recognize me from the magazine. Sassy and completely fake.

"Well, don't tell anyone." She lowers her voice to a whisper and leans down like we're old friends sharing a secret. "But I've been seeing Nate. He's taking me out to dinner and dancing tonight."

I want to laugh. I really do. But I give an award-winning performance, frowning with fake concern.

"Oh, Carly, he must not have thought to call you this morning. He had to go to New York on business. He's going to be gone for a while." I'm deliberately vague on the time line, interested to see her reaction.

I'm not disappointed.

She blushes scarlet, and her smile disappears for just a second as she processes the information, then her fake smile is back. "Oh, I haven't checked my messages this morning."

Her phone chirps from inside her suit jacket pocket, and she pulls it out to check a text message. "Oh, there he is now! Looks like an itinerary for New York. I guess I'll be joining him." She smiles sweetly. "Nevermind. See ya!"

She waves and hurries out of my office, and I'm struck dumb. Carly is going to New York? She's not even on his team. If he needs help, I should be the one to join him.

Maybe he sent for her because he knows that I have to be here in case Natalie goes into labor?

And what in the hell is up with Carly wanting me to think she's dating Nate? There's no way she could possibly know that he's been seeing me every day for the past week and a half. She knows about the no-fraternization policy. It's drilled into us during orientation. Why would she tell me, the one person she hates here, that she's dating a partner when she knows I could get her fired with that information?

Either she's really stupid, which I know she's not, or she's setting me up for something.

I'm reaching for my desk phone to call Nate and ask him about Carly when my iPhone begins ringing. I frown at Luke's name on the display.

"Hi, Luke."

"My water's wife broke!" he yells into the phone.

Ohmygod!

"You mean your wife's water broke?"

"That's what I said, Jules! Her water broke!" He's frantic. Poor, poor Luke.

I grab my purse and lock up my desk, gather my coat and make a beeline out of my office. I'll call Mrs. Glover from the car.

"I'm on my way. I'll meet you at the hospital."

"Okay. Okay." His voice changes, like he's turned his face away from the phone. "Are you okay, baby?"

I hear Natalie's calm voice in the background. "I'm fine. Calm down."

"I'm calm. I'm calm."

Christ, he keeps repeating everything. He's not calm. "Luke," I say in the most soothing voice I have. "She's fine. I'll meet you at the hospital."

He takes a deep breath, and his voice is more normal when he says, "Okay, we're on the way."

Once in my car, I realize that I didn't send that last report to Nate, and I forgot to shut my computer down. I call Mrs. Glover quickly but get her voice mail.

"Mrs. Glover, this is Jules. I've had to leave abruptly due to a family emergency, but I forgot to send Nate the report he copied you in on in his e-mail this morning. Would you please finish the e-mail at my desk and then lock my computer and text me when you're finished? I appreciate it."

I hang up, throw my phone in my handbag, and concentrate on getting to my best friend.

"JUST BREATHE."

Natalie's hand is gripping mine with a strength I didn't know she had. Jesus, is she a construction worker or something? She's going to tear my hand off at the wrist. "Breathe, honey."

I cringe as she breathes through the pain. The contractions are coming harder and faster, finally. We've been here for about seven hours, and her labor stopped progressing after about two hours.

Luke is in the waiting room updating his parents and mine, and they're calling all the siblings, keeping everyone up-to-date on Natalie's status.

"Okay, it's gone," she whispers and takes a deep breath.

"You're doing great," I say as supportively as I can muster. I'm scared to death.

"This fucking hurts, Jules. Don't ever do this to yourself. Really."

"It'll be worth it when Olivia's here." I smooth her dark hair off her face and wipe her forehead with a cool washcloth. Her beautiful face transforms into a wide grin at the mention of her daughter's name.

"We get to hold her today."

We both turn our heads toward the monitor that is keeping track of the contractions. The line starts to go up again, and Natalie grips my hand again and begins to breathe.

"Oh Jesus, Jules."

"Breathe, sweetie." I start to breathe with her, and she laughs.

"You're going to hyperventilate."

"No, I'm not. Breathe with me." Where the fuck is Luke?

"Hi, Mrs. Williams. I'm Ashlynn, your evening nurse. I'm taking over for the night. Let's check you real quick to see how you're progressing, okay?"

Natalie's contraction eases, and she smiles at the pretty nurse. "Okay."

Ashlynn pushes her hand into a glove, then shoves her hand up Natalie's crotch. *Jesus!*

"I usually require someone to buy me dinner before they can do that to me," I remark, trying to keep Natalie's mood light.

Natalie grins up at me. "Right?"

"Well, you're at about seven centimeters, and you're completely effaced, so if you keep going at this pace, it shouldn't be too much longer. I think you're ready for an epidural." Ashlynn smiles and pats Nat's leg. "I'll let the doctor know, and she will call the anesthesiologist."

"Thank God." Natalie leans her head back on the bed. "I'm going with the drugs. I'm sorry, Jules, I know we said all-natural, but I can't do it."

"Honey, you do what's best for you. These contractions are strong, and my hand may not survive many more of them. What does Luke say?"

"He said to go for the drugs if I needed them."

"Sounds like a plan then." I wipe her forehead with the washcloth again as a man with a white coat strolls through the door.

"I hear you're ready for some medication, Mrs. Williams." He's an older man with kind eyes. And needles in his hand.

"This is where I leave." I stand, but Natalie pulls me back down.

"You can't leave me here alone!"

"Um, Nat, he's got needles. I'll find Luke."

"This will only take a minute," the doctor says, and Natalie is looking at me with big, green pleading eyes.

Oh my God.

Okay. I can do this. For Natalie, I can do this.

"Sit at the edge of the bed, Mrs. Williams, and hug your pillow, curving your back for me."

Natalie does as instructed, and I kneel before her, the needles out of my view, and rub my hands up and down her bare legs.

"Thank you," she whispers, her eyes a little frightened.

"No problem." I shrug like it's no big deal and take a deep breath. He's got motherfucking needles, and he's about to stick them in her spine. I'm going to faint.

Natalie cringes as, I'm assuming, the doctor pushes the huge, gigantic, enormously evil needle through her flesh, but then it's over.

"All done," he says and packs up his tools of torture. "Go ahead and lie back. It'll take effect shortly, and you won't be able to feel anything from the waist down."

"Thank you." She's the most polite pregnant woman I've ever seen.

I help get her settled, and Luke comes back through the door.

"Hey, who was that guy?" he asks and sits next to Natalie, his hand resting on her belly.

"The anesthesiologist. I went for the drugs, baby. I'm sorry."

"Stop apologizing. We talked about this." He kisses her forehead and then her lips.

"How is everyone out there?" I ask.

"They're excited and nervous. I would have been back sooner, but Isaac and Stacy showed up, and then the rest of your brothers and Sam and Mark all wanted to hear the status update from me directly, so I was on the phone with them for a little while." He sits back and watches the contraction monitor. The needle starts to go up again, but Natalie doesn't even flinch.

"It doesn't hurt anymore?" I ask.

"I feel a little pressure, but no, the pain is gone."

"Good." I smile at them both and realize I haven't checked my phone all day. I pull it out of my purse and wake it up, frowning when I see eight missed calls and five text messages.

I check the texts first. The first one is from Mrs. Glover.

Email is sent. I hope your family is well.

I breathe a sigh of relief, knowing that Nate got the documents he needed on time, then check the messages from him.

Hey baby, breaking away for lunch do you have a minute to talk?

I'm going into a meeting, won't be available the rest of the afternoon.

Are you okay?

Please call me.

Shit. He's worried. I haven't even thought about calling him since I got the call about Natalie. I should have called him. I check the voice mail.

"I'm worried. Jenny said you ran out of the office this morning because of an emergency, but she hasn't heard from you. I can't reach you on your cell or the house line. Please be considerate and let me know you're okay. I can't pack up and go home tonight to check on you. Call me."

I hang up and glare at my phone. I don't like his tone.

"Hey, guys, I'm going to go find a quiet spot and call Nate real quick. He's been trying to reach me all day. Don't have that baby without me. I'll be right back." I kiss Natalie's cheek and walk down the hall to a small, empty waiting room. Our family must be out in the larger one near the hospital entrance.

I scroll down to Nate's name and press Send.

"Julianne." He sounds relieved and pissed at the same time.

"Hey, can you talk?"

"Yes, I'm at the hotel. Where the fuck have you been?"

"Don't yell at me. I'm at the hospital."

"What's wrong? Are you hurt?" His voice is suddenly panicked, and I feel like a shit.

"No," I respond, my voice calm now and soothing. "Natalie's in labor, Nate. I'm sorry I didn't call. I got the call this morning at the office after I texted you, and I raced here to meet them, and I've been with her ever since. It's been a long day. Still no baby."

"Is she okay?" he asks.

"Yeah, she's doing great. Luke is, too, surprisingly. It shouldn't be too much longer."

"You should have called." His voice is cold again, and I'm tired, and I do not need this right now.

"I already apologized."

"I've been worried. Also, what the fuck happened to the report I asked you to send me?"

"What are you talking about? I finished it and asked Jenny to send it for me because I forgot to hit send on the e-mail before I ran out of the office. She sent me a text and said that it was done." What the hell happened to my report?

"I got it, but it was half-assed done. That's not like you."

"That report was perfect, Nate. I don't know what the hell you're talking about." I run my hand through my hair in frustration.

"When I'm out here alone, I need to be able to depend on you to do your job in the office, Julianne."

"You're not alone. Ask Carly to fix the fucking report, Nate. She should be earning her paycheck while she's with you." Not that I really believe that Carly is there, but now I'm just fucking pissed off.

There's silence on the other end of the line, and finally, Nate responds with a deceptively quiet, "What are you talking about? Carly isn't in New York."

"She said you sent for her."

"Why would I do that?" His voice is rising, and I take a deep breath.

"Clearly, there's been a misunderstanding," I say as calmly as possible.

"Obviously."

"Look, Nate, I'm sorry. I need to get back to Natalie. I don't have time for you to get protective and bossy and needy on me today."

"That's what you think I'm doing?" he asks, and I cringe at the hurt in his voice.

"That's exactly what you're doing."

"No, Julianne, I'm not being bossy or needy. I have been worried about the woman I care about because I couldn't reach you today."

I've hurt his feelings. "Nate," I sigh and rub my forehead. "Maybe we should just talk when you get home."

"What are you saying?" His voice is hushed and nervous.

"I need to deal with this right now, and you need to focus on the deal out there. I'll be in the office tomorrow to help you from there, and I'll try to clean up the damn report mess and get it to you ASAP. We'll just talk about the rest of it when you get home. I don't have time for this relationship bullshit right now."

"That's what we are to you, Julianne? Bullshit?"

Fuck. No! This is all coming out wrong, and I need to get back to Natalie!

"I have to go."

"If that's the way you want it, fine, but know this, baby: You're only off the hook because I'm three thousand fucking miles away and can't get to you right now."

"Jesus, you're such a caveman, Nate."

"Text me later and let me know you're safe. I'll talk to you tomorrow night."

"I thought you were staying until Thursday."

"I changed my mind."

The line goes dead, and I hang my head. I shouldn't have been so mean to him.

I walk back into Natalie's room, and all hell has broken loose.

"I was only gone for five minutes. What the hell?"

Natalie's feet are in stirrups, and the doctor is sitting on a stool between her legs. There are two nurses bustling about the room, and a baby cradle with a heating lamp has been wheeled in.

"She's about ready to push," Luke says, his eyes desperate with worry and fear.

"Wow, that epidural is a miracle."

"Holy shit, I have to push." Natalie is writhing on the bed, and if it wasn't my best friend, I'd say it looks like something out of a horror movie.

"Okay, we're ready, Natalie. If you feel like you have to push with the contraction, go ahead."

"It's too hot in here." She yanks the blanket off her and throws it onto the floor, not giving two shits about being naked in front of all of us. Well, she is wearing a black sports bra, so just the bottom half is naked.

I glance down, then feel my jaw drop. It's not the fact that her hoo-ha is on display, but what's right above it that gives me pause.

"Jesus H. Christ, Natalie, you have a tattoo on your vagina!"

sixteen

"Six pounds, ten ounces!" Nurse Ashlynn declares proudly as little baby Olivia lies on the baby scale, crying angrily.

I raise Nat's camera and snap a long stream of photos, capturing the weight on the machine in the photo, in case anyone ever has the audacity to forget. Zooming in on her tiny feet and fingers, I snap more photos before the nurse wraps Olivia up in a pink and blue hospital baby blanket.

Luke is beside me, gazing down at his dark-haired daughter with such love in his eyes. When the baby was born and placed on Natalie's belly, he and Natalie were both crying wrecks, and if I'm honest, I was, too.

"Thank you for letting me be here."

Luke's blue eyes slide over to mine, and he wraps his arm around my shoulders, pulling me to his side.

"We love you, Jules. It's right that you're here."

Oh. Well, that just makes me cry again.

"God, I'm a blubbering mess."

Luke laughs at me and takes his little bundle from the nurse, kissing Olivia's tiny little forehead softly.

"She is so beautiful," he whispers.

"Hey! Can I hold her?" Natalie calls from the bed, all covered up now, thank Jesus.

I'm never having babies. My body can't do that.

Luke crosses the room and places the baby in Nat's arms and kisses her on the lips. He caresses the baby's cheek with his finger and looks lovingly into Nat's eyes.

"Thank you, baby."

"I love you," Nat whispers.

"God, I love you, too."

I raise the camera and snap more photos, capturing the most beautiful moment I've ever seen. I walk around the end of the bed, still snapping, and both Luke and Nat look up at me and grin widely, their smiles just a little tired, so proud of what they've made.

"You are a gorgeous family," I murmur, and Nat's eyes well up.

"I'm going to go fill everyone in," Luke says. He kisses Natalie passionately, earning a token eye-roll from me, kisses the baby's cheek, and pulls away. "Jules, are you going to stay?"

"Yes, I'll stay with our girls until you get back, then I'll give you some alone time with them."

"Thank you." He walks to me and wraps me in his arms, hugging me tightly. Luke's an affectionate guy, but this is different. Special. "Thank you, sweet girl," he whispers in my ear, then walks out to talk to our families.

Well, hell.

"Hey." I walk over to the side of the hospital bed and take a few more pictures of Natalie and Olivia, then set the camera aside and sit on the bed next to them. "You did good, friend."

"Thank you. So did you. Thank you for reminding Luke to breathe before he passed out."

We both laugh, and I know that's one moment I'll never let him forget. "That's what I'm here for." I tuck a spare strand of hair behind Nat's ear and grin down at the baby. "She's so pretty, Nat. I mean, how can she not be with parents who look like you guys do, but seriously, she's gorgeous."

"I think so, too. I'm a mommy, Jules."

"And I'm an auntie again! Oh my God, that's cool." We grin stupidly at each other. "Okay, so, when did you get a tat on your va-jay-jay?"

She shrugs and adjusts the blanket around Olivia. "About two years ago. And it's not on my va-jay-jay, which I'm pretty sure is not the official medical term for that part of my anatomy."

"Wanna tell me what it says?"

"Nope."

"Are you ever going to tell me what any of them say?"

"Probably."

"Okay." Enough tattoo talk. "Can I hold her for a minute before I go?"

"Of course! Here." She hands me the small bundle and scoots over on the bed a little so we can curl up together.

"How do you feel?" I ask.

"Sore, but the drugs are delightful. I am looking forward to getting my old body back."

"You didn't get any stretch marks, you bitch."

She smiles smugly. "Lots of shea butter and yoga. Remember that."

"I'm not doing babies." I shake my head adamantly. No way.

"Right, says the woman snuggling with a baby right now."

"I can snuggle with babies. They don't have to come from my body." I shake my head again and smile as Olivia makes a sucky motion with her lips. "She might be hungry."

"I'm hungry," Nat responds. "Can you call the nurse? I want mashed potatoes and gravy. Stat."

"So much for getting your old body back." I smirk and push the call button.

"Don't be a bitch. I just had a baby. I can have whatever I want."

LUKE COMES BACK with our parents while all the siblings are still waiting their turn for a quick visit, and I decide it's a good time to sneak out. I know that my mom will make sure that everyone keeps their visits to a minimum so Luke and Nat can enjoy some alone time with their daughter and so Nat can rest.

I make it down to the small empty waiting room that I called Nate from earlier, and I'm suddenly flooded with emotion. I can't stop the tears from falling, and I'm crying so hard my knees buckle.

I collapse into a chair and hold my face in my hands, my elbows on my knees, and let the tears flow.

"Hey, what's wrong, Bean?" I gasp and look up, and there's my brother Matt in the doorway. He's called me String Bean since we were kids.

I can't speak to him. Seeing his calm, kind face makes me cry harder, and before I know it, he's kneeling before me and pulling me into a big hug, stroking my back.

"It's okay. Cry it out."

I'm not a crier, but it feels like that's all I've done over the past few weeks. I don't know what to do with all of these new emotions running through me.

Finally, the tears stop, and Matt hands me a box of Kleenex from a nearby table.

"What was that all about?" he asks as I blow my nose. He sits in the chair beside me.

"I've been so worried about Natalie and the baby all day, and I'm exhausted, and I was mean to Nate on the phone, and I just love that baby so much, and I hate crying."

Matt chuckles and strokes my back again. "Hey, it's okay. Having babies is exhausting, even for the helpers. Nat and Olivia are fine, Nate will get over it, and you just need to sleep."

"Yeah, you're right." I sit back and look over at my handsome brother. Of all of us, he's the only one with darker hair, but he's as tall as my other brothers and just as built. He's a Seattle cop, and he's badass in a calm, controlled way. He doesn't have Caleb's temper or Will's arrogance. He's quiet. But he will fuck you up if he needs to.

"What are you doing?" I ask.

"I was going to pop in and see the baby, say congratulations, and then head into work."

"Working night shift?" I ask.

"Yeah, I picked up some extra shifts." He stands and helps me to my feet. "Feel better?"

"I do, thanks. I'm going to go home and sleep off this weird mood."

"Okay, drive safe, Bean."

"You, too." I kiss his cheek and head for home.

MY BED FEELS delicious. And empty. I settle in, ready to go to sleep early, and grab my phone. Should I call Nate and apologize for being a raging bitch, or just text him and talk to him tomorrow?

I choose to text and think up a really nice way to apologize when I see him.

I'm home. Baby and mom are healthy.

I lie back and start to drift when my phone pings.

Ok

Okay? That's it? I frown. This is not the Nate I know and have grown to love. He's pissed off at me, and when I think back to the way I spoke to him, I don't blame him. He was just worried about me, after all.

I decide to call him and apologize. He answers on the second ring.

"Hello, Julianne."

I don't like the cold tone of his voice. "Hi," I murmur.

"Hi."

"Nate, I'm sorry about earlier. I really am."

I hear him sigh, and I feel even more guilty, knowing how much stress he has on him over work, and I know I made him even more worried today and hurt his feelings. And I love him, I don't want to hurt him.

"I think we need to discuss a few things tomorrow night."

Oh, so apology not accepted. "Okay," I whisper and hear him sigh again. "I miss you."

"Do you."

God, I really screwed up.

"Yes."

Silence.

"Please say something."

"What do you want me to say?" he asks.

"I don't know." I feel tears threatening again, and I try to keep them out of my voice. "I just don't want you to be mad at me."

"I'm not mad. I'm disappointed and hurt, Julianne. That's twice that you've managed to hurt my feelings."

"I didn't want to hurt you, Nate. Today was hard, and I didn't know how to deal with it."

"Like I said, we have some things to talk about tomorrow. I'd rather we didn't do it over the phone. I need to see your face."

"Why?"

"Because you're too good at trying to hide what you're feeling behind that badass persona of yours, but your eyes don't lie."

Holy shit.

"I am not lying to you, Nate. I miss you, and I'm sorry that I was a bitch today."

"Don't ever call yourself a bitch again."

Jesus! I can't say anything right! "I'm going to let you go. This isn't getting us anywhere. Do you need a ride from the airport tomorrow night?"

"No."

"Are you going to come to my place?"

"No, go to my place after work."

"I don't have a key."

"Yes, you do."

Huh? "I do?"

"Yes, check your key ring. I put it on there last weekend." His voice is softer now, and I'm shocked.

"Oh."

"I'll see you tomorrow night."

"Good night."

"Good night, Julianne."

seventeen

This has been the day from hell. I was late to work this morning, after sleeping like the dead last night and through my alarm. Mrs. Glover was not pleased to see me this morning, but when I explained what happened and showed her the photos of baby Olivia on my phone, she softened up a bit and said she understood.

Thank goodness.

Not that she's my boss, but I do not want to make an enemy of her.

Nate has been in constant communication with me all day, sending e-mails requesting documents or research to be done, but nothing at all personal. As soon as I got to my office this morning, I opened the document I had Jenny e-mail to Nate yesterday and was stunned to see that Nate was right. It was half-done and riddled with mistakes. It was *not* the final draft I'd finished, saved and attached to the e-mail to go out to him. I don't know what the fuck happened, but I hope that the extra work I've put in this morning has helped straighten the mess out.

I feel shitty for making Nate think that our relationship isn't important to me. Of course it is. But there are times that he's just so . . . bossy. I know he's a strong, intelligent man, and that he wants to protect me and care for me, but I've always been so fiercely independent, I forget that I'm no longer a "me" but part of a "we."

I need to make it up to him. But how?

I'm pondering this when another e-mail comes through from Nate.

Wednesday, May 15, 2013 14:28
From: Nathan McKenna

To: Julianne Montgomery
Subject: Departing

Julianne,

I am about to board the plane back to Seattle. Once you've finished with the reports I emailed to you earlier, you are free to leave for the day.

Nate

He's still so cold, although I know that in work e-mail he doesn't really have a choice. He could have texted me with something more personal, and the fact that he didn't makes me really nervous.

Did I fuck up so badly yesterday that he's going to break it off?

Wednesday, May, 15, 2013 14:35
From: Julianne Montgomery
To: Nathan McKenna
Subject: Re: Departing

Nate,
Safe travels. See you in the office tomorrow.
Julianne

But he's not getting off that easy. I pull out my phone and send him a text.

Please travel safely. I'm excited to see you tonight.

There is no response.

Shit.

I'M LATER GETTING to Nate's than I really intended to be. I stopped by the hospital to see Natalie, Luke and Olivia, and I couldn't go empty-handed, so I shopped a little on the way. I ended up with a huge, supersoft giraffe and a tiny pink onesie that says, "Birth: Nailed It."

I don't have any idea if Nate has already made it home because I haven't heard a peep from him. I guess I'll find out when I get there.

I park in my usual space, leave my suitcase in the car in case I'm not welcome to stay tonight, and ride the elevator to his floor. As the elevator climbs, so does my anxiety level.

Based on how things have gone over the past twenty-four hours, I'm inclined to believe that things may be done between us. The thought of it makes me hurt like nothing ever has before.

I walk down to his door and put my shiny new key in the lock. I step into Nate's apartment and immediately sense that I'm alone.

He's not home yet.

It's chilly inside, so I switch on his gas fireplace to warm the space, and turn on a few lamps in the living room and the light over the kitchen stove.

Maybe I should cook for him? I wonder if he's eaten.

I'm standing in the middle of Nate's sexy kitchen, wondering what to do with myself, when the front door opens and he walks inside, pulling his small black suitcase behind him. He's wearing another dark suit and tie, and his hair is pulled back off his face.

He's still in executive mode.

"I'll be right back," he murmurs and walks through the great room toward his bedroom without sparing me a glance.

Maybe I should just save him the trouble of telling me it's over and leave now. I know he's mad, and I wasn't expecting a scene from a movie where we run toward each other in slow motion and hold on for dear life. We saw each other just yesterday morning, for Pete's sake, but I was hoping for something a little warmer than that.

My heels click on the hardwood as I walk to the couch and gather my purse and wrap, and then I head to the front door. My hand is on the knob when I hear his hard voice across the room.

"If you walk through that door, so help me God, Julianne, I will tie you to my bed."

I lower my head and sigh. I'm so confused. He wants me to stay?

"Look at me." It's not a request.

I turn around and face him. He's changed into a soft gray T-shirt and black jeans, and his hair is down. He's shed his professional clothes and is just a man standing before me.

An angry man.

"Where are you going?" he asks and crosses his arms over his chest.

"Home."

"Why?"

"You don't seem to be terribly happy to see me." I'm proud of keeping my voice steady despite the tears that want to come.

God, I'm such a girl.

Regret moves through his eyes, and he frowns and runs a hand through his hair. He doesn't say anything for a long moment, and I take that to mean that I'm right. I close my eyes and hang my head, bracing myself for the goodbye.

"It's okay, Nate. I get it. I'll go." I turn back toward the door, and before I know what's happening, Nate twirls me around and grips my shoulders in his large, strong hands, holding me in front of him, his feral eyes trained on mine. He's panting, and he's just so *angry*.

"You are not running again."

"I'm not going to stay where I'm not wanted."

"What are you talking about?"

"I've barely heard from you since last night. You won't talk to me. You're cold and distant. I'm not an idiot, Nate, I know when someone's trying to break it off."

He clenches his teeth and closes his eyes, then looks at me with such need my knees almost buckle.

"I don't know how to deal with how I feel for you. I was a wreck yesterday when I couldn't reach you. No one at the office knew where you ran off to, and you wouldn't answer me. When you finally did call me, you brushed me off and told me I'm ridiculous and that our relationship is bullshit."

"That's not what I—"

"That's what you said," he interrupts me and grips me tighter. "No one hurts me, Julianne. No one. I don't give a flying fuck what anyone thinks of me. That's what got me through fighting, and it's what's gotten me to where I am now. And then you came into my life, and you just blindsided me. I am so fucking wrapped up in you I can't see straight, and you tell me I'm a caveman for wanting to protect you and that our relationship is bullshit."

Tears are running down my cheeks at the despair and loss on his face. My God, I had no idea his feelings for me are so strong. That he feels for me the same way that I feel for him.

I've never been so relieved and devastated at the same time. How am I going to fix this?

"I don't know how to deal with it either, Nate." I cup his face in my hands. "I was so sure that you were finished with me, that I'd pissed you off so badly that we couldn't fix it. I didn't mean that our relationship is bullshit. I didn't." I stress this and look him dead in the eyes. He's watching me, listening, and I continue.

"Everything happened so fast yesterday. I was a mess, and I'm never a mess. You were gone, Carly at work was bragging to me about how she's banging you and running off to New York with you"—Nate blanches, but I keep going before he can speak—"and then Luke called, freaking out because Nat's water broke. I just left and went to the hospital, forgetting everything else." I take a deep breath and wipe my tears away with my fingers.

"When Natalie finally agreed to take the meds, I checked my phone and saw that you'd been trying to reach me, and I called you right away. I swear, I didn't mean to hurt you at all, but I was annoyed that you were annoyed with me, and I had so much going through my head. I said the wrong thing, and I apologize again."

"Jules, I'm sure I could have handled things better too, I just . . ." He swallows and looks down, carefully choosing his words. "I just hate the fact that I have this primal need inside of me to protect you. I've never felt this about anyone before, and you just don't need me. I'm so proud of you for being the independent, confident, intelligent woman you are, but you don't need me, and I want to take care of you, more than you will ever know."

He releases my shoulders and runs his hands down my arms to link his fingers in mine. He's so wrong. I do need him.

I take a deep breath, steeling myself for the words I'm about to say. I grip his fingers with mine and realize we're still standing by the doorway. I don't want to break this moment by suggesting we sit, so I look into his eyes again and bare my soul.

"You're so wrong," I whisper. He frowns and looks apprehensive again. "You once said to me that if I'd been paying attention for the past year I would have seen that I'm the only woman you're interested in." I swallow and look down at his chest.

"Look at me," he whispers, and I comply, seeing hope in his gorgeous gray eyes.

"Well, if you'd been paying attention, Nate, you would have seen that I've been in love with you since long before we first made love in this apartment." His eyes widen in wonder, and my stomach settles as calm washes over me, and I know that this is right. "I do need you. I hated that you were away yesterday. I wanted to come home to you last night and tell you all about the baby and the delivery. I need your strength. Yes, I'm a badass, but there are times that I need someone to hold me up, too, and I didn't know until I found you that that doesn't make me weak. It means that I've found my partner."

"Julianne . . ." His voice is rough with emotion, and he leans his forehead on mine, wraps his arms around me and holds me close. "Say it again."

"Which part?" I ask with a laugh.

"The good part," he whispers.

"I need you."

"The other good part."

I run my fingers down his smooth cheek and brush my lips over his, breathing him in. "I love you."

"Oh, baby, I love you, too." Nate scoops me into his arms and carries me to his bedroom, turning on the sidelight, and lowers me gently to my feet. He pulls my hair out of the tie holding it off my face and runs his fingers through it.

"I love how soft your hair is." He unzips my simple, black shift dress, letting it fall down my arms and onto the floor. My bra and panties follow it, and he steps back, enjoying the view.

"Like what you see?" I ask and smile.

"God, you're so fucking hot."

Oh. When he says it like that, my panties go all wet, and I just want to lick him.

"I want you naked, Nate." I walk to him and pull his T-shirt up over his head. He raises his arms and backs out of the shirt, making it easier for me. I unfasten his jeans and slide them, along with his boxer-briefs, down his legs and off his feet as he steps out of them.

Nate lifts me and lays me on the bed. He kisses my stomach, my breasts and collarbones as he crawls up my body and nestles his large, thick cock against my folds. I run my hands down his back to his ass and smile up into his molten gray eyes.

He kisses me, softly, tenderly, brushing my lips in that expert way of his. I lift my legs and wrap them around his hips. As I do, I feel his apa brush against my clit, and I gasp.

Nate smiles against my lips. "Like that?" he asks.

"God, yes."

"If you don't, I'll take it out."

My wide eyes find his, and I cup his face in my hands. "You don't have to do that for me."

"I'd do anything for you."

And here come a few more tears. God, when will they stop?

"Julianne, I'll do anything to make you happy." He brushes the hair at my temples off my face and gazes at me with such love it takes my breath away.

"You do make me happy. Keep the apa. I like it." I grin and tilt my hips, rubbing him against me, and moan again. "I more than like it."

Nate laughs and starts to rock his hips just a little faster, sliding the tiny metal ball against my clit with each stroke.

"God, don't stop doing that." I push my hands into his black hair and hold his face to mine, kissing him passionately as those little metal balls do amazing things to me. "Oh, honey, shit . . ."

"Yes, baby, let go." He rocks once, twice more and bites gently on my lower lip, and I fall over the edge.

He reaches down between us and guides himself inside me, slowly stretching me, and my already sensitive muscles clench around him tightly.

"Fuck, don't do that. I'll come too fast."

"I can't help it. You feel so damn good."

He cups my breast in his hand and massages the nipple as he moves in and out of me at a slow, easy pace, watching my face, smiling softly down at me. "You are amazing. I love watching your beautiful face when I'm inside you."

God, I love it when he talks like this.

"Faster, babe," I whisper, but his grin widens, and he keeps the same gentle pace.

"No, this is going to have to be slow and steady, baby." His mouth finds mine once again, and his tongue teases me. His mouth slowly moves across my own, his whole body loving mine, oh so slowly.

"I missed you so much," I whisper against his lips.

"I hated being so far from you." His hips start to move just a tiny bit faster, and I rake my nails down Nate's back to his ass and hold on. "God, you make me crazy."

"Good." I feel my body tightening, another orgasm approaching, and I cling to him, wrapping myself around him. My body shudders with my release, and Nate clenches his jaw, rests his forehead against mine and surrenders to his own climax, whispering my name.

eighteen

"**H**ow did you get fresh chocolate cheesecake in your fridge while you were gone?"

We are seated at the breakfast bar, me in panties and his gray T-shirt, and Nate just in his black jeans, the top button undone.

He looks as delicious as this decadent cake.

"I had my housekeeper bring it in." He grins and offers me a bite from his plate, and I happily accept.

"I didn't know you have a housekeeper. I never see her."

"She only comes in once a week while I'm at work. I don't need someone full time."

I put my foot up in his lap, and he starts to rub the arch.

"Okay, I'm in girl heaven. Chocolate and a foot rub. Men think we're so hard to figure out, but it really just boils down to this." I close my eyes and enjoy his thumb rubbing up and down the sole of my foot.

"So noted." He chuckles and clears our plates. "Come on."

I take his offered hand, and he leads me to the couch. He sits in the middle and motions for me to sit at the end. He pulls my bare legs up into his lap, and I turn so my back is against the arm of the couch, and he continues to massage my feet.

Oh, I love him.

"So, tell me about yesterday."

I sigh in contentment and smile at my sexy man. "The baby is amazing. It was a rather quick labor, for a first baby, and Nat did great. Luke almost passed out when Olivia's head crowned, but I talked him down from the ledge."

I laugh at the memory.

"Natalie was incredible. She's so strong. I've never seen anything like it. It was the best birth control I've ever seen. I'm doubling up on my pills from now on. I don't care if I become a mutant from the hormones."

"Baby, you're so strong, childbirth would be a snap for you."

Why is he sitting here, calmly talking about me having babies?

"Hell to the no." I shake my head vigorously. "No babies are coming out of this body."

He eyes me speculatively. "Are you saying you don't want children?"

I pause. He's being serious. "I don't know." I frown and look down at his strong hand on my foot. "I've never thought about it."

"Think about it," he suggests.

"Someday." I shrug.

"I'd like to go see them tomorrow after work." He turns the conversation back to Natalie and starts to rub the other foot, and I moan.

"They'd love that."

"You'll come with me." His gray eyes find mine, and he smiles softly.

"Okay."

He runs his hand up and down my bare leg, his eyes following his movement. "You have great skin, baby."

"Natalie has a tattoo on her va-jay-jay," I blurt out.

"What?" Nate gapes at me, his jaw dropped.

"I had no idea, but I saw it with my own eyes. It's actually right here." I point down to my freshly waxed, panty-covered pubis.

"I don't know if I need to know this. If Luke knew something like that about you, I'd kick his ass."

"I have to tell someone, and you're the only one I can tell." I laugh and link my fingers with his.

"What is it?" he asks.

"It's script in a foreign language. All of her tattoos are. She won't tell me what it means." I shrug.

"All of her tattoos? How many does she have? I've never seen any."

"I'm not sure how many she has. I don't know if I've seen them all. She puts them where you can't see them when she has clothes on. My point was"—I trace the tattoo on his forearm with my finger—"what is up with you guys letting some creep put needles in your genitalia?"

"I thought you liked it." He gives me a wolfish grin, and I laugh.

"I do, but why in the world would you do it in the first place?"

"I was a twenty-year-old kid who wanted to impress chicks." He shrugs and grins.

"Why did you keep it all this time?" I ask.

"Because I went through hell to get it. It hurt like a son of a bitch."

"Poor baby." I pat his cheek roughly and giggle when he grabs my wrist and bites my palm.

"Okay, so if we're done talking about babies and needles in sensitive places, tell me exactly what Carly told you yesterday." His face is completely serious, and his eyes look a little pissed.

I didn't mean to let that slip.

"It was nothing, really. I know she's full of shit." I pull my feet out of his lap, but he grips my calf and holds me in place.

"What did she say, Julianne?"

I sigh. "She's told me twice now that she's dating you. Once the day that your ex was in your office, and again yesterday. I know it's a lie, so I shrugged it off the first time, but yesterday it was like she was going out of her way to tell me about you two and even asked me to work her accounts for her so she could leave early for a date she had with you."

Nate scowls and clenches his jaw. "Go on."

"She seemed embarrassed when I told her you'd gone out of town, but then her phone chirped with a text, and when she looked at it, she said it was you with her itinerary to join you in New York. I don't get it. She's been a complete hag since the day she started this job, but I don't understand what she's doing with this elaborate story of hers." I watch the flames in the fireplace and pull at my bottom lip with my fingers.

"What do you mean she's been a hag?" Nate asks, his voice deceptively calm.

"Oh, she hates me."

"She seems professional enough in meetings."

I chuckle ruefully. "Honey, of course she does. It's when we're alone that her claws come out."

"Why haven't you ever said anything?"

"What am I going to say? 'Carly doesn't play nice, and I don't like her'? It's not that serious. I've dealt with morons like her my whole life." I shake my head at him.

His eyes narrow, and he cups my cheek in his palm. "She's jealous of you."

"I don't see why." I kiss his palm and lean my cheek into him. "She doesn't know about us, obviously, and she has the same job I do."

"You're gorgeous and intelligent, and she knows that you out-class her. You'll move up in our company far more quickly than she will. And she knows it." He brushes his thumb along my lower lip, and I pucker my lips and kiss it.

"Well, it'll be interesting to see how long she keeps this story up."

"Julianne, if she says anything like that again, you have to tell me. If she were to spread this rumor around the office, it would mean an investigation into me, and while I know that they wouldn't find any fault on my part, it's unnecessary drama."

"I want to kick her carrot-top ass."

"Now that, I would like to see." Nate laughs, and I smack him on the shoulder.

"You're a perv."

"I'm a guy, babe."

"So." I straddle his lap and tangle my fingers in his soft, thick hair. His hands glide up my legs to cup my ass. "You want to see other women naked, huh?"

"I didn't say that. I said I wanted to see you kick her ass. If you both happened to be naked, who am I to complain?"

I chuckle against his lips and nibble the side of his mouth. He grips my hips and pulls my pelvis more tightly against his, and I can feel his erection through his jeans.

"I want you," I murmur.

Nate growls, and suddenly I'm on my back on the couch, and he's hovering over me.

"I never stop wanting you," he responds. He pulls me up long enough to pull his shirt over my head and trails wet kisses down my throat to my breasts.

God, his lips are magical.

He pulls and tugs on my nipples, with both his lips and his fingers, and I'm writhing beneath him. I comb my fingers through his hair and hold on as he moves south, nibbles at my belly button, and nudges my legs farther apart with his shoulders. He rips my panties off and throws them on the floor.

Oh. My. God.

"You have the prettiest pink pussy, baby." He licks my core, from my anus to my clit, and my back bows up off the couch.

"Fuck!"

"Easy." He grips my ass in his hands and tilts my pelvis up toward his handsome face. He places a sweet, chaste kiss on my clit and another on my labia, and then he begins kissing me more deeply, swirling his tongue inside me, gently sucking me.

It's the most delicious thing I've ever felt.

"Oh God, Nate." I'm still gripping his hair in my fingers. He moves his mouth up to my clit and just pushes the flat of his tongue against it as he inserts two fingers inside me and pushes down gently. "Holy fucking shit."

I feel him chuckle against me, and I'm completely lost to the sensation between my legs. A thin coat of sweat covers my skin, and I convulse as the orgasm tears through me, leaving me wrecked.

Nate flips me effortlessly onto my stomach and pulls back on my hips, raising my ass in the air. He slaps me, gently, as he guides his thick, hard cock inside me, and I cry out with shock.

He fucking spanked me!

I hope he does it again.

He has a tight grip on my hips as he slams into me, hard, over and over again.

"God, I love how tight you are," he growls and continues the steady, punishing rhythm. He's so deep inside me, and the apa is pushing against that most sensitive spot, and I know this orgasm is going to consume me.

"Oh, baby." I feel my muscles tighten around him. He lifts my torso, his hands on my breasts, and buries his face in my neck, kissing me.

"Ride me, baby."

I move up and down, my hips countering his movements, and it pushes me over. I grind down on him as I'm overwhelmed by my intense climax, and he cries out as he convulses and finds his own release.

"Did I hurt you?" He pulls out of me and turns me around in his arms, cradling me close, pushing my hair off my face.

"No, why?" We're both still panting.

"I hit you." His gray eyes are wide and regretful, and if I hadn't loved him before, I would be falling now.

"You spanked me, honey. There's a difference."

"I'm sorry, I was caught up in the moment. I know I'm strong. I could hurt you."

"Hey." I take his face in my hands and kiss him, soothing him. "You didn't hurt me. It was fucking hot."

"It was?"

"Oh yeah. Spank me any time, hot stuff."

"Really?"

"Yes, please." I nibble his lips and smile at him, loving the way he's running his hands up and down my back.

He places a kiss on my forehead and takes a deep breath. "I love you, Julianne."

nineteen

"You bought Olivia Louboutins?" Natalie asks incredulously.

It's Friday evening, and Nate and I are at Luke and Natalie's place for dinner. The rest of our workweek was way too busy to manage a trip to the hospital, so Luke called and invited us over for the evening.

Nate and Luke are in the kitchen, cooking up something that smells delicious, and Natalie and I are settled on the couch with the baby, watching our men.

"Of course." I shrug like it's no big deal, but I can't stop the huge grin that comes when I look at the tiny red-soled leopard-print shoes. "They'll fit her in a few months."

"Yeah, for about a week. Jules, these are too expensive for her to wear for such a short time."

"But you can't stop looking at them, can you? Natalie, with you as her mom and me as her aunt, this baby is going to *love* shoes."

"God help me," Luke mutters in the kitchen, and I laugh.

"Just give in to it, man," Nate mutters back to him, and I am so taken aback by these two incredibly sexy men moving effortlessly about the kitchen.

"Men cooking is sexy," I whisper to Natalie, and she grins.

"I know."

"Okay, my turn with the baby."

Natalie passes Olivia to me, and I cuddle her close, kissing her dark-haired head. "Hello, little love bug. Did you miss me?" I kiss her cheek and run my fingers through her soft, fine hair.

"You're already spoiling her too much," Natalie murmurs, and watches me with happy green eyes. She looks fantastic for having had a baby this week. Her dark hair is up in a haphazard bun, and she's in jeans and a T-shirt. She's already out of her maternity clothes. Maybe there is something to be said for yoga.

"Never. We girls have to stick together, don't we, Livie? Oh my, you're so pretty." This baby is beautiful. Of course, Natalie is a knock-out, and Luke is a freaking movie star, so the gene pool in this room is pretty fantastic. "Can I walk with her?"

"Of course."

I stand and wander to the windows, bouncing lightly and swaying back and forth, so in love with the sweet baby in my arms.

"You are wonderful," I whisper to her. "And you are smart and strong and important. I'm going to tell you that every single day, so you never forget it."

"Dinner's ready," Nate says from behind me.

I turn at his voice, and I can see that he heard me, but he doesn't say anything. He smiles at me and looks down at the baby, his face softening just a bit.

"Here." I place the baby in his arms and kiss her head.

"Christ, she's little."

"Don't swear in front of the baby," I admonish him.

Nate laughs, and we walk to the dining room off the kitchen. "Right. I'll be reminding you of that, dirty mouth."

Natalie takes the baby from Nate and places her in a bouncy seat at the end of the table.

"So, any weekend plans?" Natalie asks.

"No," I respond at the same time that Nate says, "Yes."

"We do?" I look over at him in surprise, and he smiles smugly.

"We do."

"What are they?" I ask as Natalie passes me the salmon. Mmm . . . poached salmon with a garlic and cilantro sour cream sauce, roasted baby reds and green salad.

Our men can cook.

"It's a surprise," Nate responds and feeds me a bite of salmon off his plate.

"I don't like surprises."

"Yes, you do."

Okay, I do.

Natalie laughs across from me, and I glare at her. "What are you laughing at?"

"You."

"Why?"

"It's just fun to see you like this." She takes a sip of wine and winks at me, and I can't help but grin. I know what she means. She's never seen me with a man.

"So, Luke," Nate smoothly changes the subject. "When is that new Hugh Jackman movie coming out?"

"In two weeks," Luke responds and grins. "It's gonna be a good one. Lots of action."

"Movie night!" I bounce in my seat, excited.

We always go out on opening night when one of Luke's movies opens. He's no longer an actor, but he still works in the industry as a producer, securing backing from studios and wooing actors and directors. And he's awesome at it.

"I don't know if we'll make this one," Luke says uncertainly and looks over at Olivia sleeping soundly in her bouncy seat.

"Oh, she'll be fine. We'll take her with us. She'll sleep through it." I wave him off, and Natalie nods.

"She's a good sleeper. She'll be okay," Natalie agrees. "Or, your mom will be happy to come watch her for a few hours. We'll figure it out."

"Okay, movie night it is." Luke smiles like a kid.

I look up at Nate and rub my hand along his thigh under the table. "Sound good to you?"

"It's a date."

"Good. Now"—I look over at Luke and give him my sweet smile, the one I use when I want something—"when are you going to do a girl movie?"

"Uh, that's not really my style, Jules."

"I want a girl movie." I pout. "Something with Zac Efron. Have you seen him lately?" I look up at Nate, and he's scowling at me.

"Why am I asking you?" I look over at Natalie. "Have you seen him lately?"

"He was beautiful in *The Lucky One*." She sighs, and I nod. We watched that one together last month at my place.

"We want Zac Efron." I turn back to Luke and smile.

"You are so getting spanked when we get home," Nate whispers down to his plate, and my thighs clench.

Holy shit.

Natalie's eyes narrow on Nate's face, but I shake my head at her, silently telling her that this is *really* okay.

"You don't like romantic shit," Luke remarks and frowns at me.

"I don't like watching *you* lay the romantic shit on my best friend, pal. It's disgusting. This"—I gesture around the room with my hands—"is not a movie. But I do like watching Zac Efron, Channing Tatum, and a number of other hot actors lay on the romantic shit in a movie. I have a vagina."

"I'm aware," Luke says, earning a glare from Nate. "Although, not firsthand," he quickly adds.

"So," I continue, "if you could work on that, I'd appreciate it."

"I'll see what I can do." Luke smirks and drinks his wine, and Natalie winks at me.

Olivia makes a squeaky noise, and I automatically lean over to her and plug her Binky back in her little mouth.

"There you go, baby doll."

Natalie smirks at me, and I look over at her. "What?"

"No babies, huh?" she murmurs, and all three of them look at me. Nate's eyes are molten gray.

"Don't be a bitch, Nat."

"Just sayin'."

NATE AND I went to Luke and Natalie's straight from work, so we drove separately. He's following me back to his place. I thought we should stay at mine since it's closer, but he insisted we go back to his, so we stopped by the house first so I could pack some clean clothes.

I park in my spot in the parking garage and wait for him to pull in alongside me. He takes my suitcase from me, and I take his free hand, linking our fingers together as we walk to the elevator.

"Did you have a good time?" he asks.

"Of course. I always enjoy them. You?"

As the elevator doors close, he turns me into his arms and cups my face in his hands, pulling my lips up to his.

"I always enjoy them, too, but I'm very glad to have you all to myself."

"Yeah? What are you going to do with me?" I ask against his lips.

"I'm going to take a shower with you, and then I'm going to tie you to my bed and fuck you."

Holy fuck.

"You're going to tie me?" I whisper, gazing into his bright gray eyes, clutching his upper arms in my hands.

He removed his suit jacket and tie at Nat's place, and his white dress shirt is unbuttoned to the top of his sternum, and the sleeves are rolled to his elbows.

He's so sexy.

"I am." He nibbles the side of my lips, sending tingles straight down to my groin, and I moan. "I'm going to tie you up and touch you everywhere. Kiss you everywhere. You." Kiss. "Are." Kiss. "Mine."

I take a big, shaky breath and free his hair from the hair tie, running my fingers through it. "I love it when you talk to me like that."

"Do you?" he asks as the elevator doors open, and he leads me out, through the hall and into his apartment.

"You know I do."

"I know that you're sexy as fuck, and I can't get enough of you.

I know that I love how smart you are, and I know that I never know what's going to come out of that fuckable mouth of yours." He closes and locks the front door and leaves my suitcase at our feet, pulling me through the great room toward the bedroom.

I unbutton his shirt, walking backward, and push it off his shoulders, letting it fall in the hallway. He unzips my skirt, and it follows. By the time we cross the threshold into the master bedroom, we're naked, having left a trail of clothing behind us.

"Put your hair up," he murmurs against my lips and turns away from me to start the water in the bathroom.

I grab a hair tie from his vanity drawer and twist my hair up so it doesn't get wet. Nate comes out of the shower, grabs my hand and pulls me back in with him.

He pours my shower gel in his hands, rubs them together to lather them up, and begins cleaning me, my front first, down my breasts and stomach, between my legs, but only briefly, then up my sides to my armpits. I brace my hands on his hips and watch his handsome face as his eyes watch his hands roam my naked body.

"This is nice," I murmur.

"Mmm," he agrees. "Turn around, please."

I comply and hear him pour more gel in his hands, then he's rubbing my back, my shoulders and neck, massaging me. "Oh God, babe, that's good."

He chuckles behind me. "You're a little tense, sweetheart."

"I have a stressful job. My boss is a tyrant."

He slaps my ass with a soapy hand, and I yelp in surprise and then giggle. "Okay, he's a sexy tyrant."

Nate begins massaging my low back, and I support myself on my hands on the tile wall. God, he's good with his hands.

He circles down to my ass and massages my buttocks, then slips a hand between the cheeks and into my folds. "Fuck, baby, you're so wet already."

"Let me wash you."

He drops his hand, and I turn. The water is rinsing me as I soap him up and return the favor of the massage, working on his back first. When he turns, I lather up his muscled chest and six-pack stomach, over his left side, tracing the tattoo that falls down his side, over his lean hip and onto his thigh. The sleeve tattoo on his right arm also gets special attention, and I trace it over his shoulder and across his chest, around his nipple. I slide my hand down to his cock, loving how it feels in my slippery hands, and move up and down, watching those sexy silver balls in the tip as he grows in my hand.

"Enough." His voice is low and ragged. He quickly rinses his skin in the hot water, turns it off, and leads me out to the bathroom, drying us both. He's so focused on me tonight, washing me, drying me, as though he can't stop touching me.

Please don't ever stop touching me!

"Come on." He takes my hand, pulls the sash off a white terrycloth robe hanging on the back of the bathroom door, and leads me to the bed. The white headboard has slats in it, and I know that he's about to tie me up.

"I've never been tied before," I whisper.

"Look at me." He pulls my chin up so he can look deeply into my eyes. "This is new to me too, baby. Let's try. If you don't like it, just say so, and I'll untie you. I promise, I won't hurt you."

"You'd never hurt me." I stand on my tiptoes so I can kiss him softly. "Where do you want me?"

twenty

Nate wraps his arms around my shoulders and pulls me tightly against him, our naked flesh pressed together, and kisses me gently. His lips are soft, brushing over mine, and then he takes it deeper, teasing my tongue with his. I wrap my arms around his waist and hold on, enjoying his warmth, thrilled at his hard erection pushing against my belly.

I love that I turn him on like this.

His hands glide down my back to my ass, and he lifts me effortlessly up his torso. I wrap my legs around him as he walks us to the bed, wraps one arm around my bottom, and climbs on his other hand and knees up the bed.

"I love how strong you are," I whisper against his mouth.

"It does come in handy, doesn't it?"

"Hmm," I agree.

"It helps that you're so tiny," he murmurs.

He lays me down on the cool sheets and grips both of my hands in his, lacing our fingers, and pulls them above my head. I open my eyes to find him gazing down at me, his gray eyes on fire, his glorious dark hair falling around his face. "Are you okay?" he asks.

I nod, and he smiles down at me, places a chaste kiss on my lips, and pins both of my hands with one of his while he reaches for the terrycloth tie at my hip.

"Remember, if you don't like this, just say stop."

"Do we need a safe word?" I ask sarcastically.

"No, baby, not tonight."

Oh. Does that mean we will in the future?

Before I can ask the question, Nate ties one end of the sash around my wrist, tight enough that I can't pull my hand out but loose enough that I can move. He pulls it through the slats of the headboard and ties my other wrist the same way, making sure that I can't pull my hands down past the top of my head.

"God, you're so beautiful," he murmurs and sits back on his heels between my legs. I feel completely exposed and not a little vulnerable. This is all new to me, and I'm not so sure about not being able to move my hands, but the hot look in Nate's eyes keeps me where I am.

He smoothes his hand down my arm, cups my cheek in his palm and brushes his thumb across my lower lip. I bite the pad of his thumb, and his eyes narrow and darken with lust.

"Want it rough, baby?" he asks.

"I thought that's what we're doing," I respond with a grin.

"Oh, we'll get there. First, I'm going to take my time with you. I want to touch every inch of you, baby."

He braces himself on his hands at my sides, not touching me with his torso, and bends down in a push-up move to suckle my nipples. His shoulders and arms flex with the motion, and I'm mesmerized by his incredible body. He holds himself there, effortlessly, kissing and sucking my breasts, making my back bow up off the bed, trying to get closer to his chest, but he backs away and shakes his head. "No, baby, *I'm* touching *you*."

"I want to touch you, too," I whisper.

"Not tonight."

"Not at all?" I hear the pout in my voice, but I don't care.

"Not until I've had my fill of you, so keep still."

God, I love it when he's in control. I had no idea it could be so sexy. Honestly, I don't think anyone else could make it sexy. It's just him.

He trails that incredible mouth and tongue over my belly, nuzzles my navel, and peppers sweet, wet kisses up and down my ribs, making me squirm. His hands are on my hips, holding me in place, as he kisses his way south. He places two chaste kisses on my pubis, then presses my thighs even farther apart, and I expect him to start licking my pussy, but he doesn't. His lips nibble the apex of my thighs, just out of range, making me even hotter. God, I want his mouth on me.

"Nate," I moan.

"Yes, baby," he whispers.

"I need you."

"You have me, sweetheart." His hands are massaging my thighs, his lips are doing amazing things to the inside of my right leg, over the top of my knee—fuck, that's a sensitive spot I didn't even know about!—and down my calf to my foot. He sits back on his heels and bends my leg at the knee, pulling my foot up to his lips. He kisses the pad of each toe, down my arch to the heel, and then he starts the process all over again with my other foot, nibbling and kissing and massaging his way back up to the apex of my thighs, trailing damp kisses around my center, driving me crazy.

My body is on fire. I am just sensation. Electricity is shooting along every nerve-ending, and I've never felt this . . . *alive.*

"Baby, I need you inside me," I beg, and I feel his grin against my hip as he works his way back up my torso.

"Not yet, love."

"Please," I beg without hesitation. I need him.

I need him.

"No, baby, I'm not done. I'm going to turn you over." He flips me onto my belly, crossing the sash of the robe above my head, straddling my legs to hold me in place. I am completely at his mercy.

Yes, I love how strong he is. I love that he can just move me wherever he wants me. It's fucking hot.

He brushes a few tendrils of hair off my neck that have escaped the knot and nibbles his way from my hairline down my spine to the crack of my ass.

"Your back is amazing, Julianne. I love how toned you are. I love seeing the muscles flexed with your arms over your head like this." His hands are gliding up and down my back on either side of my spine, and I moan in pleasure.

"God, you're good with your hands." My voice is rough, and my skin is tingling under his expert hands.

"I love your firm ass." He kisses each cheek, biting and sucking as he does, and I lift my ass in the air. He grips my hips more tightly in his strong hands and holds me steady. "Hold. Still." His voice is harsh, and I immediately comply.

Geez.

Like he did before, he nibbles and kisses down each leg, paying special attention behind my knees, making me moan in pleasure. Finally, he's kissing his way back up, and I can't wait to feel what he's going to do next.

Suddenly, with his legs still straddling me, holding my thighs pressed together, he spreads my buttocks, exposing my anus and pussy, and his face is pressed to me, licking my folds, pressing his tongue deep inside me. I try to push my ass in the air again, but he holds me firmly in place, hands gripping my spread ass, face planted deliciously in my folds, and I come hard and fast, crying out his name.

My hands are gripping on to the sash, pulling toward my head, but it's keeping my arms above me as I come against his mouth, and I bury my face in the pillow.

He stops as quickly as he started and slides up my body, still spreading my ass with his hands and straddling my hips, and guides his beautiful, thick, large cock inside me.

"Oh fuck, Julianne, I love your tight pussy."

I feel my muscles clench at his sexy words, and he starts to move, really move, in and out of me, pushing harder with each flex of his hips, bracing himself on my ass with his fingers clenched so tightly it hurts, but it hurts in such a delicious way, there's no way in hell I'm going to tell him to stop.

Nate's thrusts are coming harder and faster, and I feel the buildup again. I arch my back, clench my fists, and every muscle in my body is flexed when I hear him say, "Yes, baby, come with me."

His words push me over the edge, and I explode beneath him, as he finds his release inside me, chanting my name as we both writhe and shudder.

He collapses on his elbows at my sides, pulls out of me and leans down, finally touching me with his chest against my ass, and kisses my spine right between my shoulder blades before resting his cheek there, laying his body on mine.

After our breathing slows and our bodies relax, Nate raises himself off of me and unties my wrists, then flips me over, brushes the hair off my face and kisses me sweetly and softly.

"Are you okay?" he asks, settling his weight at my side and cradling me in his arms. He pulls the duvet up around us.

"Hmm . . ." I answer.

"I need some verbal communication, baby." He chuckles. "I need to know that you're okay."

"I'm fine." I open my eyes and gaze up into his beautiful face. My hand glides up his tattooed arm, over his shoulder, and I run my fingertips down his stubbled cheek. "More than fine," I add.

"You didn't tell me to stop," he murmurs.

"I might have killed you if you'd stopped."

"I didn't hurt you?" he asks, his gray eyes worried and searching mine.

"Stop worrying about hurting me, ace. I'm not made of glass. You didn't hurt me." I kiss him gently, then bite his lower lip and lave it with the flat of my tongue. "I think I have a new taste for being tied up." I smile up at him shyly, and he laughs.

"I think I have a new taste for tying you up," he responds with a delighted grin.

"What are we doing this weekend?" I ask with a yawn.

"It's a surprise."

"Can I have a hint?" Damn, he wore me the hell out. I can't keep my eyes open.

"We're not staying here," he responds and snuggles me more firmly against him.

"Where are we going?" I whisper.

"You'll find out tomorrow. Go to sleep, sweetheart." He kisses my forehead, and I fall into a restful sleep.

"YOU DON'T NEED to bring all of this crap." Nate and I are standing in his bedroom with my suitcase open on the bed.

"Are you going to tell me where we're going?" I ask, hands on my hips.

"No."

"Then I need all this crap." I glare at him, secretly delighted with him, and enjoy the view. He's pulled his hair back, is wearing a white T-shirt under a black sweater and dark blue jeans. His arms are crossed over his chest, making his biceps flex.

Yum.

"Julianne, I want to take the bike."

"Okay, tell me where we're going, and I'll downsize my stuff."

"I'm not telling you where we're going."

"Then how do I know what I need? Let's take the car. It's called compromise, ace."

He sighs, rubs his face with his hands in exasperation, and glares at me when he sees my smile.

"Why are you grinning?"

"Because you're hot when you're frustrated with me."

Nate chuckles and shakes his head. "Fine, bring all your shit. We'll take the Mercedes."

"See? That wasn't so hard." I tap his cheek playfully as I walk past him to the bathroom to gather my toiletries.

"Wait, you have more shit to pack?"

"Yep," I call over my shoulder.

"Jesus," he mutters, and I laugh.

"Okay." I shove everything in my suitcase and zip it up. "I'm ready."

Nate picks up his overnight bag, which is much smaller and weighs far less than my bag, grabs the handle of my rolling suitcase with his other hand, and ushers me out of the room.

"Let's go."

twenty-one

N ate pulls his shiny black Mercedes SUV into the parking lot of his father's gym and throws it in park.

"What are we doing here?" I ask.

"I have to run in for a second to talk to my dad. Wait here?"

"Okay."

He leans over and swiftly kisses me, then hops out of the car, leaving the engine running. I watch his fine form stride through the front door of the building and sit back to wait.

Where is he taking me?

Clearly, we're not going far because we're driving, and we both have to work Monday morning. Maybe he's taking me to Portland for the weekend? That's only a three-hour drive. Or maybe up to the little resort town of Leavenworth? Or the San Juan Islands?

There's so much to do here, it could be anywhere.

I check my phone and send Natalie a text, letting her know we're going somewhere out of town in case she tries to reach me and I don't have cell service.

Just as I finish with the text, Nate climbs back in the car.

"Okay, ready?"

"Sure. Everything okay?" I ask.

"Yep, just needed to check in with Dad for a minute." He smiles over at me as he pulls out of the lot and toward the freeway.

"Okay, so are you going to tell me where we're going?" I pull his hand into my lap and lace our fingers.

"The beach."

"Really?" I feel the face-splitting grin on my face. "I love the beach!"

"Good." He kisses my hand and lays them both in my lap again. "I have a beach house in a newer little town called Seabrook. It's about a half hour north of Ocean Shores."

"You own the house?" I ask.

"Yeah, my dad and I do. He uses it, too."

"I like your dad." I really do. Rich has been nothing but sweet to me since the first time Nate took me to their gym.

"He likes you, too."

"Can I ask you a question?" I bite my lower lip, nervous to ask, and he glances over at me, then back at the freeway. Traffic is pretty light this morning.

"Of course, anything."

"Where is your mom?"

Nate signals and changes lanes. "She died when I was seven."

"I'm sorry," I murmur.

"Don't be." He squeezes my hand and smiles reassuringly. "It was a long time ago. She had breast cancer. It's been just Dad and me ever since."

"He never remarried?"

"No." He shakes his head and frowns. "I know there have been women, but he never paraded them around me. I thought he might re-marry after I was grown and gone, but he seems content with the gym and dating here and there."

"What was her name?" I ask quietly.

"Julie," Nate responds softly, and I gasp. "My dad called her Jules." He looks over at me, his eyes bright.

"Is that why you don't call me Jules?" I ask.

"Partly." He shrugs and changes lanes again. "I don't have a weird fixation on your name or anything, baby. I've called you Jules a few times."

"I know. It makes me smile, but I like that you call me Julianne."

"You do? I thought you hated it."

"I hate it when other people call me that, but it's different with you."

"Honestly, honey, I just think your name is beautiful, and it suits you." He kisses my knuckles again, and I melt.

Damn, he says the sweetest things sometimes.

"Are you getting all mushy on me, ace?" I ask, trying to lighten the mood.

"Never. I'm a man."

I laugh and squeeze his hand. "You're my man."

"And only yours, baby."

"THIS IS INCREDIBLE!" I climb out of the car and stand facing the beautiful, light blue, two-story home with lots of large windows and a wraparound porch. There are tall evergreens surrounding the house, and I can hear the waves crashing on the shore on the other side.

"I was expecting a small beach cabin." I turn back to Nate and grin as he pulls our bags out of the back of the SUV.

"I know it's bigger than I probably need, but it came up for sale last year, and I snatched it. This is a new community, and the real estate is a good investment." I follow him up the steps to the front door. Beautiful outdoor furniture sits on the porch, and the wide pine door has an oval, frosted glass window with a beach scene etched in it.

"I also work with a rental company that rents it out here and there for me, and I donate time to charity auctions."

He unlocks the door and walks in ahead of me. "Make yourself at home."

"Wow." The space is large and open and was clearly professionally decorated in a beachy theme, but in a subtle, non-annoying way. The furniture and artwork are in shades of white, blue and gray. There is a magnificent stone fireplace in the center of the space, with logs all set up and ready to light.

The kitchen and dining room are in the back of the house, facing the incredible views of the ocean. It's overcast but mild today, and the water is a deep gray-blue, beating up the shoreline. I can't wait to get out there.

"Come on, I'll give you a quick tour."

"What's up with you and sexy kitchens?" I ask, pointing to the truly sexy kitchen. It boasts all-white cabinets and cupboards, black granite countertops, and stainless steel top-of-the-line appliances. The space is large, with plenty of counter space. The adjacent dining area has a long black table with seating for ten.

"I need good kitchens to cook in." He shrugs, and I grin at him. "Let's go upstairs."

There are three good-size bedrooms with an en-suite bathroom for each, along with a spacious loft, complete with a pool table and the master suite, which I immediately fall in love with.

"Oh, this is spectacular." I walk straight to the French doors that open out to a covered balcony and walk outside, breathing in the salty air and looking out at the water. There is a one-hundred-and-eighty-degree view. "This, right here, is my favorite part."

Nate walks up behind me, wraps his arms around my middle and kisses my neck. "This is what sold me, too. There is glass to enclose this, but I like hearing the water and feeling the breeze."

"Oh, don't close it in. It's perfect." He smiles against my neck, and I turn in his arms, hugging him close. "I love it."

"I love you," he responds and tips my chin up to meet my gaze. "I love you," he repeats, his voice and eyes raw, and I feel tears prick the corners of my eyes.

"I love you, too."

Nate kisses me, gently moving his lips over mine, back and forth, nibbling at the corners of my mouth. He finally pulls back and kisses my nose, then my forehead.

"Let me show you the master suite, before I make love to you on this balcony."

"Later?" I ask as my stomach clenches at the thought of making love to Nate on this amazing balcony.

"We'll see what we can do." He smiles and takes my hand, leading me back inside. The bedroom is beautiful, with a king-size bed and the same white, gray and blue colors that flow through the whole house.

The master bathroom is simply breathtaking.

"Oh, I'm moving in," I murmur, not catching the surprised look on Nate's face as I circle the room. "I love this bathroom."

The tile is gray and blue, and the tub is large enough for two, white and claw-footed with shiny chrome fixtures. There are two white pedestal sinks with oval mirrors hanging above them.

The tub sits in a glass alcove, with the same view as the balcony.

"I love how the view is as much a part of the house as the décor is," I comment and turn to find Nate leaning against the wall, watching me.

"What?" I ask.

"What did you say when you walked in here?" His face is serious, and his arms are crossed.

"Um, that I love this bathroom?" I'm completely confused.

"Before that."

"I don't know." I shake my head and frown, and then it hits me, and my cheeks flame. "Oh."

"What did you say?" he asks again.

"I said I'm moving in here." I grin sheepishly, then wince. "It's just a girl knee-jerk reaction to this bathroom, Nate."

He shakes his head and looks down, clenching his eyes closed. What the hell?

"Hey, I'm sorry if I said something wrong." I walk over to him and take his face in my hands.

"You didn't." He swallows and wraps his arms around me, pulling me in to lean against him as he leans on the wall.

"What's wrong?"

"Move in with me."

"Here?" My voice is shrill with shock, and I know my eyes are wide.

"No, in the condo. At home."

"Nate . . ." I look down at his chest, trying to collect my thoughts. My stomach is suddenly in knots, and I can't breathe.

It's too soon.

"Look at me," he whispers, and I do.

"It's kind of soon, don't you think?"

"I don't give a fuck about that."

"Let's enjoy our weekend and talk about it when we get back." I need time to process this, but I know this is the wrong thing to say when his face falls and his eyes get cold.

"I'm sorry I brought it up." He starts to push me out of his arms, but I hold on tight.

"Stop it." My voice is hard, surprising both of us. "I didn't say no, Nate. I said let's talk about it some more. I want to be with you. Let's enjoy this beautiful home of yours and relax, just the two of us, with nothing else to worry about, for the next thirty-six or so hours."

His face relaxes into a smile, and he hugs me, tucking me under his chin. "Don't worry, baby, I'll talk you into it."

I just laugh and squeeze him tight. "Let's go for a run on the beach."

"A run?" Nate asks as I pull out of his arms and walk into the bed-room to open my suitcase.

"Yeah. I haven't worked out much this week." I know Nate goes to the gym every morning before he follows me into the office. "I need a run."

"Okay." We pull on some workout clothes, our running shoes and hoodies and head downstairs to the back porch.

"Wow." The wraparound porch that does indeed circle the entire house extends farther in the back, over a steep incline in the terrain that leads down to the sand below. There is an outdoor kitchen, and soft furniture on the covered space. The railing is made of thick rustic logs, most likely native to this area, and a long stairway leads down to the beach.

Halfway down the incline, the stairs stop at a large gazebo with more plush furniture and a fire pit. It would be a great spot to sit in the evening with a glass of wine, roast some marshmallows and watch the sunset.

Nate leads me all the way down to the sand.

"Well, the climb back up is going to be one hell of a workout," I remark drily.

He chuckles down at me. "Why do you think the gazebo is there? I don't need anyone having a heart attack on my property."

We walk down to the shoreline, where the sand is packed and wet, and silently start to run, setting a steady, even pace, running in silence, listening to the water, the birds, and our feet as they rhythmically hit the sand.

We run around driftwood, over seashells, and even spot the carcass of a sea lion, most likely washed up during the tide.

"If you want to run ahead of me, it's okay," I say, breaking the quiet. "I know your legs are longer than mine."

"I'm good."

I glance over at him, and he grabs my elbow, pulling me to the right. "Watch out."

He's steered me around a washed-up log.

"Thanks."

After about twenty minutes, we decide to turn and head back. We've run a long way down the beach, which means we have to run all the way back.

I slow to a walk when I spot the dead sea lion.

"Julianne?" Nate is out of breath.

"I'm fine, time to walk." I'm also panting, and we walk toward the house.

"I love it here." Nate's eyes are fixed on the waves as they tumble toward us. "It's like, when I'm here, nothing else matters."

I love the beach, too, and I know exactly what he means.

"Being at the beach makes me focus on myself. I forget to worry." I frown as I stare out at the water, trying to articulate my thoughts. "I guess it's my happy place."

"You're my happy place, baby."

My head whips up to meet his gaze at his softly spoken words. He just smiles and takes my hand in his as we continue along the shoreline.

"Come on, let's feed you lunch."

twenty-two

"This is nice."

Nate's running his fingers through my hair. We are lounging on the luxurious sage-green couch in the living room. Nate lit a fire in the beautiful stone fireplace, and it's warm and comfortable. After our run on the beach, I took a shower while he fixed lunch, then he joined me.

"How did your kitchen get stocked?" I ask and close my eyes, loving the way his fingers feel in my hair.

"I made some calls," he murmurs.

"Must be nice to have minions."

He chuckles and tugs playfully on my hair. "I don't have minions. I have millions."

I hear the playfulness in his voice, but I keep my eyes closed. I don't want to know how much money he has. I know he's excellent at his job, and he is clearly wealthy.

"None of my business," I murmur.

"Don't go to sleep on me."

"You like it when I go to sleep on you." Hmm . . . he's still playing with my hair, and the fire is warm. "I don't remember the last time I was this relaxed. We have to come here often."

"We can come here whenever you want, baby."

Nate turned on the satellite radio while he was fixing lunch, and the music is flowing through the whole house through the sound system. *I Won't Give Up* by Jason Mraz is playing, making me smile.

"I love this song."

"You do?" I feel him reach for the remote, and he turns up the volume.

I open my eyes and look up into his face. How did I get this lucky?

"You spoil me, you know."

"I hope so. That's the goal." His thumb brushes across my cheek.

"You don't need to. I'm happy with just you."

"This is me, baby."

I sit up and cup his face in my hands. His hair is still tied, and my fingers are itching to run through it.

"Can I take your hair down?" I ask.

His eyes flare. "You can do whatever you want."

I pull the tie out of his hair and run my fingers through the thick, ink-black softness. "Don't cut it."

"Okay." His arms are wrapped around me, and his eyes are traveling over my face, patiently watching me as I touch his hair, his face, his shoulders.

"You're so handsome," I whisper.

Nate leans down and lays his lips over mine, just resting them there, breathing me in. I never knew such a light touch could be so intimate. Finally, he kisses me sweetly and pulls back.

"I have something for you," he whispers, and I grin.

"It's about time, ace." I quickly straddle his hips and settle my center over his crotch. "This morning feels like days ago."

Nate laughs up at me as he cups my ass in his hands and pulls me closer. "Well, that's not exactly what I meant, but I love the way you think, baby."

"Oh." I kiss his cheek and nibble over to his ear. "What do you have for me?" I whisper.

"On second thought"—he wraps his arms around my middle, and before I know it, I'm on my back across the couch, tucked under him—"this is an excellent idea."

"I do have good ideas, don't I?" I ask with a sassy smile, and he grins delightedly down at me, his gray eyes shining with happiness.

"Oh, baby, you do." He scrapes his teeth along my jawline. His hands are in my hair, holding me still, and he devours me with a kiss that leaves me dizzy. My hands slip beneath the waist of his jeans and boxer-briefs, and I grip his tight, smooth ass in my hands.

"Nate," I murmur against his lips.

"Yes, beautiful."

"In." Kiss. "Me." Kiss. "Now."

He pushes back to look down at me, his eyes on fire, matching mine, and I grab for his fly. My fingers feel clumsy, and it takes me a few tries, but I finally get his zipper down, push his pants and briefs down far enough to unleash his beautiful, already hard cock, and run my thumb over the tip, back and forth over his apa.

"Fuck," he growls.

He tears the yoga pants I threw on after my shower at the crotch rather than take the time to pull them off, and pushes two fingers inside me. "God, baby, you're so wet."

"Now. I need you now."

"This is going to be fast, Jules."

"Yes, fast." I guide him through my lips to my opening, and he slides in, all the way to the hilt. He's so deep, so big, and I know this will not last long, for either of us.

Jesus, two minutes ago I was about to fall asleep in his lap!

"So beautiful." His hips are moving quickly. He's slamming into me hard, and he pulls my leg up over his shoulder, letting him sink into me even deeper. "Holy fuck, babe."

I grip on to his arms and hold on for dear life as he thrusts into me fast and hard and oh so deep. His hands tighten in my hair, and he rests his forehead against mine as I feel his orgasm work through him.

"With me," he whispers, and it pushes me over the edge, and I shatter around him.

"Wow," I whisper and kiss his nose.

"God, Julianne, I never stop wanting you." He pulls out of me and reverses our positions so I'm lying on top of him, my head on his chest. His pants are still pulled down, and mine are a torn mess, but neither of us cares.

"Back at you, ace. You are so beautiful, inside and out." I lay my hand over his heart and smile softly. "Thank you, by the way."

"No need to thank me for that, baby. It's my pleasure."

I laugh and prop myself up on my hands so I can look into his face. "Not that, smart-ass. Thanks for this weekend. We needed it."

He tucks my hair behind my ear and sighs. "Yeah, we did."

I yawn and settle back down on his chest, listening to his steady heartbeat and enjoying the rhythmic rise and fall with each breath he takes.

"Let's sleep," he whispers and kisses my hair.

I WAKE ALONE. A fresh log has been tossed onto the fire, I smell something delicious coming from the kitchen, and the radio is still on. I don't recognize the song that's playing.

I sit up and stretch. There is no sign of Nate, so I run upstairs to throw away my ruined yoga pants and change into jeans. I pick up my iPhone and turn it on as I descend the stairs.

Hmm . . . where did Nate go?

I sit back down on the couch and rub my hands over my face, trying to wake up. Naps always leave me extra groggy.

My phone starts to ring on the couch cushion next to me. I don't recognize the number.

"Hello?"

"Jules?" a woman asks.

"Yes."

"Hi, this is Marie Desmond from *Playboy* magazine. I'm sorry to bother you on a Saturday."

"No problem. What's up?" I frown and stand to pace the room as I talk. What could they possibly want?

"Well, I'm calling because we are about to do an anniversary shoot for the July issue, and we're bringing back some of our most popular girls. Do you have any recent photos of yourself?"

"Yes, I have some recent photos, Marie, but none that are nude."

Holy shit!

"That's okay. I'd love for you to e-mail a couple to me."

"I'm not even sure that I'd be interested in posing for an anniversary issue." I stop pacing in front of a wide window and watch the ocean crash on the sand below.

"Well, it pays $50,000, Jules."

"$50,000? Holy cow that's double what I got for the month I was the centerfold. Why so much?"

"We've been authorized to offer that to the veteran girls for this special issue."

"I don't know. That part of my life was a long time ago, and I'm not so sure that my father's heart could survive me posing nude again," I say with a laugh, and I hear Marie's chuckle on the other end.

"I understand. Think about it over the weekend and call me on Monday."

"Okay. Thanks for the opportunity, Marie."

"You're welcome. I'll talk to you soon."

I hang up the phone and lean my forehead against the cool glass of the window.

Holy fuck.

"Hell, no."

I twirl around at Nate's angry voice and find him standing next to the couch, leaning his hip against it with his arms folded over his chest.

"I take it you heard?"

"No way, Julianne."

"I didn't say I was going to do it."

"You didn't say no." His eyes are glacial, his jaw clenched, and he's just so pissed.

"She offered me fifty grand. That's double what centerfolds make." This is so not about the money. I don't need it. But it is such a boost to my ego to know that they still want me!

"I'll deposit a hundred grand into your account when we get home. The answer is no." His voice is so calm, but he's radiating anger, and this really pisses me off.

"I didn't ask you," I respond with a scowl.

"Julianne . . ."

"Stop." I hold up my hand and shake my head. "I am not your child, nor am I your wife. This is my decision, Nate."

I see a muscle twitch in his jaw, and his eyes narrow on mine.

"So, what you're saying is, when my girlfriend, whom I happen to be in love with, is propositioned by *Playboy* to pose nude, I don't get to have an opinion in the matter?"

"You're not giving me your opinion. You're putting your foot down and telling me that I can't. I'm twenty-six years old. I'll do what I want." I cross my arms over my chest and glare back at him.

"No discussion?" he asks quietly.

I sigh deeply and look down at my bare feet. I know I'm being stubborn and stupid, but damn it, I'm not his property!

"Nate . . ."

He crosses the room quickly and grips my arms in his hands, holding me in place. "I can't stand the thought of it, Julianne. No other man will ever see you naked again, do you understand me?" His voice is raw, his eyes pleading with me, and my brain just stops.

"Nate—" I try again, but he interrupts me once more.

"No." He shakes his head in denial. "I want to build a life with you. This isn't just an affair for me. And you get a call from someone you don't know who wants you to pose naked in a national magazine, and I don't weigh in on your decision at all? How is that supposed to make me feel?"

Fuck.

"Nate." I step toward him, and he loosens his grip on me, but his face is hard. I take a deep breath and wrap my arms around his waist, press my cheek against his chest and hold on tight. "Stop, babe."

His arms fold around my shoulders, and he hugs me to him.

I caress his back reassuringly, kiss his chest and back away, still in the circle of his arms. I look up into his uncertain, wary face and smile, my anger gone. He loves me. He wants to protect me.

"I was never going to accept their offer, Nate."

"Why didn't you just turn her down?" he asks quietly.

"Two reasons: One, because it felt nice to get the offer, and two, because ironically, I hadn't talked it over with *you*. You know I'm not interested in that. But it's really flattering that they thought of me, out of all the girls they could choose." I shrug and look at his chest. "I would hope you'd be proud of me."

"Oh, baby, I am." He kisses my forehead, and I feel the tension seep out of him. "I'm so proud of you. But I can't deal with the thought you of posing again. Please turn them down."

"Like I said, I wasn't going to accept the offer. But, Nate, you can't just dictate to me what I will and won't do. I'm not the kind of girl who will just go along with your orders."

"I know, but damn it, it pissed me off."

"So noted."

"You're not going to do it?" he asks, tilting my head back with his fingers under my chin, pinning me with his gray gaze.

"No." I run my fingers down his smooth cheek. "Besides, my brothers and Dad would freak."

"They're not alone." He kisses my forehead once again and pulls out of my arms, takes my hand and leads me toward the kitchen. "Come, I have something for you."

"I hope it's food. I'm starving."

He smiles back at me. "You'll see."

"So many surprises this weekend, Mr. McKenna."

"I like surprising you. We're going outside."

I look down at my bare feet. "Should I grab some shoes and a jacket?"

"No, you'll be warm enough. Here." He lifts me effortlessly into his arms and cradles me against his chest. I wrap my arms around his neck and kiss his cheek and breathe in his clean, Nate scent.

"You smell good. I like it when you carry me."

He smiles down at me, opens the sliding door, and walks out onto the deck. The sun is setting on the water, turning the sky orange, red and purple. It's stunning.

He walks to the stairs leading down to the beach and starts descending them.

"You don't have to carry me down all these stairs."

"You're fine," he responds and easily moves down the staircase.

We arrive at the gazebo, and I gasp.

"Surprise."

twenty-three

Nate lowers me to my feet, and I stand in front of him, his hands resting on my shoulders, transfixed. The gazebo has been transformed into a lovely romantic getaway. The fire pit in the center of the rustic space is ablaze. A table is set up on one side, filled with silver-dome-covered plates and a bottle of champagne chilling in a silver ice bucket. An ottoman has been pushed flush against one of the outdoor love seats, and there are large, colorful pillows and blankets propped on it.

White Christmas lights have been strewn along the perimeter of the space, both along the ceiling and the railing, adding a soft glow.

Added to that is the amazing orange, red and purple sunset happening over the deep blue ocean, and I've never seen anything so beautiful in my life.

"Say something," Nate whispers.

"Wow," I murmur.

Nate turns me so I'm facing him, his gorgeous gray eyes dancing with humor. "What do you think?"

"You went all mushy and romantic on me." I cup his cheek in my palm.

"Luke can give you mushy and romantic on the screen, but it's my job to give it to you in real life, baby. Get used to it." He leans down and gently lays his lips on mine, kissing me in the way only Nate can, and I sigh.

"Let's feed you," he says.

We walk to the beautifully set table, and Nate lifts the silver dome lids off the platters. The finger foods on display are too lovely to eat.

"Okay," Nate says, pointing at each dish. "We have chorizo-stuffed clams, bite-size Caprese salad on crostini." He smiles down at me. "Which means mozzarella, tomato and basil on toasted bread, crab cakes and bacon-wrapped steak."

"Holy shit, this looks delicious."

Nate hands me a plate, and we dig in, piling food on our plates. He pours us each a glass of champagne and leads me over to the lounging space. We are sitting side by side, Indian-style, our plates in our laps, facing the ocean.

"A toast." Nate holds his glass aloft, and I follow. "To you, Julianne. For making me feel alive and happy, no matter where we are."

I smile up at my man, still overcome by this amazingly romantic gesture. I've never been romanced like this. "Thank you," I whisper.

"My pleasure."

We clink glasses and sip the delicious pink champagne.

"How did you do all this?" I ask with a bite of steak in my mouth.

"Minions," he responds with a shrug, and I laugh.

"Seriously, when? This wasn't here when we went for our run this morning."

"I had it done this afternoon while you napped."

I take a bite of my Caprese crostini and watch him while I chew. His hair is loose. He's wearing a black T-shirt, showing off his beautiful tattoo, and his blue jeans fit him perfectly. Nate glances over at me, and his eyes soften. He brushes a crumb off the side of my mouth and runs his thumb over my bottom lip.

"What?" I ask.

"You look lovely with the firelight dancing on your skin, and your beautiful blue eyes look happy."

Oh. Yes, he's in über-romantic mode tonight.

"Thank you," I whisper, completely caught up in him.

I take another sip of the champagne and finish the food on my plate. "That was delicious."

"Mmm . . ." he responds as he also takes his last bite.

He takes my plate and napkin and sets them aside with his and turns back to me, opening his arms. I slide easily between his legs, leaning my head on his chest, to enjoy the view.

"It's really beautiful here, ace."

"I'm glad you like it." He kisses my hair and wraps his arms around my shoulders, hugging me against him.

"If we didn't have work, I'd never want to leave."

"Like I said earlier, we can come here whenever you want."

"We should try to come once a month. And bring Nat and Luke and the baby. They'd love it, too."

"That sounds great to me." He kisses my hair again, and I smile.

He's so kind, and I love that he likes my friends.

The sun is slipping into the water now, sending orange reflections across the surface. The sky is dark purple, and in the distance I can see some dark clouds rolling in.

"We might get lucky and get a winter storm tonight." I rub his arms where they rest across my chest.

"You like thunderstorms?" he asks.

"At the beach I do. They're awesome."

"Would you like some dessert?"

"I always, always have room for dessert, babe."

Nate chuckles as he climbs around me to the table and returns with two small individual chocolate cheesecakes.

"Oh my. Even here you manage to feed me chocolate cheesecake."

"Of course. It's your favorite."

"What's your favorite?" I ask and indulge in the decadent dessert. "Oh sweet Jesus, that's good."

"You," he responds, his eyes on fire as he watches me lick chocolate off my lips.

"You are romantic tonight." I take another bite and moan.

"Does it really bother you?" he asks with a grin.

"No. It's nice. Don't tell Natalie."

Nate laughs and offers me a bite of cheesecake from his plate, which I happily accept and offer him some of mine.

We finish our desserts this way, feeding each other, and then settle back against the cushions, drinking another glass of champagne.

"I have something for you. I've been trying to give it to you all day, but you kept distracting me." He smiles ruefully at me and digs into his jeans pocket.

"You don't have to give me anything, Nate. This whole weekend is amazing."

"Well, this is special to me, and I want you to have it. It's why we stopped at my dad's this morning." He pulls his hand out of his pocket, but holds whatever it is in his fist.

"Okay," I murmur, encouraging him to keep talking.

"I already told you that my mom passed when I was very young. I don't remember a lot about her, just mostly what my dad has told me, but I remember that she was really pretty, and she was very affectionate."

"I'm sure she was gorgeous, Nate. One look at you, and no one would doubt that."

He smiles at me and runs the backs of his fingers down my face.

"The year she passed, I gave her this for her birthday, which was today." He opens his fist, and inside is a silver chain with a pretty silver heart-shaped pendant.

He looks at me, still smiling. "I'd like to give it to you."

I feel my jaw drop, and I watch as he takes the heart in his fingers with one hand, cups my hand in the other, and places the warm metal in my palm.

"Nate . . ."

"She would have loved you," he continues. "I wish she could have known you. I want you to have this."

My eyes are searching his, and I'm just so touched. He's giving me something of his mother's. If that doesn't scream commitment, I don't know what does.

"Turn it over," he whispers.

Engraved on the back is *Love, Nate.*

Tears spring to my eyes as I rub the sweet words with the pad of my finger. I am overcome with emotion.

"I know it's not diamonds, or wildly expensive . . ."

Before he can finish the words, I climb onto his lap and wrap my arms around his shoulders, bury my face in his neck, and hold on tight, letting the tears come.

"Hey, it's okay, baby." His hands are moving up and down my back, soothing and caressing me.

"Thank you so much," I whisper into his neck, unable to look him in the eye and let him see my tears. "This is the most beautiful gift anyone has ever given me."

"Hey." He pushes back on my shoulders so I have to look at him, and he grins at me as he wipes the tears off my cheeks with his thumbs. "Can I put it on you?"

"Yes, please." I offer him a wet smile, pull my hair up off my neck, and wait patiently as he clasps it. It falls a few inches below my collarbones and shines in the soft firelight.

"It's beautiful, Nate, thank you."

"You're welcome."

There's suddenly thunder in the distance, and we both look out to the water as lightning strikes through the dark clouds moving closer to us.

"Looks like we're going to get that storm," I murmur.

"Well, as much as I wanted to make love to you here, looks like it's going to be plan B."

Nate stands and holds his hand out to me, helping me up. He passes me our champagne glasses and the champagne bottle, then lifts me in his arms and climbs the stairs.

"Seriously, Nate, I can walk."

"You don't have any shoes."

He's not even breathing hard with the effort.

Holy fuck.

"What about the food and the fire?" I ask.

"The catering company is coming back in a few hours to clean up."

"Oh."

He sets me down at the top of the stairs and kisses my cheek, takes his glass and the bottle out of my hands and leads me inside and up the stairs to the master suite. We walk into the bathroom, and Nate turns on the water to fill the tub and lights some candles throughout the spacious room, then turns off the lights so the space is bathed in soft candlelight.

He pulls a remote out of his back pocket—I didn't know he had that!—and turns on the sound system, and Jason Mraz's *I Won't Give Up* is again coming through the speakers.

"Did you do that on purpose?" I ask.

"No, it's just a coincidence," he murmurs.

He lowers our glasses and the champagne to the floor next to the tub, and when everything is ready, he turns back to me and slowly walks toward me in time with the song.

Nate starts to sing along, softly, "I won't give up on us, even if the skies get rough, I've given you all my love, I'm still looking up . . ."

He pulls me against him, one arm wrapped around the small of my back, and takes my hand in his, and begins to sway with the music, dancing me across the beautiful bathroom in the candlelight, while the sky explodes in lightning outside. He lowers his face next to mine and just barely touches me with his cheek, turns his face, and brushes my cheek with his nose, sending shivers down my spine and through my arms and legs.

"I won't give up on us," he whispers in my ear, and I feel tears prick my eyes again.

Where did I find this beautiful man? And how did I resist him for so long?

When the song is finished, Sade begins to croon about this not being an ordinary love, and Nate pulls back, his eyes alive with love, and he gently brushes my hair off my face. "I love you, baby."

"I love you, Nate."

THE WATER IS warm and smells like lavender. Nate is sitting against the end of the tub with me between his legs, resting on his chest.

The sky outside is dancing in light and rolling black clouds, reflecting on the choppy water below. I love that the tub sits in a glass alcove so we can watch the show.

"Where did you learn to dance like that?" I ask.

Nate squirts my shower gel in his hands and rubs them together until he's happy with the lather. "Sit forward a bit."

I lean forward, and he starts to rub my back and shoulders, massaging my muscles, and I melt into him. "Holy Moses, ace, you're good with your hands."

He chuckles behind me and continues the delicious massage.

"I've never had a dancing lesson. I guess martial arts taught me rhythm." His hands slip below the water line, and he rubs my lower back in slow, relaxing circles.

"Mmm . . . I love the way you move," I murmur.

"You do?" I hear the smile in his voice.

"Mmm hmm . . . I could watch you move all day."

He kisses my neck and pulls me back against him again, his hands circling up to my breasts.

"I love your breasts," he whispers.

"I thought about enhancing them when I was young and posing for the magazine, but now I'm glad I didn't."

"You don't need to enhance them, baby. They're perfect as they are." He brushes his thumbs across my nipples, making them pucker, and I brace my hands on his thighs and arch my back, pushing my breasts into his hands.

His left hand slips down my torso, between my legs, and he sweeps his finger lightly over my clit.

"God, babe."

"Shh, I've got you," he whispers against my ear and tugs the lobe between his teeth.

I can feel his erection against my back. His hands are wreaking havoc on my sensitive skin, and the water is warm and fragrant. Trees sway in the wind outside, and rain is beating on the windows now, reflecting the lightning that's shooting across the stormy sky.

I turn in Nate's arms and straddle his hips. I kiss him, gently at first, my hands in his hair, and then deepen the sweet kiss, tangling our tongues. His hands lift my ass, and he pulls back, his eyes on mine, his mouth open as he pants.

"I need to be inside you, baby."

I reach between us and wrap my hand around his cock, pull up and down once, then guide the tip to my folds and lower myself onto him.

"Fuck, you're so small," he growls.

"Fuck, you're so big," I respond and smile, my forehead resting on his.

He grins wolfishly and begins raising and lowering me over him steadily, ignoring the water splashing over the side, and we are in a whirlpool of lust. I can't get enough of him. I'm squeezing around his length, his piercing is brushing along that most sensitive spot, and I feel the familiar tightening of my muscles around him.

"I'm going to come," I whisper.

He grips my hips and pulls me against him, grinding into me, his feral gray eyes on mine, and growls, "Let go."

And I do.

twenty-four

I wake early, before Nate for a change. We are naked, tangled in soft white sheets. Nate is on his back, one hand thrown over his head, covered from the waist down, and I brace my head on my elbow, admiring the view of his amazing tattoos, long hair, and dark chin stubble. His arms, chest and stomach are deliciously toned, even in sleep.

Fuck, he's a feast for the eyes.

I sit up and stretch, glancing outside. The storm has passed, leaving the beach just a little messy with debris. I get up to answer nature's call, throw on some capris jeans and a sweatshirt, pull my hair up in a knot, grab my flip-flops and head down to the water.

I should let Nate know that I'm going out, but he's so sleepy, I decide to leave him be and make him breakfast when I get back.

When I get to the gazebo, I'm amazed to find that the caterer did indeed come back and clean up. The space has been returned to its original state. Amazing, I didn't even hear them.

I reach the bottom of the stairs and kick off my flip-flops, wiggling my toes in the sand, and take a deep, deep breath. The air is salty and just a bit musty from the storm. Seagulls are flying around, scouring the sand for food, and the water is crashing on the shore in white clouds, then pushing out onto the sand in sheets of wet glass.

I can't wait to put my feet in it.

I walk down to the edge of the water and stand still, waiting for the water to rush forward and engulf my feet and ankles. Oh my, it's so cold! I giggle and do a little dance in the water, splashing about, getting used to the cold, looking down at my toes.

I need a pedicure. Maybe I'll call Nat and see if she wants to go with me after work this week.

Work. I'm not ready to go back.

"There you are."

I hear Nate call from behind me, and I turn to smile at him. He's pulled on his jeans and a sweatshirt, but he's not smiling. He looks pissed.

Great.

"What's wrong?" I ask and walk toward him.

"You were gone when I woke up again."

"Uh, you were asleep, Nate. I just came down to the beach for a bit. Where else would I go?"

"I hate waking up and finding you gone. Bad memories." He hugs me to him and kisses my hair. "I'm sorry."

"It's okay. I'll wake you next time and tell you I'm up." I pull out of his arms but link my fingers in his. "Take your shoes off. I'm not done wading in the water."

"It's cold." He frowns down at me. "I don't want you to get sick."

"Oh stop, I won't get sick. C'mon, it's fun."

Nate removes his shoes, rolls his pants to his knees and we walk through the water down the shoreline.

"I'm not ready to leave," I murmur and take a deep breath of salty air.

"We don't have to head back until this evening if you like." He kisses my knuckles and smiles at me.

"I know. I guess I'm not ready to go back to work tomorrow either." I shrug. "Probably not something I should admit to my boss, I know, but there it is."

"What aren't you telling me?" he asks.

"Oh, nothing." I wave his statement aside. "There's no drama. I'm just not a great actress, and the whole 'you're my boyfriend at home but just my boss at work' thing is tiresome. By the end of the week I'm exhausted from being afraid that I'll say or do something inappropriate."

"You know, baby, if you ever decided you didn't want to, you don't have to work."

I laugh and kick the water, splashing. "Right. I do have to work, Nate."

He pulls us both to a stop and looks down at me with serious eyes. "No, you don't."

"Yes, I do." I shake my head and rub my forehead. "I like my job. I'm good at it. And, yes, I've been smart, and I have a nice-sized nest egg, along with a bit of an inheritance, but I do have to work, babe."

"I can take care of you," he whispers.

Oh, I love him.

"But you shouldn't have to, that's the thing." I start walking again through the water, and Nate follows me. "Besides, what would I do if I didn't work? I'd go crazy. I'm not crafty. I hate TV. I need to do stuff."

"You are, too, crafty. What about making more signs like the one you gave Natalie for the nursery?"

"Oh no." I laugh up at him and shake my head. "That was a one-time thing. It was fun, but I'm not artistic."

"I thought it was great." He kicks water up, splashing my legs, and I giggle.

"Well, it's not a career."

"What if you had kids?" he asks, and I immediately shut down inside.

I do not want to have this conversation. I'm not ready.

"Don't go there."

"It's a valid question."

"Kids aren't even on my radar, Nate."

"What is on your radar, Julianne?"

We aren't looking at each other. We're just walking, hand in hand, through the water, watching the waves and the birds.

"You. Work. Family." I shrug. "That's plenty for now."

"As long as I make the list, baby."

"You're at the top these days, ace." I smile sassily and try to lighten the mood. "In fact, I like it when you're on top."

He laughs, a full-on belly laugh, and splashes my legs again. "Okay, funny girl."

PEDICURES TONIGHT AFTER *work?*

I send the text to Natalie and resume reading a report on my desk. I have so much to do! Three reports to write, Nate sent me a list of items he needs researched, and we have a meeting in just a few minutes.

My phone pings with a response from Natalie. *Sure! I'll bring Liv. She'll sleep.*

Perfect! Can't wait to see you both. Will call when I'm on my way to pick you up.

I smile and gather my coffee and things I need for the meeting. I'm so excited to see Nat and the baby. It's just what I need.

We all file into the conference room and sit in our usual places. We don't have assigned seats, but we are people of habit. There are six of us: Nate and I, Mrs. Glover to take notes, and the other partner, Mr. Luis, and his team, Carly and Ben. Mr. Luis is in his mid-forties, graying and pot-bellied. He's a shrewd businessman, and is not at all friendly in the office. He's all business.

Ben is much the same way. He's about my age, not much taller than I am, thin and wears glasses. He's handsome and very intelligent. He's not rude. He's just all about business, which I can respect and even admire.

I have no idea if either man is married or what their private lives consist of, and that's just fine by me.

Carly sits across the table from me, dressed in a green shift dress, her red hair pulled back in a bun. She looks over to me and offers a fake, brittle smile.

I don't reciprocate.

I glance casually over at Nate, and he's watching our exchange, running his forefinger over his lower lip in thought.

My fingers unconsciously touch the silver heart at my neck. My birthday diamonds are in my ears, and I'm wearing my birthday tennis bracelet. I'm draped in my man, he's sitting three feet from me, and I can't touch him.

It's a little weird.

When everyone is settled, Mr. Luis begins the meeting, bringing us all up-to-date on account statuses, what needs to be worked on and what's not working at all, then he turns it over to Nate.

He passes around some reports. "Miss Montgomery put these reports together this morning. I'd like to go through them now, since I have you all here."

As he methodically works his way through the reports, I find myself able to focus on the work, and it makes my stomach settle. I was worried that we'd ruined this for me, that it would always be a struggle, and I'm relieved that I answer his questions appropriately and professionally, and no one would ever guess that we are anything but colleagues.

As we all begin to file out after the meeting, Nate says to me, "Miss Montgomery, I'd like to see you in my office in ten minutes, please."

Huh. "I'll see you then." I nod and head back to my office, close the door, and exhale. Another meeting accomplished without any screw-ups.

Win.

"YOU CAN GO on in, Miss Montgomery." Mrs. Glover smiles warmly at me as I walk past her desk toward Nate's office.

"Thanks." I knock once and walk into his office. "You wanted to see me?"

I close the door behind me and smile over at my hot executive boyfriend. He's in another one of his dark suits with a white shirt and gray tie, his hair pulled back.

He's effing hot.

He steps out from behind his desk and crosses to me, and I'm suddenly crushed to his chest in a big hug. He smells fantastic, all fabric softener and coffee and Nate.

He reaches behind me and locks the door quietly, and I pull back to look into his eyes. "What's wrong?"

"Nothing, I just missed you this morning."

"I've been right down the hall." I chuckle and kiss his chin.

"I know, it's not the same. Mondays suck, for more reasons than one."

I know exactly what he means. We've just had the whole weekend together, and now we're back where we have to pretend.

"Hey, before I forget, I made plans with Natalie for after work. We're getting pedicures. So I won't be at your place when you get home."

"Okay. Are you coming over when you're done?" he asks.

"I think I'll just go home, Nate. I have a mountain of laundry to do, and I've barely been there over the past few weeks. One night apart won't kill us, you know."

He frowns and runs his fingertips down my face. "I'll go to your place tonight."

"You don't have . . ."

"I don't want to sleep without you, Julianne."

"Okay, I'll meet you at my place then. I need to make you a key."

"No need." He smirks down at me. "I'll talk you into moving into the condo with me soon enough."

"Pretty sure of yourself, aren't you, ace?"

"Yeah, pretty sure," he whispers and kisses me softly.

Yeah, I'm pretty sure, too.

"OH, THIS FEELS so good."

Natalie and I are at our favorite nail spa near Alki Beach. We've been coming here for years. I have Olivia on my chest, snoozing away, my feet in hot water, and my best friend to my right.

Life is damn good.

"We need to get back on our pedicure schedule," Natalie remarks and sighs as she dips her feet in the hot, fragrant water.

"Definitely." I kiss Olivia's head and pat her little diaper-covered bottom. "She's so sweet, Nat."

"I know." Natalie smiles at us. "Here, give me your phone, I'm going to take a picture."

"Oh good!" I hand her my phone and smile as she takes our photo and then hands the phone back to me. "Oh, look at us, Livie. We're beautiful." Without hesitation, I send the photo via text to Nate.

"Can we paint her toes, too?" I ask Natalie, and she giggles.

"Sure. Let's do pink."

The nail tech finds the tiny brush she uses to hand-paint designs on nails and paints each of Olivia's tiny toes baby pink. She sleeps right through it.

"Adorable."

My phone pings, and I check the text from Nate. *Gorgeous girls. Kiss her for me.*

I sigh and show it to Natalie.

"He's very sweet. I'm surprised."

"I know. He can be rough around the edges, with his motorcycle, and the fighting, and the tattoos. I had no idea. But at work he's exactly the opposite, all professional and rich businessman." I kiss Olivia's head and breathe in her baby smell. "And this weekend he was incredibly romantic and sweet."

"So, someone's in love." Natalie grins at me.

"Yeah, I won't deny it."

"I'm so happy for you."

"But it's so complicated, Nat." She frowns and tilts her head, and I continue. "We can't tell anyone at work. Ever. We'd both lose our jobs. It's not easy to pretend."

"Don't pretend, just be you. You've always gotten along well with him at work. Just keep doing that."

"Easy for you to say. You're not the one who wants to lick him every time you see him."

"Well, no, Luke might have issues with that." We laugh, and then she's serious again. "Just be who you are, Jules. Enjoy him. The rest will work its way out."

"I hope you're right." My phone pings again, and I check the text message.

Hey baby, I'll be late tonight. Unexpected teleconference.

I frown but then shrug. *Okay. Still coming over when you're done?*

I'll be there.

Okay, see you later. xo

"Nate's working late," I murmur and stow my phone back in my handbag. "Are we on for Friday movie night?" I ask, changing the subject.

"We are. Luke's mom is going to watch the baby at our place. I'm a bit nervous to leave her for the first time, but she'll be in good hands."

"I'm so excited. A night out is exactly what we all need. Let's go to that newer bar by the theater that has a live band on Fridays. We can dance, and the guys can shoot pool." Olivia starts to squirm, and I give her her pacifier.

"That sounds good to me. I'm warning you, though, I'll be texting Lucy all night for updates."

"I don't mind." I grin at her over Olivia's soft head. "I'm just thrilled that you're no longer pregnant and we can have a margarita."

"Or three." She smirks. "I guess there's one upside to not being able to breast-feed."

"You know, Nate's birthday is only a couple months away." I pat the sleeping Olivia's back as an idea forms in my head. "Since he's working late tonight, why don't you and I spend some time in the studio after we leave here?"

"Oh, that would be fantastic! I'm itching to get back to the studio."

"Then it's a plan."

We grin at each other and sigh as the technicians begin to rub our calves and feet.

"I FORGOT HOW fun this is with you," Natalie murmurs and presses the shutter aimed at me.

Luke met us at the house to pick up Olivia, so it's just Nat and I, like the good ol' days, playing around with pretty lingerie, makeup and her camera.

Sexy dance music is pumping through the speakers, and I can't help but move my body with it.

"You're so good at this, Nat. I'm so proud of you."

"Okay, no mushy shit tonight. Think sexy."

Natalie backs up and surveys the scene. I'm on her king-size, white satin-sheet-clad bed in the middle of the studio. Because it's dark outside, she has her lights on. My long blond hair is down and wavy around my face, in that just-fucked state that men find so sexy.

"Lie on your back with your head facing me and arch your back and put your legs in the air, knees together."

I comply, making sure my silver heart is nestled seductively in my cleavage, and cross my ankles, legs straight up in the air. I'm wearing white thigh-highs with a white garter and a lacy white push-up bra.

"Nice, Jules, hold that. Put your hand up at the side of your face. Good."

The shutter clicks some more, and I close my eyes, imagining that Nate is looking at me, that he's the one behind the camera, and I start to move.

Natalie comes around the bed, taking different angles of the same shot, then I turn over onto my stomach and flirt with her some more.

"Take the bra off now, but then keep your torso flat against the bed."

"Yes, ma'am." The sheets are cool and soft against my breasts, and I feel my nipples pucker.

"Do you want some nudes as well?"

"Hell, yeah, it's his birthday." I grin wickedly, and she presses the shutter.

"He's gonna go crazy when he sees these." Natalie grins, and I giggle.

"Here's hoping."

I sit at the side of the bed and remove the stockings, the garter, the thong, with Natalie all the while taking photos. I know that when she edits them she'll make them look incredibly seductive. A woman taking her clothes off for her man.

"Okay, naked girl, on your back again."

I lie down and arch my back, looking to my side at the camera, cup my breasts in my hands and bend my knees, pointing my toes.

"God, Jules, if I swung that way and wasn't married to the hottest man in the free world, I'd so do you right now."

I laugh at Natalie, completely at ease with her, and we move about the bed and the room in different poses, trying on different pieces of lingerie and jewelry.

Natalie's studio is a blast for a girlie girl like me.

When we're finished and locking up the studio, I see lights coming on in the main house.

"Nate's here. We'd better get inside so he doesn't know what we've been up to."

Natalie smiles. "That was fun. We should do it more often."

"I know, I've missed you. *Playboy* called this past weekend. They want me to pose in an anniversary issue."

"What did you say?" Natalie asks as we walk through the back door and into the kitchen area.

"I told them I'd think about it, but then I called them this morning and declined."

Nate walks in the room, clearly looking for me, and smiles widely at me before pulling me into his arms and kissing me deeply.

"Well, hi, hot stuff," I say.

"Hi. Did I hear you say you turned them down?"

"Yeah, this morning."

"Good. Hi, Nat."

"Hey." Natalie grabs her camera, purse and jacket and kisses Nate on the cheek as she passes by.

"What have you two been up to?" Nate asks, eyeing Natalie's camera. "And where's the baby?"

"Luke came and got her so Natalie and I could indulge in some girl talk." I smile sweetly at him and bat my eyelashes, but he narrows his eyes, seeing through me.

"Uh huh," he responds.

"Well, speaking of Livie, I'd better go. See you guys on Friday." She waves and then is gone.

"What were you really doing?" he asks.

"I can't tell you."

"Why?" He kisses my cheek and then my ear, and I lean into him with a sigh.

"Because you'll find out soon enough. You aren't allowed to ask questions like this within three months of your birthday."

"What?" He pulls back and grins down at me. "What do you mean?"

"No questions so close to your birthday, ace. Just trust me, we were having fun and I was thinking of you."

"Well, that's all I can ask, baby." He kisses my forehead and pulls out of my arms, takes off his suit jacket and rolls his sleeves, exposing that sexy tattoo.

"Are you hungry?" I ask.

"Starving. Come on, I'll make you dinner, and you can tell me about your day." He heads for the kitchen, and I grin. Nate cooking is a sight to behold.

"You already know about most of my day." I sit at the breakfast bar and gratefully accept a glass of white wine from Nate.

"Did you and Nat have fun getting your feet done?" he asks.

"Definitely. It was a good treat, both the pedi and seeing her and the baby."

"She's getting big already," Nate comments and seasons two steaks to place under the broiler. "The picture you sent me was beautiful."

"She's awesome," I murmur.

"Thank you for turning *Playboy* down, Julianne," Nate says softly, and my gaze shoots up to his hot gray one. He's cutting up baby red potatoes, and his face is serious.

"I told you I was going to."

"I know." He sighs and shakes his head as if shaking off a mood and then shoots me his sexy grin. "How do you want your steak, baby?"

"As soon as possible so I can get you naked."

Nate laughs. "I can do that."

twenty-five

N ate smacks my ass, making me jump.

"What did I say?"

"Stop talking about hot dudes," he growls, and I giggle.

We've just left the movie theater after watching Luke's newest movie, *Never Surrender* with Hugh Jackman. We're walking on the sidewalk toward the bar.

"What's the big deal? If you told me that you thought Scarlett Johansson was a hot piece of ass, I'd agree with you." I push my arm through his and lean my head on his shoulder as we walk. Natalie and Luke are walking ahead of us, hand in hand.

"Besides, you're the only hot dude I want, ace."

"Gee, I'm so happy to hear it," he mutters drily, making me laugh again.

"Has Lucy turned her phone off yet, Nat?" I call to her. She's texted the poor woman ten times already.

"No, smart-ass. But she just sent me the cutest picture of Liv and Sam sleeping on the couch." She shows it to me, and we both ooh and aah over the sweet photo.

"I need a beer," Luke says. "Nate, can I buy you a beer?"

"Yes, please. I need it, too."

"You both know you love looking at that baby." I smirk.

"Yes, but we're men, Jules. We keep our feelings to ourselves." Luke nuzzles Natalie's neck, and I make a gagging noise in my throat.

"Keep your hands to yourself, pal, and we'll be fine. Jesus, why do I come out with you?"

"Because you think I'm cool and handsome and witty."

"And modest," I quip, and we all laugh.

I do enjoy these people.

Oasis, the bar we're trying out tonight, is fairly busy, darkly lit, and loud with rock music. The cover band is playing a Maroon5 song and doing a pretty good job of it, which is a good sign for us as Natalie and I are big Maroon5 fans. We find an empty booth and all have a seat.

"This is fun," I say as I look around the busy bar. The dance floor is a good size and fairly full of dancers in various stages of intoxication. There are two pool tables in the opposite corner from the stage, both in use at the moment. The bar itself is long and big, with three bartenders running back and forth filling orders.

A cocktail waitress in a tight white T-shirt and short black skirt with black apron approaches our table to take our orders.

"Hey there, ladies and gentlemen, what can I getcha?"

Luke orders beers for himself and Nate, and Natalie and I a margarita each. He knows how we like them.

"The music is great! Get a couple drinks in me, and Natalie and I will be bustin' some moves." I smile shyly at Nate.

"You are beautiful tonight in this red dress," he murmurs in my ear.

We always dress up on premiere night. It's tradition.

I'm wearing a halter-style red chiffon dress that flows down to my knees. The back exposes my shoulder blades, but all in all, it's pretty modest. My hair is up in a twist, and I went a little more dramatic with my makeup tonight. I am wearing black Louboutin stilettos.

I'm rocking this dress.

Natalie is also gorgeous tonight in a black one-shoulder dress, also chiffon, that floats to her knees. She's wearing her pearls and red Louboutins.

Luke is movie-star handsome in his black slacks and white button-down shirt with black jacket, and Nate is just delicious in black slacks and black button-down with rolled sleeves.

I trace his tattoo with my finger and smile up at him through my eyelashes. "You look mighty fine yourself."

Nate leans down farther with a smile and whispers, "I can't wait to get you out of that dress and fuck you senseless."

My thighs tighten at his words, and I lean over to whisper back in his ear, "No need to get me out of it, ace. I'm not wearing any underwear."

I lean back and grin as he clenches his eyes shut and whispers, "Fuck."

I laugh as the waitress delivers our drinks, and we settle in to discuss the movie.

"Okay, so we've established that Hugh is hot." Nate narrows his eyes at me, and I smile innocently and take a sip of my drink. "But what did we think of the movie?"

"Action, sex, blood, stuff blew up . . . it was fantastic." Nate salutes Luke with his beer and takes a sip as we all laugh.

"I liked it, too." I nod. "I'm getting used to the blood, but I'm not sure if that's a good thing. The sex was hot, as was Hugh."

Nate tickles my ribs, and I laugh. "It's just too easy to tease you!"

"I thought it was pure producing genius," Natalie adds. "Obviously, the man who produced it was intelligent, sexy, and incredibly handsome."

"Well, that goes without saying, baby." Luke kisses her neck, and I roll my eyes.

"Puke."

"Are you saying I'm not sexy?" Luke asks me with a raised eyebrow. "If I remember correctly, your opinion was very different the first time you met me."

"Well, now that you've had your hands—and other things that make me throw up in my mouth—all over my bff, you can never be sexy to me again. Besides, you were Movie Star Luke then. Now you're just Luke, my seriously cute brother-in-law."

"That's the sweetest thing you've ever said to me." He wipes an imaginary tear from the corner of his eye, and I throw an ice cube at him.

The waitress delivers refills on all our drinks, and Luke changes the subject.

"So, I hear you have a beautiful home on the beach, Nate."

"I do." Nate laces his fingers in mine and kisses my knuckles, then rests our hands on the table between us. "Julianne and I would love it if you three would join us there for a weekend next month."

I smile up at him, delighted with him, and he kisses my forehead.

"I would love that! I love the beach." Natalie nods enthusiastically. "I'll bring my camera and take some photos of you guys, too."

"Cool." I grin over at her. "Maybe we should set up an appointment with you in the studio."

Natalie's eyes go wide, and then a lazy smile spreads across her face. "Anytime, sweetie."

"Uh." Luke frowns over at me. "Is that a good idea?"

"What are you all talking about?" Nate asks, and I giggle to myself.

"Have you told Nate what kind of photos I take, Jules?" Nat asks and sips her drink, not giving any indication that we were just in the studio earlier this week.

I shake my head at her and wink.

"Well?" Nate asks me.

"Can I show him?" I ask Natalie.

"Sure." She shrugs, and Luke grins as I pull out my iPhone and scroll through my photos until I come to the ones that I snapped of the canvases hanging on the studio walls, specifically the ones of the naked couples in various sexual positions, and show them to Nate.

His eyes go wide, and then he thumbs through each of them, then back through them again, and hands my phone back to me.

He takes a long gulp of his beer, not looking any of us in the eye. We're all watching him, smiling, and finally he looks at Natalie and says, "If I weren't so in love with my girlfriend, and didn't respect your husband like I do, I'd attack you right here on this table. Those are fucking hot."

We all bust out laughing, Luke high-fives Nate, and Natalie blushes just a bit.

"However," Nate continues, "I don't think I'm comfortable with anyone, but especially you, Natalie, taking photos of me making love.

We'll keep it in the bedroom, thanks."

"Well," I add, "not just the bedroom . . ."

"Ew." Natalie wrinkles her nose, and I smile smugly at her.

"Not as pretty from the other side, is it, friend? Okay, no sex pictures. But I could use some studio time."

"Absolutely. When?" Nat asks and winks, enjoying our deceiving banter, then looks over at Nate with a frown.

I look up into cold gray eyes. "What?"

"Why?"

I squeeze his fingers and lean in to whisper in his ear, "Your birthday is coming up, ace."

"Next week work for you?" he asks Natalie, making us all laugh again, and I'm relieved to know that he's going to love his birthday gift.

Suddenly, the band breaks into another hot Maroon5 song, and Natalie and I grin at each other.

"Shall we?" I ask her.

"Sure," she responds.

The boys let us out of the booth, and I take her hand as we stride out to the dance floor. We join the sea of bodies and begin to move. Natalie's body is gorgeous, curvaceous and naturally graceful, and she moves with ease on her tall stilettos. I'm thankful for many years in martial arts classes that gave me balance, and a natural rhythm, and I swing my hips and arms with the song. I close my eyes and turn in a tight circle, getting lost in the music.

When I open them again, the boys have joined us. Luke wraps himself around Natalie and moves against her, all tall, blond and sexy, and suddenly Nate is pressed to my back, his hands on my hips, his face in my neck.

"You are so fucking hot, baby," he growls against my ear.

I grin back at him, and he leads me through the rest of the song, then through two more, his body pressed close to mine, sending fire through me.

Finally, the band plays a slow Matchbox Twenty song, and Nate wraps me in his arms and sways me back and forth, his hands on my hips. He kisses my forehead, and I lean against his chest, enjoying the slow music and being in my man's strong arms.

When the song ends, Natalie and I decide we need to get off our feet for a bit, and the guys decide to try their hand at some pool. They escort us back to the table and then go claim an empty pool table.

"Damn," I mutter as I take a sip of my drink and watch Nate lean over the pool table to take a shot. His ass fills out those slacks so nicely.

"Our men are hot," Natalie comments with a grin.

"Very hot." I nod, and we giggle. "I'm so glad we did this. I've missed you."

"Me, too. Who knew a year ago that our lives would be so different?"

"Right? I know that it's all good stuff, and I'm thankful, but I miss you."

"Well, we'll have to make the effort to see each other more." Natalie checks her phone, and I smile at her.

"Why don't you just call her?" I ask.

"I'm sure they're fine," Natalie responds as her phone pings. "Oh! She texted me. Yep, they're fine." She smiles widely.

I glance over to the pool table and find Nate's eyes trained on me. I grin at him, and the side of his mouth turns up in a lazy smile, and I feel the hit straight to my loins.

Jesus, he does things to me.

"Well, hello, gorgeous."

My head twirls and there is DJ, a man I was briefly involved with two years ago, standing at the end of our table. I was so caught up in Nate, I didn't even notice him.

"Hi, DJ," I respond unenthusiastically.

"Nat." He winks at Natalie, and she glares at him.

Things between DJ and I did not end well.

"So, how you been, Jules?" he asks with a cocky grin.

DJ is handsome: tall, toned and dark-haired. He works at the gym I used to work out at and was my trainer for a while.

"I'm great, DJ."

"Glad to hear it. And to see that you're maintaining that sweet body of yours."

He winks at me, and my stomach rolls. He's an asshole. I want him gone, and I pray that Nate is too busy with his game to notice him.

"Thanks for stopping by, but Natalie and I are enjoying our drinks, DJ. Have a good night."

"Mind if I join you?"

Jesus, no one ever accused him of being smart.

"Yes, we do mind. Goodbye, DJ."

"Oh, c'mon, don't be like that." He runs his fingers down my cheek, and I catch his wrist in my hand and pull it away from me.

"Don't touch me. Just go away."

"Or what, Jules?"

"Or I'll have to kick your ass," Nate murmurs quietly behind him.

twenty-six

F uck.

I look over, and Nate and Luke are both standing behind DJ, Luke with his arms crossed over his chest, watching, and Nate glaring at the back of DJ's head, his gray eyes hard and narrowed.

DJ turns and offers Nate his cocky smile, the one he thinks is charming, and winks at him. "Hey, dude, I got this. I fucked her a few years ago, and if I play my cards right, I'm hoping to fuck her again later tonight."

I hear Natalie gasp, and then everything happens in slow motion.

Nate bares his teeth and grabs DJ by the shirt and physically drags him away from our table, past the bar, and right out the front door, with Luke right behind him.

Natalie and I look at each other for a heartbeat, then scramble out of the booth and follow them outside.

Enraged, Nate has DJ up against the wall of the building, his face inches from DJ's.

"Who the fuck taught you manners, asshole?"

"Fuck you," DJ spits out and kicks Nate in the shin.

Nate grunts but doesn't lose his grip on DJ's shirt. His arms are flexed tight in anger.

DJ looks over Nate's shoulder at me and smirks. "Hey, baby, did you miss this?" He grabs his cock through his jeans and laughs at his own joke.

"You have no idea who you're fucking with," I murmur.

Nate hasn't moved a muscle. He's glaring at DJ, breathing hard, but he's completely controlled, and obviously isn't hurting the other man, given that he's able to make rude gestures at me.

"What do you want me to do, Julianne?" Nate asks softly.

DJ smirks. "Gotta ask your girlfriend for permission, pussy?"

"Kick his ass, Nate."

"Thought you'd never ask, baby."

Nate takes a step back, releasing DJ, and turns his back on him, and I know what his strategy is: Let DJ take the first shot.

Nate is not disappointed.

DJ grabs Nate's shoulder and pulls him around to face him and punches him, square in the jaw. Blood spatters from the corner of Nate's mouth, making me wince and want to run to him, to comfort him, but I stay where I am.

"What do you think of that, asshole?" DJ sneers.

"I think you have a pathetic right hook, moron."

Nate punches DJ twice, once in the nose, then in the gut, sending DJ to the ground, but the other man is stupid and gets back up, swinging. Nate weaves out of the way and counters with another right hook to the jaw, then grips DJ's shoulders and pulls him down against his knee, right to the gut, and throws him to the ground again.

"Stay down," Nate growls.

"Fuck you!" DJ stands, more shaky this time, and rubs his stomach. He lunges for Nate again, fists flying, but Nate crouches and catches DJ around the torso and lifts him, slamming him against the wall with his strong shoulder, and drops DJ to the ground again.

Holy fuck! I knew Nate was strong, but seeing him like this is just amazing. Not only could he really hurt someone, he could kill someone.

"If you know what's good for you, you'll stay down, motherfucker."

DJ wheezes and coughs, wincing in pain. I'm sure his ribs are bruised, if not broken. He gets up to his knees, and Luke speaks for the first time.

"Are you learning-impaired, dude? Stay the fuck down before he puts you in the hospital."

DJ is clearly embarrassed as he falls back to the ground, sits on his ass and winces again. A small crowd has gathered to watch the show, mumbling and laughing at DJ. He looks up at me and glares.

"I should have beat the shit out of you when I had the chance. You're nothing but a fucking whore anyway."

Nate rears back to kick DJ in the face, but I yell, "Don't!"

He stops and whirls on me, his eyes raw with rage. "What?"

I shake my head and look back down at DJ. I offer him a sweet, fake smile, walk sassily over to him, and squat in my heels so I'm close to him.

"You tried to kick my ass, remember, DJ? And I beat you bloody. I'm pretty sure that nice scar there by your left eye is thanks to me."

I stand and walk away from him, and he calls out, "Cunt whore!"

"Do it," I mutter to Nate as I walk past him, and I hear DJ's low grunt, then his head hitting the pavement, after Nate punches him one last time in the face, knocking him out.

"WELL, ONE THING I will say about our nights out, they're never boring." Natalie turns in the passenger seat of their Mercedes and looks back at Nate and me.

"No, never boring," I murmur and kiss Nate's bruised and swollen knuckles. "Are you okay?" I ask him.

"I'm fine," he mutters. He won't look me in the face, and aside from me touching him, he's hardly laid a hand on me.

Luke pulls into my driveway, and Nate and I get out of the back seat. I lean in Nat's window and kiss her cheek. "Kiss Livie for me. I'll call you tomorrow."

"Okay. Bye, Nate. You kick major ass." She winks at him, Luke waves at us both, and they pull out of the driveway.

"Let's go in." I walk toward the front porch, but Nate runs a hand through his hair and stands still.

"Maybe I should just go back to the condo tonight."

"What?" I turn back to him, confused and a little scared. "Why?"

He shakes his head and looks at his feet. "You said yourself that one night apart won't kill us."

I'm completely thrown. This cold, distant man is not *my* Nate.

"I don't want to sleep without you," I whisper, and my stomach rolls when he winces and turns away from me.

"Look, Nate, I'm sorry about DJ . . ."

Nate whirls back to me, his gray eyes angry and face taut. "Don't you apologize for that motherfucker, Julianne."

"Okay." I step back and fold my arms over my chest. I don't know what to say. I don't know what's wrong.

"You didn't do anything wrong."

"Okay," I repeat and lick my lips nervously. "So why are you punishing me?" I ask quietly.

Nate hangs his head, plants his hands on his hips and takes a deep breath. "That's not what I'm trying to do."

"Talk to me, Nate."

"I'm fucking pissed, Jules. Beyond pissed. I wanted to keep punching him, over and over, until he was a bloody pulp. I have too much adrenaline and anger running through me right now to trust myself to not hurt you. I would never intentionally hurt you, but I'm not feeling gentle." He pushes his fingers through his hair roughly and paces away in frustration.

"Don't run away from me." I throw his words back at him. His back is to me, and he's gazing down my dark driveway. "You won't let me run, well, back at you, ace. If you're pissed, fine. If you're frustrated, fine. But you'll be those things with me, not while running away from me."

We stand like this for what feels like long minutes, but it may only be seconds.

Finally, I hear his low voice. "Why did you ever let that idiot near you?"

"Fuck," I mutter and rub my forehead.

"Seriously, Julianne, I don't get it." He turns and stares at me, his eyes unreadable.

"Nate it was *years* ago. Years."

"And?" He raises an eyebrow.

"I used to go to the gym he works at. He was—probably still is—a trainer. I was young and stupid enough to think he was cute. We went out on two dates, Nate. I had sex with him one time, and he went stalker-crazy on my ass. I told him I wasn't interested in seeing him again, he raised a fist, and I knocked a couple of those pretty teeth out."

I walk to Nate and reach out to touch him, but he backs away from me.

"Stop this," I whisper.

"You don't understand. It makes me sick that he ever touched you." He runs his hands through his hair again and looks up toward the sky and then back at me. "I know that you weren't innocent when I met you, but I don't ever need to meet anyone who has been *inside* you. Even if he hadn't been an asshole, I still would have wanted to kick his ass."

"Nate, he means less than nothing to me. You saw that yourself. I told you to kick his ass."

"Yeah, that was new, too. I've never asked permission to protect someone before."

So that's what this is about.

"Do you know what it means to me that you had the control to take care of me before you took care of him?" He frowns at me, and I keep talking. "You'd never hurt me, babe."

I take a deep breath before I continue. "Besides, I came face-to-face with the woman who still has your last name, Nate. I wanted to pull her heart out of her asshole but maintained my composure. I won't do it again."

"I told you, I don't have anything to do with her anymore."

I just tilt my head to the side and stare back at him impassively until he sighs deeply and shakes his head.

"Point taken."

"If I let myself think about the fact that you were married, or think about the women you've been with, Nate, it'll kill me. I refuse to think about it. I'm with you now, and I know I'm the only one with you now, and that's all that matters." I step toward him again and cup his face in my hands, run my fingers through his hair, and he doesn't move away, but he doesn't touch me either.

"Thank you for tonight, for protecting me, and making me feel so loved."

"I do love you," he whispers, and I smile up at him, so in love with him.

"I know," I whisper back, and Nate's arms come around me, pulling me into him.

He tucks my head under his chin and just hugs me close. I wrap my arms around his torso and cling to him as he rocks me back and forth, kissing my hair.

"So, um, does this mean you'll stay?" I ask, and my stomach settles when I feel him chuckle against my cheek.

"Yeah, I'll stay, baby." He kisses my hair once more, and I pull back. Nate grips my chin in his fingers and tilts my head back. "You are mine."

A slow smile spreads across my face. "Ditto."

"Jesus, you're beautiful."

I'm suddenly cradled in Nate's arms, and he's fumbling with the keys, unlocking the front door, and carrying me inside. He sets me down in the foyer, closes and locks the door, and stalks toward me slowly as I back up toward the stairs.

"Do you know what you do to me?" he asks, his voice low and rough, his eyes narrowed and his hands in fists at his sides.

"What?" I ask breathlessly.

"You make me want things I've never wanted before. You make me want you. You make me fucking hard."

My heels hit the bottom step, and I climb the stairs slowly, backward, unable to stop looking at him. I get about five steps up when he mutters, "Stop."

He unbuttons his shirt as he climbs the steps below me and peels it off his shoulders, letting it fall to the floor. He reaches the fourth step and is eye level with me. I'm gripping the handrail for balance, mesmerized by his beautiful gray eyes. He's still not touching me, yet my skin is humming in anticipation.

"Touch me," I whisper.

He leans in and brushes his lips across mine, lightly, and pulls back again, watching me.

"Please touch me," I whisper again.

His eyes travel from my hair, over my face, down my dress to my shoes and back up again. "Sit on the stairs," he commands.

I frown, and he narrows his eyes. "Sit."

twenty-seven

I lower myself to the stairs and look up into his face, wondering what the fuck he's going to do next. He unbuckles his belt and opens his slacks, and just when I think he's going to free his cock so I can go to work on it, he kneels in front of me.

I feel my eyes widen and roam over this angry, beautiful man. He's kneeling before me, still not touching me.

"Lean back on your elbows," he whispers, and I comply.

"Pull your skirt up around your hips." Again, I comply, and I feel my breathing quicken. I feel completely exposed, because I am, from the waist down. I wasn't lying when I said I wasn't wearing underwear.

Nate's eyes dilate, and he sucks in a deep breath. His eyes are narrowed on my pussy, and his hands are flexing in and out of fists, and I know he's dying to touch me.

"Touch me, babe," I whisper.

His molten gray eyes find mine as he reaches up and tucks a stray curl of hair behind my ear, sending shivers through me.

"You are so beautiful, Julianne."

"Touch. Me," I whisper again, and he clenches his eyes closed for a heartbeat and looks back down my body again, raking me with his gaze.

"Nate." I get his attention with the strength of my voice. "You won't hurt me, my love."

He growls and plants his fists on the stairs at my hips and pushes himself up to kiss me, slipping his tongue in my mouth, tangling and sliding along mine. This kiss is urgent and needy. I wrap his hair in my fingers to hold him to me, but he backs away, panting, eyes on fire and says, "Elbows on the stairs."

"Oh."

Finally—FINALLY!—he slides his large hands up the outsides of my thighs to my hips and pulls me forward to the edge of the step and lowers his head. He blows on my center, raising my skin in goose bumps. He spreads my thighs wide, spreading my labia in the process, and licks me from my anus to my clit and back down again.

"Holy fuck!" My head falls back as my hips come up off the stairs.

Nate holds my hips firmly, presses his face into my pussy and kisses me, plunging his soft, talented tongue inside me, swirling around and around, and presses his nose against my clit.

Electricity is shooting through my core, up my spine, and out my limbs. I look down at him, and his hot gray gaze is pinned on my face, alive with lust.

"Oh God, babe, I'm gonna . . ." I can't finish the sentence.

He moves that tongue up along my lips to press on my clit and roughly pushes two fingers inside me, pressing down, and I come apart, my muscles pulsing and milking his fingers, my clit throbbing against his tongue.

He kisses and nips at the insides of my thighs and my pubis, and then pulls his fingers out of me and sticks them in his mouth, sucking my sweetness off of them.

"You're delicious," he whispers. He reaches up and loosens my halter straps, letting the bodice fall around my waist, exposing my naked breasts. "Jesus."

Nate leans in and circles one nipple with his nose. My breathing is still erratic from the mind-blowing orgasm he just gave me, and that nose on my nipple sends fire straight to my core, and I moan his name.

He wraps his lips around the tight bud and worries the other with his fingers. I reach up with one hand and tangle my fingers in his hair, and he backs up and glares at me.

"Elbows on the stairs," he repeats.

"No, I want to touch you."

"I'll restrain you if I have to. Elbows on the stairs."

Fuck.

I comply, completely turned on by his need to control me. To control this.

His mouth covers the other breast, and he sets about making me crazy again, writhing beneath him.

He suddenly pulls back, grips my hips and lifts me, and flips me onto my knees.

"I need you," he growls, and I hear him push his pants down his hips. "Now."

He slams into me, hard, and I cry out in surprise and just a little pain. The apa feels larger than usual, pressed against the very core of me.

"Jesus, baby, you're so wet and tight." He moves out and in once again, as hard as before, and I moan.

"Yes," I whisper.

"This is gonna be rough, baby."

"Good," I respond.

"Tell me if it's too much."

"Just do it, babe. Fuck me."

He spanks my right ass cheek and grips my hips roughly and begins to pound in and out of me in a fast, desperate rhythm. He spanks me again, twice, and I moan at the pleasure of the sting, loving that he is crazy with lust for me, that I can make him lose himself in me.

"Fuck, baby." He tightens his grip on me and slams into me one last time, his release pushing through him, and takes me over with him.

He's panting and shaking behind me. He doesn't pull out of me. He leans over and kisses between my shoulder blades and rests his cheek there, his hands planted on the stairs by my elbows.

"Are you okay?" he whispers, making me smile.

"I'm fantastic. Are you okay?"

"Did I hurt you?"

"No, babe." I kiss his bicep. "You rocked my fucking world."

He chuckles and pulls out of me, making me gasp as I feel that apa pull along the walls of my pussy.

"Jesus, I'm glad you're not afraid of needles." I turn and sit my bottom on the stairs and look up into his bright gray eyes.

He's relaxed now, the anger and frustration seemingly released with rough sex and a hot orgasm.

"You'd look amazing with a tattoo," he murmurs.

I narrow my eyes at him. "You were inside me less than thirty seconds ago, and now you're being cruel."

"I'm not being cruel. I'm being serious."

I tilt my head and run my eyes over his sexy tattoos, and for the first time in my life, I consider it. "Yours are hot."

"I have an excellent artist, if you ever change your mind." His eyes are warm and filled with lust, his lips in a half smile looking down at me, and something shifts in me.

"Let's go talk to him tomorrow."

Nate's jaw drops, and his eyes widen. "Seriously?"

"Seriously. I'll consider it." I shrug, trying not to show how nervous I am at the thought of someone coming at me with needles in a gun thingy, but he sees right through me.

He always sees right through me.

"You don't have to do that for me," he murmurs.

I shake my head. "Adding permanent artwork to my body and undergoing torture at the hands of a needle is not something I'd do for any man. Maybe it's time to face a few of my fears."

He laughs and pulls me to my feet, throws me over his shoulder and slaps my ass, then climbs the stairs.

"Shower," he says with a smile in his voice.

"Good idea."

"ARE YOU SURE about this?" Nate asks.

"No."

"Do you want to leave?" He grips my hand harder and kisses my temple.

"No."

"What the hell, McKenna?" The tattoo-covered man smirks at Nate and smiles kindly at me. He's the guy with the weapons of mass destruction. "You're gonna be fine, sugar. What you're getting is tiny, and it'll take me all of ten minutes, tops."

"I can't believe I'm doing this." I close my eyes and lean my head back in the tattoo chair. Mr. Tattoo leans the chair back so I'm lying flat.

"Okay, pull your pants down."

"Fuck, dude, really?" Nate glares at him, and it makes me giggle.

"Just a perk of my job, man." He smiles and shrugs, and I relax until I see him pick up a gun-like thing and come toward me.

"Wait."

He stops with his eyebrows raised.

I lick my lips. "Um, how many tattoos have you done?"

"Thousands," he responds.

"Are you good with that gun thingy?" I ask, and he glares at me.

"This is not a gun. It's a machine."

Oh.

"Are you good with your machine?" I ask, and a wolfish smile spreads across his handsome face. Nate swears under his breath again.

"Honey, you have no idea."

"I'm serious."

"Okay." He sits forward, elbows on his knees, and looks me in the eye. "I've been doing this for almost twenty years. I majored in art in college, so I'm pretty good. I've never had an unsatisfied customer. You saw the portfolio earlier."

I nod and take a deep breath. Besides, he's right. What I've chosen is super small.

"Sweetheart, we wouldn't be here if I didn't think he's the best." Nate squeezes my hand reassuringly again, and I relax a little.

"Okay." I unbutton my jeans and shimmy them down so my left hip bone is exposed. I point out where I want the tattoo. "Right there."

"No problem, just sit back and take some deep breaths." Tattoo Guy—I've forgotten his real name in my panicked horror—rubs the stencil on my skin, pours the ink into tiny plastic jars, and picks up his *machine.*

When he turns to me with it in hand, I feel my eyes go wide. "You're going to try to kill me with that thing, aren't you?"

"No." He laughs hard and shakes his head. "This is going to be quick, really."

"Look at me," Nate says, his voice full of humor.

I look up into his soft gray eyes and grip his hand more firmly as I feel Tattoo Guy grip my hip with one hand.

"Just focus on me, baby," Nate says. "What do you want to do when we leave here?" He brushes my hair off my face and smiles down at me.

The *machine* starts up, and I flinch.

"Um, I don't know."

"Let's go for a ride on the bike," he whispers in my ear, and I close my eyes and focus on his voice.

"That's appropriate. Tattoos and motorcycles," I whisper back.

He laughs softly and kisses my cheek.

"Here we go," Tattoo Guy says, and I feel a slight sting on my hip.

I clench my eyes closed tightly, and suddenly Nate is kissing me, softly, teasingly, running those soft lips over mine, nipping the sides of my mouth, and then taking the kiss even deeper. He's still holding my right hand in his tightly, and his other hand is cupping my face, holding me to him.

The stinging is persistent but not too bad. Nate's lips are the perfect distraction.

"You're doing great," he whispers against my lips, and I open my eyes to look into his. "He's almost done, Jules."

"How do you know?" I whisper back.

He smirks and kisses me again, with more fervor, until finally, I hear someone clearing his throat loudly.

"I think he's done," I whisper against Nate's lips, and he smiles down at me.

"All done," Tattoo Guy announces and sits the chair up. "Take a look before I cover it up."

He hands me a hand mirror, and I look down at the new little piece of art on my left hip. It sits low, so a bikini will cover it up. Only Nate and I will know it's there.

"So, what does it mean to you?" Tattoo Guy asks.

"It's the ace of hearts," I murmur. It is a small red heart with an A above and to the left of it, like in the corner of a playing card. "It's Nate."

I look up and find Nate staring at my hip, his eyes dilated. His breathing has gone ragged, and my breath catches. Jesus, he's all turned on and just looks so . . . primal.

"Are you okay?" I ask him.

"Fine."

"Don't you like it?"

Without looking at me, he says to his friend, "Cover it up so we can get out of here."

Shit, he doesn't like it.

I wanted to get something that reminded me of Nate, without actually having his name tattooed on my body. The ace of hearts made sense. I call him ace all the time, and he has my heart, just like I wear his around my neck every day.

After my new tattoo is covered and I've been given instructions on how to care for it until it heals, Nate pays his friend, and we walk over to his motorcycle.

"Where do you want to go for a ride to?" I ask and reach for my helmet, but Nate stops me, grabbing my hand and pulling me to him.

"Jules, I . . ."

"What's wrong?" I lean my belly against him and gaze up at him. "I'm sorry if you don't like the tat, Nate . . ."

"I love it. It's sexy as fuck, and I love seeing part of me on you. I'm just surprised that it's what you chose." He looks down at me with a frown, looking a little confused, and a knot forms in my belly. Maybe it was presumptuous to get this particular tattoo this early in our relationship?

"I should have talked it over with you first." I close my eyes and look down. "It just seemed like the right thing to do." I shrug and grin. "And I love it. I think it looks sexy. Natalie is going to wig out when she sees it."

"It's kind of a commitment," he murmurs, and I swallow. "Like moving in together."

Shit.

He tilts my chin up with his fingers, making me look him in the eye, and I calm at his loving, happy expression. He's right. I've committed to having a piece of art that reminds me of him permanently displayed on my body. Why am I fighting the idea of living with him?

"Okay," I whisper.

"Okay what?" he asks, gazing intently into my eyes, as if he's trying to read my mind. His hands tighten at the small of my back, and I smile shyly.

"Okay, let's move in together."

"Seriously?" He's still searching my eyes, hope and love moving across his face, and I've never been more sure about anything in my life.

"Yes. Seriously. Let's start looking into it this week."

Suddenly, Nate's face splits in two with the widest grin I've ever seen on him, and he lifts me and spins me around with a loud, "Hell yeah!"

We're both laughing as he sets me back on my feet. He cups my face in his hands and kisses me gently but deeply, lovingly, and I melt against him.

"Thank you," he murmurs. "Come on, let's go for that ride." He hands me the helmet, and I frown down at it.

"Can't I ride without this? I like the wind in my hair."

"Hell no. Safety first."

He fastens the helmet on my head and then puts his own on, and we climb on the bike. I snuggle up behind him, wrap my arms around his belly and lean my cheek on his back, between his shoulder blades. "Where do you want to go, baby?" he calls back to me.

I take a deep, contented breath and smile. "I don't care. Just go."

And he does, taking off out of the parking lot and toward the freeway, driving fast but not recklessly. I know he's more careful when I'm with him, and it makes me feel safe. He merges onto the freeway heading north but exits about five miles later and takes us on a ride around Lake Washington on little roads I didn't even know were there. The view is amazing, and I watch the pretty boats on the water, and it occurs to me that it's almost the end of May already, and the weather is warming.

The motorcycle hums loudly, drowning out the noise that seems to constantly surround us, and I just lean against my man and enjoy the wind, the view and the feel of him against me.

A few hours later, we pull into Nate's parking garage, and he helps me off the back of the bike. "How was that, Miss Montgomery?"

"Awesome. It was an awesome way to spend the day. Thank you." I stand on my tiptoes and kiss his lips. "Now, let me feed you."

"What do you have in mind?" he asks.

"I'll forage through your kitchen and come up with something."

He leads me into the elevator and pulls me to him, wrapping his arms around me, as the elevator makes the climb to the thirtieth floor.

"You can start leaving lists for the housekeeper. She'll get whatever you want."

"That's kind of . . . awkward." I scrunch up my nose and look up at him.

"Why?"

I shrug. "I don't know. I don't mind doing the shopping."

"Julianne, buying groceries is part of her job. It's fine. Besides, if you're going to live here with me, you need to get used to it."

I look up at him again and search his face. He smiles and kisses me lightly. "I can't wait to have you here, permanently."

I grin up at him, and none of the nervousness or fear at the prospect of living with Nate settles in my belly. Instead, I'm excited and happy at the thought of being together.

"I'll start a list tonight."

twenty-eight

"What do you want to do tomorrow?" I ask, basking in post-orgasmic bliss.

We are cuddled up in bed, the blankets wrapped around us, my head on his chest. Nate's fingers are thrumming up and down my back.

He fucked my brains out in the shower, and then dirtied me up again when we got to the bed.

I'm not complaining.

"How do you feel about going down to Pike's Market? I'd like to get some fresh produce and cook for you tomorrow night."

"Sure, sounds fun. I love downtown."

"You're moving in with me," he whispers, and I grin.

"I am."

"Tomorrow," he says simply.

I giggle and kiss his cheek. "I think I have some phone calls to make, some packing to do, and you and I need to talk about logistics."

"I'm ready for your things to be mingled in with my things. Your clothes in our closet, and you, in our home, every day."

"God, you say the most sweet, mushy things to me, babe."

"I'm serious."

"So am I. This is new to me." I run my fingers through his impossibly soft, long black hair and sigh. "It feels like we're moving really fast."

"No, Jules, we're playing catch-up. I've wanted this with you for the better part of the last year. I screwed up last summer with you. I won't let you go again."

"I'm not asking you to let me go. I don't want you to let me go." I kiss his chin. "I love you so much. It feels fast, but it feels right. I want those things, too."

I sigh and bury my face in his neck and breathe him in. He wraps his arms around me and hugs me close, and I know, without a doubt, this is where I want to be, in his arms, for the rest of my life.

"Go to sleep," he whispers and kisses my hair.

"READY?" NATE ASKS, smiling down at me.

We just stepped onto the sidewalk outside his building, which happens to be just a few blocks up from the market and waterfront. We're going to walk down today.

He's delicious in faded blue jeans and a long-sleeve, white button-down shirt with the sleeves rolled up his forearms. The weather is finally warming in the late spring sun, and we're taking advantage of it today.

"Ready," I confirm, and he twines our fingers as we stride toward downtown at a casual pace.

"You look beautiful today," he murmurs and kisses my hand.

I'm also in blue jeans, black ballerina flats, and a red tunic top cinched at my waist with a thin black belt.

"Thank you. So do you." I lean my head on his warm, muscular shoulder, then kiss it as we wait at a crosswalk. "So, what are we shopping for today?" I ask.

"Greens and veggies for a salad and fresh lobster." He pulls our linked hands around to the small of my back and leads me across the street, watching for crazy drivers.

I love how he protects me, and watches out for me, while still making me feel like we're partners.

"Sounds delicious."

"Anything you want to grab while we're there?" he asks.

"Tiny doughnuts and Starbucks."

Pike's Market boasts the very first Starbucks café ever built, just across the street from the vendors. There is also a booth that serves delicious, fresh doughnuts that melt in your mouth. They are both must-haves when I visit.

"Let's do that first." Nate's hand tightens around mine as we descend the steep hill leading to the Market.

When we reach the cobblestone street below, I take a deep breath and look around. This is the heart of Seattle. Businessmen and blue-collar guys, families and couples, and people of all shapes and sizes and colors. Musicians are on the sidewalk, singing and playing instruments for change, and they are incredible, drawing quite a crowd.

I love the sights, sounds and smells.

"I'm so glad you suggested this." I smile up at my man. "I haven't been down here in ages, and I love it."

"Me, too." Nate kisses my forehead and leads me into Starbucks. We order our drinks and wander through the Market, starting at the end with my tiny doughnuts, so we can munch on the hot, soft goodness while we wander.

"SALMON!" someone yells, and a large gray salmon goes sailing through the air in front of us. A man in orange pants held up by brown suspenders catches the fish and throws it back to a guy in the same outfit behind the fish counter.

Nate and I smile at each other and watch the fish-throwing show for a few minutes, sipping our coffee and eating our doughnuts, soaking up Seattle.

More fish sail back and forth, the men yelling and putting on a fun show. Nate and I pick out two large lobsters, and they are packaged in a box with a handle for easy carrying.

With Nate's hands full of lobster and coffee, I push a bite of doughnut into his mouth, and we continue through the Market, winding through a sea of people. It's impossible to shop here in a hurry. There are too many people, especially on a weekend.

Nate and I choose our salad veggies, and he buys me a bouquet of fresh tulips and gerbera daisies.

"Thank you, babe. These are gorgeous." I bury my face in them and breathe in their sweet fragrance and smile up at him.

"Like you." He kisses my nose, tosses his empty coffee cup in a nearby garbage can, and presses his hand on the small of my back, leading me out of the Market and onto the sidewalk.

I look up and freeze. Fuck.

"What's wrong?" Nate asks and follows my stare. "Shit," he whispers.

Not twenty feet away is Carly from the office. She's turned away from us, looking at a handmade scarf. She pays the vendor and turns her head our way, and her eyes catch mine. I hold my breath, waiting for her to say something, but she doesn't. Nothing in her expression changes, and it's as though we're strangers. She gathers her shopping bags and walks in the opposite direction without looking back.

"She saw us," I whisper.

He kisses my forehead and nuzzles my ear with his nose. "Don't worry," he whispers.

Suddenly, a little brown-haired boy about three years old stops in front of Nate, crying, and looks up at him. "Daddy?"

"Hey, buddy." Nate sets the lobster on the ground at his feet and kneels before the little guy, who is obviously lost. "Are you looking for your daddy?"

The boy nods and continues to cry. Nate pats his little shoulder reassuringly and smiles gently. "What's your name?"

"Bwian."

"Brian?"

He nods again.

"Okay, Brian, let's find your daddy."

Nate hands me the lobster box and takes Brian's tiny hand in his and looks around. He doesn't have to look far as a panicked man comes running over to us.

"Brian! You can't wander away like that!" He pulls the boy up into his arms and kisses his cheek and smiles ruefully at Nate. "Thanks. I swear, you turn your back for a second . . ."

"No problem." Nate smiles back. "I'm glad you found him."

I've taken in the whole scene with a bit of awe. Nate is so easy with kids. They just seem to be pulled to him.

And for the first time in my life, the thought of having kids doesn't scare the shit out of me. Nate would love us, protect us, and just be . . . Nate.

Could I be a wife and a mom full time, not consumed by work?

Maybe.

Nate turns back to me and smiles, takes the lobster box out of my hand, and laces our fingers together with his free hand. "Ready to head home?"

Oh. My. God.

Yes. I could definitely make a family with this man. And it renders me speechless.

"Baby?" He frowns when I just stand here, staring at him.

I shake myself out of my trance and grin. "Yeah, I'm ready. Let's go home."

twenty–nine

"**W**ake up, baby."

I'm on my stomach, and my arms are under my pillow, cradling my head. Nate brushes my hair off my face and kisses my cheek.

"What time is it?" I mumble.

"Six," he murmurs and kisses my shoulder.

Mmm . . . that feels good. I'm not ready for Monday.

"I don't want to get up." I keep my eyes closed.

"I know," he whispers and runs the flat of his hand down my spine to my ass and back up again, and I groan. Nate kisses my cheek and nibbles my earlobe, and my body comes awake. "Grab the pillow, baby."

I pull my arms out from under the pillow and grip each end in my fists. I open one eye and gasp at the sight of my sexy man, long black hair loose, tribal tattoo down his right arm and another down his left side, looking all sleepy and sexy and *mine.*

"You're sexy," I murmur.

"I want you," he whispers.

"I'm right here, ace."

He plants a wet kiss on my shoulder and whispers in my ear, "Don't let go of the pillow."

One of his hands glides back down my spine to my ass, and he strips the covers off me to the end of the bed. He moves between my legs, pushing them apart with his knees, braces himself above me with his fists on either side of my torso and kisses his way down my back to my ass.

"Nate," I whisper.

"Yes, baby." He licks and nips each of my cheeks and slides a hand up my inner thigh, finding me wet and waiting for him. "Fuck, Julianne, you're so wet."

"I need you inside me, babe."

"You'll have me. You can let go of the pillow."

I do, and he flips me to my back and then covers me with his long, muscular body again, kissing me deeply and passionately, as if he can't go another minute without his lips touching mine.

I wrap my legs around his hips, the soles of my feet resting on his thighs and push my fingers into his hair.

"Grip the pillow again," he whispers against my mouth, but I shake my head no.

"Nate, I need to touch you this morning." I do. I can't explain why. I just need to have my hands on him.

He pulls back a bit so he can look at my face, his bright gray eyes searching mine. "What is it?" he asks.

"I don't know. I just need to feel you."

"Okay, baby, touch me all you want. I love it when you touch me." He kisses me again, more gently this time, working that talented mouth over mine and sinking onto me. He lowers his torso, letting me feel his weight. "I'm right here," he whispers.

I wrap my arms around him and run my hands up and down his back, from his ass to his long thick hair, and back down again, while I rub his thighs with the soles of my feet. I can't stop touching him, rubbing myself against him. "You feel so good."

"Let me make love to you, baby." He nibbles my lips, along my jawline and over to my left ear.

I tilt my head, giving him easier access to this sensitive spot, and he licks under my ear, where he knows it makes me crazy.

"I love how you smell, Julianne. So soft and clean and sweet." His teeth clench gently onto my earlobe, and I squirm under him. "You feel so damn good, sweetheart. So smooth and firm and small."

His words are intoxicating me, making love to me as thoroughly as his body is, and I feel my heart rate speed up and my breathing quicken.

"Nate," I whisper.

"I can't get enough of you." His hips start to move in a slow circle, rubbing his hard, thick cock along my folds, the silver ball of his apa massaging my clit, and I arch my back, pushing against him.

"Nate, I need you." I grip his firm ass in my hands and pull him against me, almost coming undone at the sensation of his long shaft rubbing my lips and the head of his cock, along with the piercing, making my clit pulsate, an orgasm working its way through me.

"So beautiful," he whispers against my neck and pushes his forearms under my shoulders so he's cradling me, his hands cupping my neck and fingers pushed up into my hair. He holds on and pushes harder, faster, rubbing himself against me. "I love making you come like this."

"Oh God," I whisper. Our voices are soft, we're panting quietly, making love almost reverently. I feel tears pool in my eyes, and I close them, the tears spilling down my temples.

"Shh, baby, don't cry." He settles his lips on mine again, rubs them back and forth, caressing me and then kissing me sweetly, softly. "Come for me, honey."

I come apart, silently, my body quaking and pushing against him. He deepens his kiss and pulls his hips down, finding my opening with the tip of his sex, and pushes into me, so, so slowly, letting me feel the apa as it slides against the walls of my pussy, and he fills me so completely. He sinks into me to the root of his amazing cock and stops.

"Open your eyes."

His gray eyes are on fire, looking down at me with such love, and I feel more tears leak out of my eyes.

"Your eyes are the most brilliant blue I've ever seen, and they're even bluer when I'm in you. I love it when you look at me like this."

"How am I looking at you?" I whisper and push my fingers into his thick hair, loving how it feels to have my head and shoulders cradled in his arms and his body draped over mine, filling me up.

"Like I'm all you see," he whispers back to me.

I run my fingers down his face and cup his cheeks in my hands, looking him square in the eye, not paying any attention to the tears on my face.

"You are all I see."

He growls softly and kisses me desperately. His pelvis begins to move, slowly sliding in and out of me. I grip his ass in my hands again, and I feel the orgasm building up in me once more. He must feel it, too, because he moves faster and pushes into me a bit harder with each thrust.

"Let go, Julianne," he murmurs.

"Come with me," I whisper.

He breaks the kiss on a groan and pins me with his raw gray eyes, his mouth open as he pants, and he pushes into me twice, three times, and then grinds his pubis against my clit as he spills into me, and I come apart beneath him, not taking my gaze from his, as my body shudders around him.

"Oh my God," I whisper as my body calms.

He collapses onto me and buries his face in my neck.

"Hey."

He lifts his head at my voice.

I kiss his cheek. "I love you, Nate."

"God, I love you, Julianne."

WORK TODAY HAS been . . . well, weird. Mrs. Glover keeps looking at me speculatively each time I walk past her desk, which makes me nervous and curious about what she's thinking. I haven't heard from Nate all day. I came to the office first while he went to the gym and followed me in about an hour later, as per our usual schedule. But he hasn't sent me any work requests at all, nor have I heard from any of my colleagues.

So, I've been in my office for most of the day, working on some reports that needed reworking and doing some research on a client Nate is considering bringing on.

At two o'clock, there's a knock on my door.

"Come in," I call out.

Mrs. Glover pokes her head in the door. "You are being asked to join a meeting in the conference room, Miss Montgomery."

"Okay, thanks. Any idea what it's about?" I ask as I gather my iPad and walk toward the door.

"No, but they've been in there all day."

"They?"

"Yes, both partners, the CEO and the head of human resources."

My stomach falls to my feet.

Fuck.

I follow Mrs. Glover to the conference room. She knocks on the door and steps inside.

"Miss Montgomery," she announces and ushers me into the room.

Nate and Mr. Luis are seated behind a long conference table, along with our CEO, Mr. Vincent, and a woman in a black suit, presumably from HR.

Nate doesn't meet my eyes when I enter the room.

"Miss Montgomery, please have a seat." HR Lady motions to the seat opposite them at the table.

Great, I get to sit by myself in front of all of them.

Shit.

I take my seat and lay the iPad on the table before me, then link my hands together in my lap, looking back and forth between each of the people before me. Their faces are completely impassive, not giving any indication as to why I've been asked in here, but I know.

Carly must have told.

"Miss Montgomery," Mr. Vincent begins. I've met him only once before, but he seems like a kind man. He's older with gray hair and kind eyes. His eyes are still kind as he looks at me, his hands folded on the table, leaning toward me. "I have a question for you."

"Yes, sir," I respond, proud of myself for sounding confident and professional.

"How long have you been with my company?"

I frown slightly and glance over at HR Lady. Surely they have this information?

"Three years, Mr. Vincent," I respond.

"And in that time, have you been given information regarding our policies and procedures?" he asks.

"Of course."

"Good." He nods and looks down at papers spread before him. "So you're aware that this company has a no-fraternization policy."

"I am."

I will not wilt and crumble before these people. I knew this could happen, and I took the risk. I feel all four pairs of eyes on me now, and I look at each of them, Nate last. His face is cold, his eyes gazing at me with no emotion. It's the way he looked at me for eight months, after the first time we made love in his apartment and until he talked me back to his place right before my birthday.

"We have received information that you have been involved with another member of this company," Mr. Vincent continues.

"You must have received a statement from Carly this morning," I respond coolly, not breaking eye contact.

Mr. Vincent's eyes widen, and then he frowns and looks at his colleagues. "Actually, no. Why would you suggest that?" he asks.

I frown and immediately hate myself for my big mouth. "It was just a hunch."

"So you don't deny this?" he asks.

"No, sir."

Mr. Vincent sighs and leans back in his chair. "Miss Montgomery, you have an excellent employment record here. You've done very well in your three years with us."

"Thank you, sir."

"But policy is policy."

I glance over at Nate, and his demeanor hasn't changed. Isn't he going to say something?

"We know that you and Mr. McKenna have been seeing each other for some time now. As a partner, Mr. McKenna is too much of an asset for us to lose. Unfortunately, I can't break the rules of this company and keep you on as well, Miss Montgomery."

He stops talking, and all four of them stare at me. The only person who has spoken since I came in the room is Mr. Vincent. They are all so calm, impassive. Cold.

Especially Nate.

I look at him again and stare at him for a long minute. He doesn't flinch. He doesn't waiver. He's not going to defend me or offer to quit. And that hurts more than the fact that I'm losing my job.

Miss HR speaks for the first time and hands me a check. "We have drafted up your final paycheck, cashing out your vacation and sick time, and Mr. Vincent has approved three months' severance pay. You'll be receiving information in the mail about rolling over your 401(k). You have fifteen minutes to gather your things."

Seriously? My eyes haven't left Nate's while she speaks. I stand and turn to leave, but Mr. Vincent's voice stops me, and I turn back to the table.

"Miss Montgomery, you have truly been an asset to this company. I will personally be happy to write you a letter of reference should you need one."

I nod at him. "Thank you."

I walk on numb legs to my office and shut the door. *Holy fuck.* Did that just happen? Did I just get fired, and my boyfriend did nothing about it? He just sat there and looked at me like I'm a stranger?

Like he hadn't been inside me less than six hours ago?

I've never kept many personal items in my office, so I grab my purse, throw in my iPad, phone, a tube of lip gloss out of my desk drawer, and my coffee mug, and walk out of my office, mentally congratulating myself for keeping it together.

"Miss Montgomery."

I turn at Mrs. Glover's voice and see Nate standing at her desk, staring at me. His jaw is clenched, but that's the only emotion on his face.

"Best of luck to you, dear."

And that's all it takes to bring tears to my eyes. I don't respond. I just walk straight to the elevators and push the call button.

Carly appears at my side. "Oh my gosh! I just heard the news. Are you okay?"

She had to have been behind this, had to have reported what she saw to HR first thing this morning, probably while Nate was making love to me.

I don't look at her. I just watch the numbers above the elevator doors. I feel Nate's eyes on my back.

Fuck him.

Fuck all of them.

"Jules, are you okay?" Carly asks again in her disgustingly fake sweet voice.

The elevator pings, and the doors open. I step inside and turn, my eyes meeting Nate's, and I answer Carly without looking at her.

"Fuck you."

thirty

"Hello?"

"Will, it's Jules." I clear my throat and change lanes, heading toward my house.

"Hey, what's up?"

"I need to come stay with you for a while."

Silence.

"What's going on?" Will's usual happy, flippant voice has lowered, and I know he's ready to kick ass for me.

"I just got fired and lost my boyfriend in the process. I need to get away and get my head on straight. Can I crash with you?"

"I'll put clean sheets in the spare room. Are you okay to drive?"

"Yeah, I think I'm still in shock. I'll fall apart when I get to your place."

"I'll get the Kleenex ready, too. Love you, kiddo."

"Love you, too."

I hang up and call Natalie. I need to get the phone calls out of the way now, before the tears start. Because once they start, I don't know if I'll be able to stop them.

"Jules?" Nat answers. "Why aren't you at work?"

"I got fired."

"Fuck, someone found out."

"Yep." I pull into my driveway, cut the engine, and stride quickly into the house and up to my bedroom.

"You sound calm."

"I'm pissed as fuck, mostly at Nate. He didn't get fired, and when

I was in front of him and the other members of the firing squad, he didn't defend me."

I hear Olivia fussing in the background. "Do you need me to come over?" Nat asks.

"No, I'm packing. I need to get away for a little while."

"Come here," Natalie offers, but I know that's not an option either.

"Thanks, but I'm going to Will's. I really want to go off the grid for a while and figure out what I'm going to do next."

"Okay, but if you need anything, you know where to find me."

"Thanks, Nat." I feel tears starting, but I swallow them down and focus on throwing clothes into my biggest suitcase. I'm taking just about everything because I don't know how long I'll be gone.

I'm tossing toiletries into a smaller suitcase when I hear my front door open and slam shut and heavy footsteps running up my stairs, two at a time. Suddenly, Nate is in my doorway, panting, his hair down, in just his white button-down shirt and slacks. He eyes my open suitcases and then pins me with narrowed gray eyes.

"Where are you going?" he asks.

"None of your business." I turn to go back into the bathroom, but he lunges for me and grabs my elbows.

"Let's talk about this, Julianne."

I pull out of his grasp and wrap my arms around my middle, so livid, so hurt, so confused.

"Don't touch me. There is nothing to talk about, Nate. You threw me under the bus."

He steps toward me again, but I back away, and he plants his hands on his lean hips. "That's not what happened."

"You sat in that room and let them fire me without saying one word in my defense."

"You weren't in that room all morning when that's exactly what I did. I offered to quit if they'd let you stay."

"But you didn't threaten to quit if they fired me."

His jaw clenches shut, and he runs a hand through his hair.

"I didn't think so," I mutter and stalk into the bathroom, gathering my shampoo, razor and shower gel out of the shower and dump them into the suitcase with my makeup bag.

"Julianne, it doesn't do us any good if we're both unemployed."

"Fuck that! Nate, I knew when I stepped foot in your apartment for the first time that this could happen. I *knew* what I was getting myself into. And you know what? I chose you. I CHOSE YOU!" I poke my finger into his chest and pace around the room. I am on fire. "If those people had asked me, I would have told them that I loved you and they could kiss my ass if they didn't like it. I didn't lie when he asked me about our relationship. But you sat six feet away from me and didn't even show any goddamn emotion!"

"Jules—"

"No," I interrupt and pace back toward him. "I don't give a fuck about that job right now. I'll get another. What I care about is that I didn't even know you today. The man who defended me with every fiber of his being Friday night wasn't there. The man who makes sure I don't get hit by cars in downtown Seattle and makes me feel safe wasn't fucking there."

"Goddamn it, Jules, what was I supposed to say?"

"Oh, I don't know, maybe something along the lines of, 'It takes two to tango?' or 'If you fire her, I'm out, too?'" I throw underwear and shoes into my bag, not even caring to see which ones they are exactly, and I zip the bags shut.

"If you'll calm down, I'll tell you what happened before you came into the damn room, Julianne."

I take a deep breath and hang my head and rub my forehead with my hand. I love him so much and feel so betrayed by him. I know that I can't be around him right now.

"I have somewhere I need to be." I pull the suitcases off the bed and extend the handles to drag them behind me.

"Where are you going?" he asks again, crossing his arms over his chest.

"Don't worry about it, Nate. Just forget about me." I start to move past him, but he steps in front of me, blocking the way to the door.

"I will not forget about you." His eyes are feral, his face taut in pain, and it hurts to look at him. Everything just hurts. I close my eyes and feel a tear escape down my cheek. "Baby, don't cry."

Nate leans down and kisses me softly, and I let him, knowing that this is our last. I wrap my arms around his neck and pull him to me, putting everything into this kiss. I run my hands through his hair and finally pull away, brushing my fingertips down his face, memorizing everything about him.

"You and I were probably never meant to be," I whisper, staring into his beautiful gray eyes, "but I loved every single second that I spent with you."

I pull out of his arms as he swallows hard, and I cup his palm in mine, laying the silver heart he gave me at the beach in his hand. I grab my bags and walk out the door, down the stairs and out to my car.

"Julianne, wait."

"Just lock up when you leave, Nate."

"Goddamn it, wait!"

I push my bags into the back seat of my car and open the driver's side, and suddenly Nate is next to me. "Look at me."

I raise my tear-filled eyes to his and swallow. His gaze lingers over my face. His eyes are sad, and he starts to say something but stops himself. Finally, he kisses my forehead and whispers, "I love you."

I don't respond as I get behind the wheel and pull away.

WILL OPENS HIS front door and pulls me into his arms, hugging me close. All of my brothers are tall and muscular. We all come from the same extraordinary gene pool, after all. Will has dark blond hair and sapphire-blue eyes and is only two years older than I am. He and I have always been very close.

I take a deep breath and let him hold me in his doorway, my cheek nestled in his soft Seahawks T-shirt, and the enormity of this afternoon's events washes over me. I feel the tears and honest-to-God temper tantrum start to surface, so I step back and murmur, "Bedroom."

"This way." He leads me through his beautiful Seattle home, but I don't really pay attention to the rooms. I follow him upstairs, and he opens a door. "This is your room, kiddo, for as long as you need it. I'm just across the hall in case you need me."

I nod and step into the beautiful room. The bed has been freshly made. "I forgot to get my bags."

"I'll get them."

"I think I'm going to cry, Will."

"Do you want me to stay or go?"

"I don't know." I shake my head and sit on the edge of the bed. God, I wish I could get that numb feeling back. It was so much better than this piercing pain that's running through me.

"I'll go get your bags and give you a minute, and then I'll be back, okay?"

I nod and look blindly at my brother. He looks concerned and a little mad. "Are you mad at me?"

"No, kid, I'm worried. I've never seen you like this."

"I don't think I've ever been through this." I touch my fingers to my lips and remember kissing Nate goodbye fifteen minutes ago, and the tears start to fall. I hang my head in my hands and give in to the crushing grief. I start to rock back and forth, sobs wracking my body. I've never cried this hard. I've never been this devastated.

I hear my own voice, keening and mumbling. I'm a fucking mess, and I can't stop it. My body has taken over, exorcising the hurt through tears and snot and spit.

Will comes back into the room, wheeling my bags behind him. He pulls some tissues out of the box by the bed and hands me a wad to clean up the snotty mess on my face, and stands before me with his hands on his hips. "Are you able to talk?"

I shake my head no.

"Do you want me to kill him?" he asks, his voice low.

I shake my head no again, then think twice about it and shrug. A smile tugs at the corner of Will's lips.

"What do you need me to do, Jules?"

God, I love this man. I'm so glad I came here.

"Just don't tell anyone but the family that I'm here. If Nate calls, you haven't seen me."

He raises an eyebrow and crosses his arms over his chest. "He really fucked up."

"Yeah, he did."

"Another woman?"

"No." That brings more tears, and I break down again.

"Okay, we won't talk about it tonight."

"Am I ruining any plans for you?" I ask through my tears.

"No, but you know I'd change any plans for you, kid."

I just nod, and he shuffles from bare foot to bare foot and finally walks around to the other side of the bed, climbs on, sits against the headboard, and says, "Come here."

He pulls me into his lap, and I curl into a ball and cry. Long, loud and messy sobs. Will keeps handing me tissues, rubs my back soothingly and holds me, letting me cry.

"Isn't it yucky holding your sister like this?" I ask.

"Not when you're this sick," he responds, and he's right.

I'm sick.

Sick with fear, anger, sadness, betrayal and longing.

"WAKE UP, JULES."

Someone is jostling my shoulder and squeezing my head with a vice. I try to open my eyes, but the light is too bright.

"Go away," I croak.

"It's almost noon."

I moan and turn onto my back. My body is sore from stress and grief. My eyes are swollen from crying, and my head is killing me.

"Here." Will holds out a glass of water and some pills. "Take these and get in the shower."

"I think I'll just stay in bed." I frown and look around. I'm still in my work clothes from yesterday, and I don't remember climbing into bed. I just remember crying, long into the night, and Will holding me.

"No, you won't."

"I'll do whatever I want," I respond defiantly.

"You're not going to bury yourself in this bed for days, Jules. You're stronger than that."

"No, I'm not," I whisper as yesterday's events run through my head. I don't need to cry anymore, but I'm drained.

"Yeah, you are. Come on, get up. Shower, get some food in you, and then you can go to the gym with me and beat the shit out of something."

Beating the shit out of something sounds really good. I take the pills he's holding out to me and climb gingerly out of the bed. "I'll be down in fifteen."

thirty-one

"**S**o let me get this straight," Will says as he jogs next to me on a treadmill. "They pulled you into the room, the CEO confronted you with the whole fucking-around-with-your-boss thing, you got the ax, and Nate didn't say one word in your defense the entire time?"

We are at his gym, an exclusive training center for Will's team. It's the off-season, so many of his teammates have left Seattle for their hometowns, but there are a few guys working out in the state-of-the-art facility.

"That's pretty much the way it went," I confirm and boost the speed on my treadmill. "Then he came to my place while I was packing."

"What did he say then?"

"He told me to calm down and he'd tell me what happened before they pulled me into the room."

"And?" Will asks and takes a swig of his water.

"And nothing. I didn't let him talk." I feel Will's eyes on me, and when I meet his gaze, his eyebrows are raised. "What?"

"Why didn't you let him talk?"

"Because I didn't want to hear it, Will. It doesn't change that he sat in that chair without saying one word to me and let them fire me. He had no emotion in his face at all. It was like I was a stranger who was being fired for sexual harassment."

"Has he tried to call?" Will asks.

"I don't know. I haven't checked my phone since I left the house yesterday."

"Maybe you should hear him out."

"Maybe not." I shake my head and increase my speed again. "I don't want to be with someone who doesn't have my back."

"Maybe—"

"Maybe not, Will. Shut it!" I glare at him, done with the conversation, and he rolls his eyes at me.

"Fine, brat. You're a complete pain in the ass. But if you want me to have him killed, I'm sure I know someone who knows someone." He grins at me, and I find myself grinning back.

"I'll keep it in mind. For the rest of today, I just want to put it out of my head."

"Okay. How about if I kick your ass in the pool, and then I'll take you to dinner and a movie?"

"That's the best offer I've had all day."

We slow the treadmills down to a walk and finally climb off them. After changing into swim wear, we walk out to the pool area to swim laps.

"Hey, Montgomery, who's the honey?" A very tall, very muscular man with mocha skin and long black dreadlocks approaches us, looking me up and down in my bikini.

"This is my sister, dude." Will frowns at him and stands in front of me, and I snicker.

"I'm Jules."

"Trevor Miller."

I shake his hand and smile kindly. Any other day I would have been flattered by the attention and definitely would have flirted with the handsome football star, but I can't help but think about how pissed Nate would be if he saw me standing here, in my bikini, being ogled by these men, and it makes me somber.

Damn Nate.

"Nice to meet you. Shall we?" I ask Will, and we dive in, swimming the length of the long pool several times. I tire out long before Will, so I boost myself up on the side of the pool and dangle my feet in the warm water, spreading my toes, enjoying how it feels.

I wonder if Nate has tried to call or text. I miss him. It hasn't even been a full day, and I miss him.

It's disgusting.

Will finally pulls himself out of the water next to me, and we sit there while Will catches his breath.

"When did you get the tattoo?" Will asks.

I gasp and look down, noticing that my bikini bottom has slipped, exposing my tattoo.

"On Saturday."

"You're not supposed to be swimming until it's healed, you know."

"Oh." I hadn't thought of that. "Well, I won't swim again then."

"What does it mean?" Will asks and looks down at me.

I avert my eyes and shake my head, not wanting to answer him. I don't regret the tattoo, but it's a sore spot for me right now, literally and figuratively.

"Are you ever going to talk to him again?" Will asks.

Oh God. The thought of never talking to Nate ever again makes my blood run cold. Is that the decision I've made? I said goodbye yesterday. I gave him back his mother's necklace.

It's over.

"Fuck," I whisper.

"I'm sorry, kiddo. Take a few days and calm down. Maybe you'll be able to give him a chance to explain things. If you don't like what he has to say, fuck him. Maybe he'll be able to give you some insight." Will shrugs and looks down at his feet. "I probably shouldn't tell you this . . ."

"What?" My gaze whips up to his, and he scowls and shakes his head.

"He called me last night."

"What? How do you know? You were with me all night."

"No, I wasn't. When you fell asleep, I tucked you in like a good big brother and let you sleep. He'd left a message earlier in the evening."

I don't respond. I don't know if I want to know what Nate said. I don't know if I can take it. I'm missing him so much, and I'm starting to feel weak in my resolve, and I don't like this new quality in my personality.

"Don't you want to know what he said?"

"No."

"Jules." Will laughs and looks down at me with humor. "You're so fucking stubborn."

"Learned it from you, big brother."

"You really don't want to know?"

"No."

"Let me just say this, kid. And this is coming from me, your big brother, who would fucking kill for you. Take your few days to lick your wounds and be pissed. You have a right to them. But then give him a chance to explain."

"Let's go to dinner." I start to pull myself up, but Will stops me with his hand on my arm.

"Jules . . ."

"I heard you. I'll think about it." I kiss his cheek and pull away. "I'm hungry."

"Let's go then."

WILL TAKES ME to one of our favorite burger joints in North Seattle called Red Mill Burgers. It's nothing fancy, but the food is to die for. We place our order and find a seat, waiting for my name to be called so we can go collect our food.

"I haven't been here in ages." I look around the restaurant and back at Will and giggle when I see him pull his baseball cap down lower on his face. "Do you really think that's much of a disguise? Dude, you're like six-four, all built, and your ugly face is on a billboard downtown. People are going to recognize you."

"Shut up," he murmurs, making me laugh again.

"Jules?" I look to my left and see a gorgeous, petite woman smiling down at me with beautiful hazel eyes and long auburn hair with chunky blond highlights.

"Meg!" I quickly jump up and pull her in for a big hug. "Oh my gosh, I haven't seen you in years! How are you?"

Meg steps back and smiles at me, then glances nervously over at Will. "I'm doing very well, thanks. It's great to see you."

"Will, this is Megan McBride, a friend from college. Meg, this is my brother, Will."

Will stands, towering over her, and offers his hand. Meg's face sobers, but she shakes his hand politely. "I know who you are."

He just nods and takes his seat again.

"What have you been up to?" I ask her.

"I'm a charge nurse in the cancer unit at Seattle Children's Hospital." Meg smiles shyly, the dimple in her left cheek winking at me, and I grin back at her.

"That's awesome! Good for you, girl. Are you still singing?"

"Uh, no." She shakes her head and blushes, looking down at the table. "Not since college."

"You sing?" Will asks.

"She has a fantastic voice," I reply and smile encouragingly at Meg.

"Thanks, but you know how it is. Life takes over, and things get busy." She shrugs and smiles at me again.

Will catches my eye, and he raises an eyebrow.

Yes, she's hot, moron.

"Are you married?" I ask her.

She giggles almost cynically. "Hell no."

"Can I get your number?" Will asks, straight out, and I frown at him.

Meg gapes at him for a moment, but then glares at him. "Hell no," she responds coldly.

Wow, what got her panties in a twist?

Will's jaw drops, and he smirks, then shakes his head. "Excuse me?"

"I don't think I stuttered." Meg puts her hand on my shoulder and grins at me. "It was great to see you. Take care, girl."

"You, too, Meg."

"What the hell was that all about?" Will asks, bewildered.

"I don't know." I shrug and then smirk at him. "You just have such a debonair way with women."

"Shut up, brat."

IT'S WEDNESDAY, BUT the whole family is at my mom and dad's for dinner, despite it being the middle of the week. I know it's because everyone wanted to make sure that I'm okay, and it makes me feel loved and secure knowing that they care enough to want to check on me in person.

But my heart just isn't in it. It's been two days since I last saw Nate, and it's killing me.

"Jules, honey, would you like some dessert?" my mom asks, smiling at me.

I'm completely stuffed from her delicious fried chicken and mashed potatoes, which will earn me another killer session at the gym, but I always have room for dessert.

"What do you have?" I ask.

"I made your favorite," she says with a wink. "Chocolate cheesecake."

And just like that my world falls apart all over again. At first, all I can do is stare at her as tears fill my eyes, and the next thing I know, I tip the chair over in my haste to get out of it and run out into the backyard. The tears are falling in earnest, and I just can't control the shudders working through my body.

Suddenly, strong arms wrap around me, and I'm cradled in my dad's arms. He rocks me back and forth, his big hand running up and down my back.

"Shh, baby girl, it's okay."

"No, it's not okay," I sob and cry harder, gripping on to his shirt with my fists.

"I take it Nate gave you chocolate cheesecake?" he murmurs with humor in his voice.

I nod.

"Sounds like he likes to spoil you."

"I can't talk about him," I mumble through my tears. "I don't even know why I'm so upset."

"Because you love him, and he disappointed you, darlin'."

I lean back and look up at my dad. "I thought I knew him."

"What exactly happened, honey?"

I shake my head and pull out of his arms, but he leads me to a near-by bench and makes me sit. "What happened?" he asks again.

So I explain what happened on Monday, and as I work my way through the events, my dad listens with narrowed eyes, nodding, exhaling loudly, and when I'm done, he looks at me with a sober face.

"Julianne Rose Montgomery, I'm disappointed in both of you."

"Huh?"

"You need to let him explain."

I start to shake my head, but he lays his hand on my forearm, catching my attention.

"People screw up, Jules. He has some explaining to do, but you wouldn't let him talk. Let the man talk."

"You and Will are two peas in a pod."

We stand and walk back into the house. It's quiet inside. Everyone looks so somber waiting for us to return.

"You okay?" Isaac asks quietly.

"I will be," I respond.

Natalie is burping Olivia, and I hold my hands out. "Baby. Mine."

Natalie smirks and hands her over to me. I cuddle Olivia close and smile at Nat. "Thanks."

"So, no cheesecake. How about apple pie?" Mom winks at me, and everyone starts chattering around me again.

I kiss Olivia's head and look over at Luke, who grins and takes a sip of a beer.

"SO, WHY DID I have to call Will's phone to reach you?" Natalie asks from the facial bed next to mine.

We decided to cash in my birthday spa day. Our heads are wrapped in white towels, our bodies draped in cozy white sheets, and we both have mud masks freshly brushed on our faces with cucumbers over our eyelids.

It's freaking heaven.

"Because I haven't checked my phone in four days," I murmur.

"Why?" she asks again.

"Because I don't want to know if Nate's called or texted," I respond and sigh as the technician begins to massage my hands.

"But . . . why?"

"Trying to de-stress here, Nat. You're not helping."

"I'm sorry. I'm trying to understand."

"If he has called," I say patiently, "I'm not sure I want to hear his voice or his excuses. If he hasn't called, it'll hurt."

"Okay." She doesn't sound so sure, but she drops it, and we stop talking and enjoy our delicious facials.

We decided to go for the whole princess treatment today and indulge in one-hour massages, mani-pedis and waxing, too.

"That was fantastic." I link my arm through Natalie's as we leave the spa and take a deep breath of early-summer air. "Tell Luke thanks for me. It's so nice having an obscenely rich brother-in-law who loves nothing more than spoiling his gorgeous wife, and therefore, his gorgeous wife's bff gets spoiled, too."

"I will tell him." Natalie laughs and leads me down the street to our favorite café for lunch. I look over at my friend and smile. She's is beautiful, with her freshly polished face and chestnut hair back in a loose ponytail.

We order our usual of soup and sandwiches and find a table.

"So, I think you should turn your phone on, friend," Natalie says with a raised eyebrow. She pulls off her thin green scarf and drapes it on the back of the chair next to her.

"No." I sip my Diet Coke.

"I dare you." Her lips turn up in a soft smile, and I glare at her.

"Don't be a bitch, Nat."

"Don't be a pussy, Jules."

Fuck.

I hate how well she knows me. She knows I can't resist a dare. I have four older brothers who got me into all kinds of shit growing up because of their dares.

"Goddamn it, Natalie," I mutter and pull my iPhone out of my Gucci handbag. "You turn it on."

I pass her the phone, and she fires it up, watching the screen and twirling a strand of her hair with her fingers.

"Does it seriously take this long for that piece of shit to fire up?" I ask.

"Yes." She laughs up at me and keeps watching the screen. "Looks like ten voice mails and twenty-two texts."

"Holy fuck. I don't know that many people."

"Here." She tries to hand the phone back to me, but I wave it away.

"No. You check them."

"No, Jules. Jesus, grow a pair and check your phone."

I take a deep breath and continue to glare at my best friend. God, I hate her right now.

"Okay, give it to me."

She hands it to me, and I check the voice mail first. The first six messages are from my family, wanting to know if I'm okay. The seventh and eighth are Natalie wanting to meet up for a spa day and threatening to call Will.

The ninth is Mrs. Glover telling me that I forgot a personal item in my office that she'll mail to me.

The tenth is Nate. It was left this morning.

"Julianne . . ." He pauses and sighs, and I grip the phone tighter, pressing it harder against my ear as if I'll be able to hear his voice more clearly this way. "I hope that four days is long enough. I can't go another day without hearing your voice. Please, baby, call me. Talk to me. I love you." There is another long pause, and then the message ends.

I'm staring at Natalie with tears rolling down my face. I'm not sobbing or making a scene, but the tears began to fall when he said my name. I tap the button to play it again and pass the phone to Natalie so she can hear.

She listens avidly, her beautiful green eyes on mine. Her eyes also well with tears as she passes the phone back to me.

"Wow, Jules."

"Damn it," I mutter.

"What are you going to do?" she asks.

"Write you out of my will," I reply and wipe my cheeks.

"Seriously."

"Oh, who am I kidding? I'll probably call him later today." The waitress sets our lunches in front of us, and we dig in.

"He's been calling me, you know."

"Jesus, he's been calling everyone. Will said he called him, and Mom told me last night that he'd called her."

"He hasn't been able to find you, Jules. It's making him crazy."

"Good."

"My best friend once gave me good advice when I was mad at my husband. She said, 'Don't play games with him.'" Natalie frowns at me, and I squirm.

"I'm not playing games."

"Yeah, you are." She shrugs and sips her soup. "I get it, though. He was an idiot on Monday. But I get why he was."

"You do?" I ask incredulously.

"Yeah, we all do. We're all talking to him, bonehead."

I sit back in my chair and stare at her, my mouth open and eyes wide. "You've all been *talking* to him?"

She nods and takes my hand in hers. "Just talk to him, Jules. I hate to see you hurting when you don't need to be."

"You weren't there . . ."

"Nope, I wasn't. And you have every right to be angry. But doesn't he have the right to explain?"

"I just . . ." I shake my head and look down, blinking tears from my eyes. "I just keep seeing myself sitting in that chair, with those people looking at me impassively while they took away my job. A job that I was so good at and dedicated so much of myself to. And Nate knew,

Natalie. He knew how much I loved my job, and how good I was at it."

"You'll find another job, Jules."

"I know, but while they so flippantly took my job away, the man I love so much, and professed to loving me so much in return, sat in his chair and looked at me like he didn't even know me. There was no emotion in his face. In his eyes. He was just . . . blank. And that's what tore me up the most."

I pull my hand out of hers and lean back again, shaking my head. "You were there Friday night, Nat. You saw how he kicked DJ's ass. You know how protective he is of me, yet I'm telling you, that man was not sitting in the conference room on Monday. And it tore my heart out."

Natalie frowns and looks down at her plate and then looks back up at me. She looks like she wants to say something but stops herself.

"What?" I ask.

"Jules, maybe he didn't have a choice."

"What do you mean?"

She shakes her head slowly and looks out the window to watch the cars pass.

"Nat, what do you know?" I hear the desperation in my voice, but I don't care.

"Honestly, I don't know anything about that meeting. Nate didn't say anything about it. But what you're describing . . . It just . . ." She frowns again and looks back at me. "Honey, I don't think he had a choice."

What? We stare at each other for a long minute, and my brain churns with what-ifs.

"Do you think . . . ?" I stammer.

"I don't know. Just do what he's asking, sweetie. Call him."

thirty-two

After Natalie and I say our goodbyes, I drive back to Will's house and pack my bags. It's time to go home.

"Leaving me so soon?" Will asks drily, leaning against the doorjamb with his arms crossed over his chest.

"It's time to go home and pull it together."

"Good call, sis." He smiles at me, but his eyes still look worried.

"I'll be okay," I reassure him.

"I don't doubt it. But if you need anything, I'm here. We all are."

"I know." I throw the last of my things in the bag and zip it closed. "Thank you, Will. Really."

"I do have my moments, you know. Just don't let the press know." He winks at me, and I walk over to him, and he opens his arms to give me a tight hug. "Gonna call him?"

"Yeah, when I get home."

"Good." He kisses my head, and I pull back. "Come over for dinner next week. I'll cook."

"Gag." I roll my eyes. "I'll cook. You'll poison me."

Will grins and lifts my suitcases and follows me out to my car.

I HAVEN'T BEEN home in four days, and it feels good to be here. I grab a water from the fridge and unpack my things, knowing that I'm procrastinating. I want to call Nate. I want to hear his sexy voice. But I don't know what to say.

Finally, when laundry has been done and put away and there's nothing left to do, I pick up my iPhone and sit on the couch, staring at it. I bring up Nate's number on my Favorites list, and my thumb hovers over his number, but then I power down the screen.

This needs to be done in person.

I climb the stairs to my bedroom and carefully choose an outfit of dark denim wide-leg jeans, a cornflower-blue blouse that matches my eyes, and a black belt, cinching the blouse around my waist. I add my birthday diamond earrings and black Louboutin stilettos.

I paint my clean face with a small amount of makeup, accenting my eyes and lips, and curl my hair in loose waves, framing my face.

I drive to Nate's without giving it too much thought so I don't chicken out and go back home. His car and the bike are both in their parking spots, telling me that he's home.

Good.

I use my usual parking space and take the elevator to his floor.

I pause at his door, my stomach suddenly full of those mutant butterflies again. God, what if he's decided he doesn't want to see me?

Instead of knocking, I use the key Nate gave me a few weeks ago and open the front door, stepping inside. The lights are on in the kitchen and living areas, and there is a fire roaring. There are several bouquets of pink roses throughout the space, on the breakfast bar, on the dining room table, by the sofa.

No Nate.

Then I hear the voices.

I walk back toward the bedrooms, and the voices get louder. They're coming from Nate's office. I stop, just out of sight, and listen.

"This is it, Audrey. This is the last time."

"Sure." She snorts. "You won't be able to stay away from me for long, baby."

"After this, I want you to change your name."

"Change my name?" she asks incredulously. "What the fuck?"

"I don't want you to have it anymore. I'll make the arrangements. You'll just have to sign the papers."

He's making her change her name!

"Is this about that blond tramp you've been fucking?"

And . . . that's it.

I turn the corner so I can get a look into the room, and I'm transported back to Nate's office last month. Audrey is perched on his desk. He's scowling up at her, and she's about to run her perfectly manicured hand down his face.

"Touch him and see how fast I have you on the ground," I warn quietly.

Both of them whip their heads toward me in surprise. Nate's face registers shock, hope, and then wariness as he realizes what I've just witnessed.

Audrey grins and lets the palm of her hand make contact with his face.

I grin back. Nate backs out of Audrey's touch and stands quickly.

"Goddamn it, Audrey . . ."

"I warned you," I murmur as I stalk toward her.

She hops off the desk and faces me head-on, her brown eyes glaring at me. "I'm not afraid of you."

I smile and cock my head. "You should be."

Her eyes go wide for a moment, and then she glares at me again. "Nate doesn't want you. You left him, remember?"

I slide my eyes over to Nate just as he balls his hands into fists, his molten gray eyes on mine, and I know.

"Audrey, Goddamn it, shut the fuck up . . ."

I pivot on my heel before he can finish the sentence and stalk out to the living area.

"Julianne!" Nate's voice is panicked as he follows me, but I ignore him. I hear Audrey's heels click on the hardwood as she follows after Nate.

I walk into the kitchen and open the fridge. Chocolate cheesecake and lobster are staring back at me along with my favorite champagne. I turn and take in the room, the flowers, the fire, and I look into Nate's gray eyes for a long minute.

Audrey is fuming, shooting daggers at me, then gazing longingly at

Nate, and I almost feel sorry for her.

"I understand," I tell her calmly. "I understand how easy he is to love, Audrey."

Nate swears under his breath and pushes a hand through his hair. Audrey's lip quivers.

"But none of this"—I wave my hand at the room—"is for you. He isn't yours. I suggest you take whatever he offered you and run with it, because it's all you're going to get."

Her eyes narrow, and she smiles slyly. "He just offered me his cock, like always."

"What the fuck, Audrey!"

I walk casually over to her and look her straight in the eye. "If you ever touch him again, I'll rip your tongue out of your pretty little head."

Audrey looks over at Nate. "This is who you want?"

"With every breath I take. Get the fuck out of our home, Audrey."

The breath leaves me as I stare at him. *Our home?* He stares back at me, his jaw clenched, his gray eyes burning with need and love.

Audrey looks at us both and sneers at me. "At least I got you fired."

"Get the fuck out, Audrey!" Nate yells, and she jumps.

She snatches up her purse and jacket and stomps moodily to the door, slamming it behind her.

I can't move. I just feast on him with my eyes. He's in his jeans and black T-shirt, showing off his beautiful tattoo. His hair is loose. His hands are in fists at his sides, and every muscle in his gorgeous body is tight.

"Are you really here?" he whispers.

"I'm here," I whisper back.

"Why?"

Why?

I walk toward him and suddenly feel calm. This is where I'm supposed to be. But he still has some explaining to do.

"Because I'm done running."

"Jules, what happened on Monday . . ."

"We'll get to that. I have a question first."

His eyes narrow on mine. "What is it?"

"Can I have my necklace back, please?"

Nate's whole body sags as he sighs and closes his eyes in relief. He reaches in his pocket and pulls out the necklace. "I've been carrying it around for four days."

He holds it out to me, but I shake my head and turn around. "Will you please fasten it?"

I pull my hair out of his way, and he fastens the lovely silver heart pendant around my neck but doesn't touch me.

Not yet.

And that's okay, because once he starts, I'm not going to let him stop, and I need to hear what the fuck happened on Monday.

"Let's sit." He leads me to the sofa, and we sit.

I kick off my shoes and pull my legs up under me and turn to face him. He brings one leg up on the cushion and faces me, too. We sit like this for a minute, just looking at each other, until I feel tears pool in my eyes.

"Don't cry," he whispers. "I can't stand it when you cry."

I shake my head and look down at my hands, then take a deep breath and look back up at him, the tears under control.

"I'm listening."

"Where did you go?" he asks, his voice low and eyes fierce.

"I was at Will's."

"Are you okay?" he asks.

"I'm getting there," I respond.

"You're done running, Julianne." He clenches his eyes shut for a moment and then looks at me again, his eyes sad and filled with longing. "I can't take it when you run away from me."

"Nate, Monday was . . ."

"I know exactly what Monday was, and you would, too, if you'd listened to me."

"It hurt," I whisper. "I needed you more Monday afternoon than I've ever needed anyone, and you weren't there for me. You didn't fight with me, for us. It made me feel insignificant and like everything we had was nothing."

"I know, baby." His voices softens, and he reaches a hand out to run his knuckles down my cheek, but I pull back out of reach. He flinches. "Jules."

"Just tell me what happened."

"You won't let me touch you? Does that mean that you just want an explanation so you can leave for good?"

I swallow hard and look at his beautiful hands and shake my head slowly, but I can't talk. Not yet.

"Monday was a clusterfuck, Julianne." He pulls a hand down his face and suddenly looks very tired. "I was pulled into Vincent's office as soon as I got to work. He told me that they'd received an anonymous phone call telling them that I'd been having an affair with you. He said that they didn't have any proof, so at first I denied it."

"Audrey," I state, and he nods.

"It was Audrey. She saw us at the Market on Sunday."

"How does she know about the no-frat policy?" I ask, confused.

Nate sighs and shakes his head. "I don't know. I have a feeling she's probably made it her business to look into most everything about me. She's a nosy woman."

"So it wasn't Carly?" I'm so confused.

"No, but she was just a ticking time bomb, too. After you asked about her in the meeting, Vincent had us do some checking into her computer and office. She had extensive notes on you, Jules. She's the one who sent me that incomplete report in New York. Jenny admitted that she asked her to hit send on your computer after you called that day, and Carly set you up. She was trying to figure out a way to get you fired."

"Why?" I ask.

"Who knows?" He shrugs and shakes his head. "To move up in the company faster, maybe she just didn't like you, the possibilities are endless. When confronted, she denied it, but we had enough evidence to fire her."

"So Carly's gone, too?"

"Yes." He exhales deeply.

"What happened that morning?" I ask.

"Vincent told me that he was going to fire you whether I copped to it or not. He said he didn't need proof, which is true. This is a no-fault state. They can fire anyone for any reason. So I called over to HR to have a representative present, and I told them that, yes, you and I are in a relationship." He swallows and shakes his head.

"Then Vincent told me that he'd let you stay if I broke it off and transferred you to the New York office."

I gasp and feel my eyes go wide.

"I told him to go to hell. I told him that I would stay on with the company if he offered you a severance package and cashed out your sick time as well as your vacation time."

"Nate, it wasn't about the money . . ."

"I'm not finished, Julianne."

Oh, that's right, this is Nate.

"All right."

"Then I left his office and went to mine and started making calls. At noon, I was asked to go to the conference room so Vincent could discuss some things with Luis and me about how we'll handle the accounts with you gone."

He looks me in the eye. "It was killing me. The thought of having to fire you and planning how to divvy up your work was killing me."

"You looked just fine in the meeting, Nate."

"Yeah, well, looks are deceiving. When they pulled you in the room, I wanted to hold you and protect you. But I had a plan, and I couldn't show you any emotion. I knew you'd be strong and that you would tell the truth, and you didn't disappoint me, baby."

"I didn't have any reason to lie. I knew what I was doing when we started our relationship, Nate."

"I know. We both did. But we don't have to worry about it anymore."

"No, we don't."

"I mean, there's more." He smiles at me, a wide, beautiful smile, like he has a gift for me. "After you left the building, I made a few more calls, and then ran after you. You know what happened then."

"Yeah," I whisper.

"Well, the following day, I handed in my resignation."

I gasp again and search his face. He looks happy. At peace.

"Nate, God, you didn't have to . . ."

"Yeah, I did, Jules. But here's the best part. You know I've done well in this business. I've been smart. I'm a very, very wealthy man, sweetheart."

"Okay." I narrow my eyes on his face, not sure where he's going with this.

"Well, as of this morning, you're looking at the CEO of McKenna Enterprises, LLC. We have clients on board, and Mrs. Glover is coming with us, too."

"Us?" I ask, in shock.

"Of course, us. It's going to be a busy year ahead, but I know you're not afraid of a little hard work."

Oh my God.

"Are you offering me a job?" I ask, still not entirely grasping what he's asking.

"No, my love, I'm offering you a partnership. This is *our* company."

"Holy shit."

"Is that your way of accepting the position?" he asks with a grin.

"No-fraternization policy?" I ask.

"I'm not fond of those," he replies.

"You did this for me?" I whisper, in awe.

"I would do anything for you, baby. When are you going to figure that out?" His face is so serious, so sure.

"Oh, Nate." I launch myself into his arms, and he pulls me close, buries his face in my neck and holds on tight.

"I love you so much, Julianne. Don't leave me again. Please."

I run my fingers through his hair and soak in his warmth. "I'm here."

He pulls back and gazes down at me, brushes his knuckles down my cheek and kisses my forehead. "Your skin is so soft."

"Natalie and I had my birthday spa treatments today."

"You deserved them," he murmurs.

"Nate?"

"Yes, baby."

I pull my fingers down his face, so in love with this sweet man. "When can I move in?"

"I'll call a moving company in the morning."

epilogue

"**A**re the arrangements all made, Jenny?" I ask my assistant.

"Yes, sir, everything is ready." Jenny winks at me, and I smile back. Bringing her with Julianne and me to the new company was one of the best moves I've ever made.

"Thank you. You can go ahead and go home for the weekend."

"Great, I'll do that. Happy birthday, Mr. McKenna."

"Thank you, Jenny."

Jenny pulls her purse out of her desk just as Julianne comes out of her office, looking fucking amazing in her red dress and black heels, hair all loose around her gorgeous face.

God, I love her.

"Are you heading out, Jenny?" she asks in her soft, sweet voice.

"Yes, Miss Montgomery, unless you have anything else for me?"

"Oh, no, that's fine. Have a good weekend." She smiles at Jenny and then crosses to me, a happy smile on her lips. "I think I'm ready to call it a day as well, Mr. McKenna."

"You read my mind, baby." I take her in my arms and rest my lips on her soft forehead, breathing her in. She always smells like sunshine and vanilla. "I have a surprise for you."

She looks up at me with wide eyes and then frowns. "But it's *your* birthday. I have a surprise for you."

"Will it travel?" I ask and rub my hands up and down her lean back.

She purses her lips, and her eyes widen a bit in surprise, and then she says, "Yeah, I guess so."

"Good. Grab your things and let's go."

"Are we going home first?" she asks.

I love it when she says home like that. It's our home now, and has been for two months, but it still sounds new when it trips off her sweet tongue.

"No, we don't have time."

"But, I didn't bring anything for a weekend trip."

"It's been taken care of, Julianne. Trust me."

She gathers her things, and we lock up the office, then I hold my hand out for hers, lacing her fingers in mine, and we ride the elevator down to the parking garage.

"Where are we going?" she asks, her big blue eyes looking up at me expectantly.

"You'll see soon." She sticks her bottom lip out in a pout, and I laugh and lean down to nibble and kiss her lips. "You taste good," I whisper.

"I had a Hershey Bar before we left," she whispers back.

I chuckle as the elevator opens and lead her to the Mercedes. I'd really like to take the bike this weekend, but we have too much stuff to bring with us.

After stowing our things, we're soon on the freeway heading south out of Seattle. Julianne runs her fingertips up and down my thigh, sending shivers through me and making my cock twitch. I catch her hand and kiss her fingertips, and then rest our hands in my lap. She smiles sassily. "Later," I murmur.

"Okay, spill it. Where are we going?"

"To the beach house."

"Oh good! We haven't been in a while." She beams at me, and I smile back.

"I know, we've been too busy building the business. We deserve this weekend away." I kiss her hand again, and she leans over to kiss me.

"Yes, we do."

"HEY, BABY, WE'RE here." I brush the back of my hand down Jules'

soft cheek, waking her from her nap. She fell asleep thirty minutes into the car ride here, and I just let her sleep. She looks like an angel when she sleeps, and we've worked many sixty- to eighty-hour weeks lately, exhausting both of us.

"We're here?" she asks sleepily and sits up to stretch, pushing her breasts out against that sexy dress, and my cock immediately stirs to life.

I didn't realize until I pulled in the driveway how nervous I am about tonight. Telling her that I have a surprise for her was the understatement of the year. This could be one of the most important nights of our lives, and I just pray to God I don't fuck it up.

Jules grabs her handbag, and I pull the large suitcase containing our clothes for the weekend out of the back seat and join her on the porch, unlock the door, and follow her inside.

The rental company I use to care for the house in our absence has been here like I requested, and I take a quick look around. There is a fire burning in the fireplace, the logs not burned too far down, telling me they were here recently.

Perfect.

The dining room table is set for dinner, and there are chafing dishes on the counter with our dinner being kept warm.

Jules drops her bag on the couch and turns to look at me, her pretty eyes wide and her mouth dropped.

"What is this?" she asks.

"I knew we wouldn't want to cook." I shrug, pretending that it's no big deal.

"More of your minions?" she asks, making me laugh.

"Yes, my minions."

I leave the suitcase at the foot of the stairs, planning to carry it up later, and flip on the sound system, satisfied as John Legend starts to croon out of the speakers.

Jules has walked over to the fireplace, looking at the flames, her arms folded over her chest. The light is bouncing off her beautiful blond hair and pale skin, and I can't resist her. I wrap my arms around her from behind and bury my nose in her neck, breathing her in.

"You are so sexy, Julianne."

"Hmm," she murmurs. "You're not so bad yourself, ace."

I smile at her silly nickname for me, then kiss her soft neck. "Come on, let's eat."

"Okay."

We pile our plates full of delicious-smelling pasta and white sauce, salad and bread, and I open a bottle of her favorite champagne.

"Wow, you went all-out."

"Wait till you see what's for dessert," I respond.

"Chocolate cheesecake?" she asks with a grin.

"You guessed it," I respond. *You so did not guess it, baby.*

Goddamn it, I'm nervous. I'm thankful that my hands are steady as I pour the pink champagne into flutes, and we sit at the table to eat.

"To you." I hold my glass in the air, and she follows suit. "The most beautiful woman in the world."

"I'll drink to that." She winks and sips her champagne, and I can't help but chuckle at her.

When our food is consumed, Jules jumps up and kisses me square on the mouth, and before I can grab on to her and pull her on my lap, she draws back, flashes me that sexy grin, and says, "Wait here. I'll be right back."

She leaves out the front door with her keys in hand, and then returns less than thirty seconds later with a large black box in her arms.

"What the hell is that?" I ask.

"Your birthday present," she responds with a grin.

"Baby, you didn't have to give me anything."

Just please don't say no. That's the only gift I need.

"Uh, duh. Nate, it's your birthday. Of course I got you a gift." She clears our dinner plates and sets the box on the table before me. "Open it."

I pull the lid off and peel back the silver tissue paper to find one framed photo resting on a photo album.

I pull the frame out and stare in awe at the photo. Jesus Christ, it's her. It's Julianne, but she's not wearing any clothes. She's lying on a bed, on her belly, and she's smiling at me the way she does when she knows that I'm hot for her.

Fuck, I'm hot for her right now.

"Say something, ace."

I look up into her uncertain eyes and grin. "You're so damned beautiful."

She smiles sweetly in relief, and I lean over to kiss her, wrapping a hand in her long, soft hair. She pulls back and whispers, "Open the album."

There are pages and pages of her, in the sexiest lingerie I've ever seen, wrapped up in a sheet, stark-ass naked, all in different poses. All sexy as hell.

I close the album and scoot my chair back and then pull her into my arms, her ass resting in my lap, and kiss the shit out of her. I run my fingers down her soft face, and over her breast, feeling the nipple harden as I play with it between my fingers. With a soft moan she stands, hikes her skirt up around her hips and straddles me.

"Right now, fast and hard, ace." Her blue eyes are on fire with lust, and who the fuck am I to say no? She's my every fantasy.

I rip her underwear in two and throw it on the floor as she smirks.

"I'll buy you more next week."

"Yes, you will."

She unfastens my pants, and I yank them down around my thighs, and suddenly she's on her knees, my dick in her sweet little hands, and her pink mouth is wrapped around it, sucking hard.

"Fuck, baby." I gently grab her hair and guide her head up and down as she jacks me off with her fist. My balls tighten, and before she can make me come in her hot mouth, I yank her up by the shoulders, and she straddles me again, guiding me inside her, and all conscious thought evaporates. All I can think about is pounding in and out of that sweet pussy.

"Oh, Nate, yes." She throws her head back, and I kiss her neck as she rides me, thrusting up into her wet softness.

"Christ, you're so wet, honey."

"Mmm . . ." she moans, and her muscles tense around my shaft, and I can feel the orgasm building in her. She's going to take me with her, and I start to move faster, cupping her ass in my hands and bringing her down on me harder.

"Oh, Nate, I'm gonna come, babe."

God, I love hearing my name come out of her like that when I'm inside her. I look down to watch her, to watch *us* and see her red tattoo, and I'll be damned if it doesn't make me even hotter.

"Come for me, my love," I whisper to her and watch in awe as she bites her bottom lip, clenches her eyes shut, and grips on to my hair as she explodes around me, grinding down so hard on me that it almost hurts, and I feel my own climax take me as I still, pushed all the way inside her heat, and spill myself inside of her.

She collapses onto me, her arms wrapped around my shoulders and face buried in my neck, breathing hard.

"Happy birthday," she murmurs, and I laugh.

"God, honey, you're amazing."

She's so fucking amazing.

"I take it you like the pictures?" She leans back and grins down at me.

"I love them. Natalie?"

"Yeah, Nat took them."

"Remind me to thank her, too."

"I hope you just send her a thank-you card or something, rather than thank her this way."

"Um, yeah, that sounds like a good plan." I brush her hair off her cheek and pull her down for another kiss. "I have something else for you," I whisper against her lips.

"You do?"

"Yes, come on." I lift her off me and tuck my dick back in my pants, while she shimmies her skirt back down, and open the back door.

"I'm not wearing any shoes."

"Here." I lift her easily, and she wraps her arms around my neck and kisses my cheek.

"Thanks."

"Anytime."

When we get down to the gazebo, I nod my head in satisfaction. It's decorated exactly the way it was the first time I brought her here, when I gave her Mom's necklace.

"Oh, Nate, this is beautiful."

"I'm glad you like it." I pour her another glass of champagne from the bottle the catering company left down here, and we settle on the plush couch.

"Julianne." I take her hand in mine, and the nerves are back. Fuck. I take a long pull off the champagne.

She's looking at me curiously, her head cocked. "Nate, it's okay."

My eyes dart to hers, and my stomach immediately settles. That song she loves, *I Won't Give Up,* starts to play through the speakers, and I know. This is my moment.

I clear my throat and look down at our linked hands, and then back up into her perfectly blue eyes, searching for the words I've practiced every day in my head for the past two months.

"I love you, Julianne. I've loved you for a long time. You and I are a team, in every way. You amaze me with your strength, with your kindness, and the love you show everyone around you, including me." Tears leak out the sides of her eyes, and I reach over to catch them with my fingertips.

"Don't cry, baby," I whisper. I can't stand it when she cries. "Jules, we *were* meant to be. I knew it the minute I first saw you." I kneel before her and pull the red Cartier box out of my pocket and open it so she can see the vintage-style diamond engagement ring I picked out for her a month ago.

More tears fall out of her wide eyes as she stares down at it and then back up at me in awe and surprise and love, and I don't need to search for the words anymore.

"Marry me, Julianne. Share my life with me. Be mine for the rest of my life."

Her lips tremble before they spread into a wide smile, and she launches herself into my arms, holding me tightly around the neck, her face buried against me.

"Honey, I need to hear the words," I murmur with a chuckle.

"Yes." She pulls back and holds my face in her hands, looking deeply into my eyes. "Yes, Nate, I'll marry you."

I rest my forehead on hers and breathe a long sigh of relief.

"Thank you," I whisper. "Can I put this on you now?"

"Hell yes, ace." She laughs and wipes her tears away as I slide the ring on her tiny finger. She holds it up and admires it. "You did good, babe."

"I'm so glad you approve," I reply drily.

"I do." She smiles sweetly at me, and my gut clenches in love and lust, and she hugs me tightly again. "I love you, Nate."

"I love you, too, Julianne."

"Did you say something about chocolate cheesecake?"

The End

The With Me In Seattle Series continues with Will and Meg's story in the third book, PLAY WITH ME. It is available now.

Note from the Author:

I hope you enjoyed Nate and Jules' story. Nate McKenna has been, and continues to be, one of the most beloved of my characters by my readers, and as such, I had many requests to write the prologue from Nate's point of view.

So I did.

Here is what I came up with. I hope you enjoy it!

prologue

Nate

Summer

I grip her round ass and lift her against the wall of the hallway outside my bedroom. I can't wait another minute to feel her sexy, long legs wrapped around my waist. Julianne wraps her arms and legs around me and holds on tight as I bury my face in her neck and breathe her in.

God, she smells good. She's all vanilla and clean sunshine, and she's just so fucking sweet.

She pulls my hair out of the tie and pushes her fingers through it as I lean back to just look down into her bright, lust-filled blue eyes.

Fuck me, she's beautiful.

She's panting and clinging to me, and I rock my pelvis against hers, reveling in how hot her center is, even through my slacks. She offers me a sassy little smile. God, I love her smart attitude.

"Do you know how beautiful you are, Julianne?" I whisper against her lips. I can't get enough of her lips. Soft and perfect, I nibble them again, and when she rocks those hips, pushing herself against my cock, I can't take it any longer.

"I need you naked, now." And I do. I lift her easily and carry her into the bedroom, not bothering to stop and turn on the light. If I'm not inside her, now, my dick will explode.

We make quick work of our clothes, pulling at each other, stripping the offensive fabric away and flinging it all about the room until we're naked, and now I have unfettered access to her gorgeous, slim body. I can't stop touching her soft skin, her firm breasts, her sides, her back.

I can't fucking believe she's here, finally. She's my every fantasy.

I push my fingers into her amazing blond hair and pull her lips to mine, kissing the shit out of her. Jesus, her lips are incredible, and if I don't slow this down, I'm going to make a fool of myself before I even get her on the bed.

I lift her, cradling her in my arms, and lay her gently on my bed.

Licking and kissing my way up her body, I cover her, settle my pelvis between her legs, and return to kissing those amazing lips. Her hands are all over me, running up and down my torso, my shoulders, my arms.

I love how eager she is to touch me, and I kick myself in the ass for not turning the light on. I'd love to look into those baby blues and watch her response to me. Watch her eyes go wide as I sink inside her. Watch her legs tremble when my mouth is on her.

I can't stop touching her hair, brushing it off her face, as I kiss her tenderly and let her run those small hands over me, exploring my body. God, she makes me fucking crazy.

Finally, I lean on my elbow at the side of her head and run my fingers down her face, her neck, and finally to her breast, and tease the nipple in my fingertips. It pebbles up, and I have to taste it, pull on it with my teeth, and kiss it again as my hand continues the journey down her flat stomach and to that sweet spot that I can't wait to bury myself in.

Fuck, she's so wet! I slip past her hard clit and plunge two fingers inside her warm, wet, tight-as-fuck pussy, and circle her clit with my thumb.

"Oh God!" Her back bows off the bed, and she pushes her pelvis against my hand. Damn, she's so tight. There's no way in hell she's a virgin, but she's also clearly not had sex in a while.

Thank Christ.

"Oh, you are so wet. And so fucking tight. How long has it been for you, honey?" Fuck, I'm going to hurt her. There's no way around it.

The only other option is to not make love to her, and that's just not an option.

No fucking option at all.

I've waited too long to have her here with me, in my bed, and by God, I'm keeping her here.

She stills for a moment at my question, making me grin. "Longer than I care to think about." She lifts her hips against my hand again, and I groan.

"Shit, I want you. I've wanted you since I first laid eyes on you." My lips find hers again, more demanding now. I can't get enough of her. I need her like I need to breathe.

"We shouldn't do this," she whispers.

Fuck yes, we should.

"Why not?" I whisper back and nibble over to her ear, teasing her earlobe with the tip of my tongue before I grip it firmly in my teeth, making her squirm against me.

"Because . . . Oh God, yes, right there." Her hips are circling, pushing against my hand rhythmically, and she skims her hands down my back to my ass, pulling me to her, and I know that she wants me as desperately as I want her.

"You were saying?"

"We could both be fired. No-frat policy."

"I don't give a fuck about anyone's policy right now." I clench my lips around her other nipple, lick and lave it, and work my way down her amazing little body, teasing her navel with my tongue, and then I find her wet center, spread her thighs wider, plant a kiss on each soft thigh and then sink into her.

Fucking hell, she tastes good. She's sweetness, and I know, right now, I will never, ever get my fill of her.

She is mine.

"Fuck!" She bucks her hips up off the bed, making me grin. I grip her hips tightly and hold her to me, then spread her legs farther apart, pull my fingers out of her and make love to her with my tongue, swirling and pushing around her clit and lips, and finally plunging deep inside her.

She grips my hair in her hands, and I briefly consider making her hold on to the headboard, but change my mind. She's not ready for that yet.

Next time.

Her legs are starting to tremble, and she's writhing and squirming against my mouth. God, I love how responsive she is.

I lick up to her clit and push my flat tongue against that tiny nub while I push a single finger inside her, hitting that little, rough spot, and send her into oblivion.

Her pussy tightens around my finger, milking and pulling at it, as she cries out, and I can't wait to bury my cock deep inside her.

I open the condom and lick and kiss my way back up her incredible body, paying special attention to her nipples, loving the sound of the breath catching in her throat. Finally, my lips are on hers again, where they fucking belong, and she's wrapping herself around me, eagerly pressing against me.

It's almost my undoing.

I raise up on my hands, braced above her, my cock cradled in that glorious wetness, and want so desperately to plunge inside her and fuck her, hard, until she screams my name.

God, I want this woman.

But I can't move. I'm staring down at her, wishing again that I could see her eyes. Her hands travel down my back, up my sides, and back down again.

"Nate, I want you," she murmurs in her soft voice.

"I know." Fuck, I want you, too.

"Now, damn it." I grin at her impatience.

"You are so fucking hot." I softly kiss her forehead and breathe her in again. Jesus, is she really here? Am I dreaming?

"Inside me!"

I'm about to laugh at her impatience, but she wraps that hand around my dick, and I'm about to explode like a fucking teenager. She gently pushes up and down, not too tight, just exploring me, and it's the most incredible thing I've ever felt.

Then she gets to the tip and stills. "Holy shit, what is that?"

I chuckle softly and kiss her lips, trying to distract myself from her magical fingers tracing the head of my dick and flicking against the piercing.

"It's an apa."

"A what-a?" she whispers.

I can tell she's a little shocked, and a lot curious, and my excitement just skyrocketed.

Just wait until you see the tats, baby.

"An apadravya. Fuck, honey."

"Why would you get this?" she asks, her voice full of curiosity and lust.

"You're about to find out." I roll the condom on and plunge my fingers into her hair again, holding her face to me as I kiss her, devouring her mouth. She wraps her arms around me and lifts her hips until the tip of my dick is resting on her lips.

Dear God, she's going to be the death of me.

I slowly, gently slip inside her hot core. She's so fucking wet that she easily accepts me inside her, and I don't stop until I'm buried balls-deep in her.

"Fuck, I love how tight you are," I whisper against her lips, and she tightens around me, pulls me more firmly against her with her legs and grips my hair in her hands. She doesn't want me to go anywhere, and damned if I plan to.

I want to stay here forever, buried inside her.

I start to slowly move, plunging in and pulling out in a long, slow rhythm. I feel the metal balls dragging against her walls, and her body's reaction to it is astounding. She's quivering and pulsing against me, clenching me. Fuck, she's so strong.

Getting that fucker was the best damn thing I ever did.

She's not going to last long, thank God, because neither am I. I pick up the pace and twist my hips, just a bit, and I feel her begin to shudder beneath me.

"Come on, honey, let go," I whisper against her lips.

She cries out as she grips me like a vice and comes around me, shuddering and shaking, her pussy milking me, and I have no choice but to follow her over the edge.

"Oh, fuck!"

"ARE YOU OKAY?" I ask and pull her against me, settling us into the bed.

"Yes."

"Do you need anything?" I run my fingers down her soft cheek and sigh contentedly.

"No, thank you."

I can feel her withdrawing, regretting this already, and it fucking pisses me off.

"Do you want me to turn on the light?" I ask calmly and reach for the lamp beside the bed, but she stops me with her hand firmly on my arm.

"No, it's fine."

"You don't sound like yourself. Are you sure you're okay?" Talk to me, baby.

"I'm tired. Probably too much wine."

Bullshit. She didn't drink that much. I noticed. I notice everything about her. I hate myself for being such a pussy and not making her talk to me, tell me what's going on in that beautiful head of hers, but I know that she won't open up to me right now, and if I push it, she'll run. I just want to hold her in my arms all night long. We can talk in the morning and discuss where we go from here.

Because the job can kiss my ass. She's mine. And, God knows, I'm hers.

I kiss her forehead and turn her away from me, curling around her back, tucking her against me. She fits perfectly.

"Go to sleep. We'll talk in the morning."

I tighten my arms around her and fall asleep with my nose buried against her hair, breathing her in.

I WAKE BEFORE the alarm, as usual. I run my hands down my face and then I remember. Julianne.

I reach for her, but the bed is cold and empty, except for me. I frown and sit up. Did she already get up? I hope she made some coffee.

But I don't smell coffee, and unease settles, unwelcomed, in the pit of my stomach.

Not bothering to pull on underwear, I hurry to the living room, but she's nowhere to be found. The condo is empty, showing no signs of her. Her purse and clothes are gone. My heart drops into my stomach.

She fucking left.

Son of a bitch.

It took me a year to get her here. How long is it going to take me to get her back?

65553879R00157

Made in the USA
Middletown, DE
28 February 2018